"Playing the truant, are you, my girl?"

Susan began to rise, suddenly realizing he must think her one of the maids.

"No," he ordered abruptly, "don't get up. I don't wish to spoil your fun." He leaned casually against the trunk of an apple tree.

The temptation to play the role of the maid was too great to resist. Susan rose and dusted off her grimy pinafore, then imitated the soft lilt of one of the housemaids as she informed the earl that she truly must return to the house.

"You aren't quite the child you looked, are you?" Carlton remarked lightly, his eyes running lazily over her body.

Susan turned pink and decided that the little game had proceeded quite far enough. She started for the house but Lord Carlton caught playfully at her hand.

"Come," he teased, "there must be some reward before you take to your heels if you wish me to remain silent about your truancy."

Susan drew herself up and opened her mouth to let him know in no uncertain terms who she was and that this silly game was done, but before she could do so, he had taken her hands and pulled them behind her back. Startled, she twisted in his arms, her eyes blazing with indignation.

"Hush, my girl," he murmured huskily, as he claimed her lips with his own . . .

THE BEST IN REGENCIES FROM ZEBRA

PASSION'S LADY (1545, $2.95)
by Sara Blayne
She was a charming rogue, an impish child—and a maddeningly alluring woman. If the Earl of Shayle knew little else about her, he knew she was going to marry him. As a bride, Marie found a temporary hiding place from her past, but could not escape from the Earl's shrewd questions—or the spark of passion in his eyes.

AN ELIGIBLE BRIDE (2020, $3.95)
by Janice Bennett
The duke of Halliford was in the country for one reason—to fulfill a promise to look after Captain Carstairs' children. This was as distasteful as finding a suitable wife. But his problems were answered when he saw the beautiful Helena Carstairs. The duke was not above resorting to some very persuasive means to get what he wanted . . .

RECKLESS HEART (1679, $2.50)
by Lois Arvin Walker
Rebecca had met her match in the notorious Earl of Compton. Not only did he decline the invitation to her soiree, but he found it amusing when her horse landed her in the middle of Compton Creek. If this was another female scheme to lure him into marriage the Earl swore Rebecca would soon learn she had the wrong man, a man with a blackened reputation.

DANCE OF DESIRE (1757, $2.95)
by Sarah Fairchilde
Lord Sherbourne almost ran Virginia down on horseback, then he silenced her indignation with a most ungentlemanly kiss. Seething with outrage, the lovely heiress decided the insufferable lord was in need of a royal setdown. And she knew the way to go about it . . .

Available wherever paperbacks are sold, or order direct from the Publisher. Send cover price plus 50¢ per copy for mailing and handling to Zebra Books, Dept. 2076, 475 Park Avenue South, New York, N.Y. 10016. Residents of New York, New Jersey and Pennsylvania must include sales tax. DO NOT SEND CASH.

KAREN LAHEY
A NOBLE AMBITION

ZEBRA BOOKS
KENSINGTON PUBLISHING CORP.

ZEBRA BOOKS

are published by

Kensington Publishing Corp.
475 Park Avenue South
New York, NY 10016

Copyright © 1987 by Elizabeth Albright

All rights reserved. No part of this book may be reproduced in any form or by any means without the prior written consent of the Publisher, excepting brief quotes used in reviews.

First printing: May 1987

Printed in the United States of America

Chapter 1

With a gentle sigh, Miss Caroline Phillips closed the pages of the novel she had been reading and gazed at her sister, a rapt expression in her blue eyes.

"Oh, Susan," she breathed, "if only you could meet such a man as the count."

Susan Phillips, who at nineteen was the elder of the two by three years, raised amused eyes from the mending in her lap and regarded her entranced sibling.

"Don't be a goose, Caro," she said with a small chuckle. "Do you suppose counts simply walk about hoping to be introduced to penniless American girls?"

She snipped the thread from the shirt she had been mending, laid it aside and picked up a second.

"Pooh," said Caro with a pout. "We may not be well fixed but we are not penniless. Besides, we have the Phillips name and in England, at least, that stands for something." A triumphant smile crossed her lips. "When you go to London to visit my aunt and uncle, who knows but what royalty may not come your way."

"Now Caro," began Susan gravely, abandoning her work for a moment. "It's not at all nice in you to talk that way. You know Aunt Henrietta wouldn't approve if she thought you were interested in how the family is situated and as for the other—" She paused a moment, letting her gaze wander to the window of the small parlor in which they were sitting and then to the tiny garden, brown and barren under a weak January sun, which lay beyond. "You know quite well that nothing has been settled. My uncle has not yet invited me to London, and even if he does, I'm not at all convinced that I should go."

"Not go?" cried Caro indignantly. "How can you say such a thing, Susan? Why, only think of the adventure you shall have, the balls and assemblies, to say nothing of the theaters and even . . . masquerades. And no matter how much you may shake your head at me, you might very well become acquainted with a dark, handsome, count. Our uncle is, after all, a baronet, and quite wealthy, so he must know all the right sort of people. I'm persuaded that my count need only set eyes on you to become enamored and then . . . why . . . he shall ask for your hand at once."

"Dear Caro," Susan said with a quiver of laughter, "you really must try for a little more conduct if you ever wish to be presented into society. Besides, if I do go to visit my uncle, it shall not be for the purpose of making an eligible connection, I can assure you."

Caroline thrust out her lower lip and glowered at her sister, who had once again calmly returned to her needlework. "You know you could make a perfectly Splendid Marriage if you but lifted your little finger . . . and . . . and just think how that would help me when it came my turn to be presented."

Susan raised her brow, intending to remind her sister that she should not be rushing her fences, but upon observing the hurt in Caroline's eye, dropped her mending and went to her side.

The two sisters looked very much alike although Susan was the taller of the two by several inches and was accredited the greater beauty. Her form was graceful and her complexion of a creaminess which could only be enhanced by her black curls and dark blue eyes. There was more to her beauty than simply the perfection of her features, however. She had an openness of expression, a gleam of irrepressible humor in her eyes, and a sunny disposition quite without any conceit.

That gleam of amusement was apparent as she placed her arms about the dejected figure on the sofa and gave her a quick hug. "I've quite overset all your grand plans, have I not?"

Caro nodded. "I think it would be very poor spirited in you to refuse to go to London, Susan."

"I should hate to be poor spirited, my love," smiled Susan, "but you must know I should be compelled to refuse if I thought Aunt Henry couldn't spare me. Her constitution isn't strong and I don't wish to be a cause of concern to her."

"But Susan," her sister broke in indignantly, "how can you even think of refusing when we know it was Aunt Henry herself who wrote to my uncle suggesting that you go? Certainly she would feel nothing but pleasure if Sir Peter were to invite you to England, and as for her constitution, why she'll be in the best of hands with Robert and me to cosset her."

Susan smiled to herself as she pictured her fourteen-year-old brother's reaction to this idea. "Well," she finally responded, "even with Aunt Henry's letter, which I'm not at all certain was well advised, I really haven't the least expectation that my uncle shall ask me to come. After all, why should he? I've never even met him."

"Susan," cried Caroline, her eyes sparkling with indignation. "I vow you're trying to vex me. Why shouldn't Aunt Henry write to Sir Peter? I'm sure it was quite unexceptionable in her to do so for you know he and Papa had it set since we were born that we should make our come-outs under his protection."

"Perhaps," Susan said as she resumed her seat and picked up her mending, "or perhaps he'll feel that we're the sort of encroaching relatives one cannot like."

Caroline gazed at her elder sister in consternation. "He couldn't be so mean, Susan, he simply couldn't."

Susan shrugged, "The pact he made with my father was done long ago. Depend upon it, he has forgotten all about it."

And it would not be all surprising if he has, Susan reflected as her sister, unable to refute this piece of logic, reached gloomily for a shirt and bent her dark head over her work. Indeed, she mused pensively, how could Uncle Peter welcome into his household the daughter of one who could only be construed as the black sheep of the family.

The silence in the parlor was complete, and as

Susan plyed her needle, she recalled the story she had heard several months ago when, in anticipation of a possible journey to London, she had pressed her Aunt Henrietta for an explanation of the deep division she sensed within the Phillips family. Although Henrietta had primed up her lips, remarking that it was hardly a story fit for a young lady's ears, Susan had persisted with determination, explaining quite reasonably that as her father's eldest, she had a right and, indeed, an obligation to be made familiar with the facts.

Susan's aunt, Henrietta Ashley, was a pretty little woman on the shady side of forty with light gray eyes and a figure which could only be described as plump but whose smile was sweet and disposition compliant. She had a quantity of dark, shining hair, which she had for a number of years kept hidden under a series of becoming caps, the donning of that first lacy, beribboned cap coinciding with the day she had firmly and finally set the thought of marriage from her mind.

Henrietta wasn't educated nor even particularly intelligent but she had a generous, loving nature, and when her sister had died quite suddenly of a congestion of the lungs, she had comforted and protected her nieces and nephew, reassuring them that they should make a home together. That the task of caring for a lively young family might be heavier than she could wish never entered her mind, and indeed, she and her sister's children had dealt quite well together. She truly loved her nieces and nephew and wished only the best for them and to that end had nurtured the hope that Sir Peter would one day realize his obligation and help the orphans.

Although her mind was not of a particularly brilliant nature, it had not taken her many moments to see the truth in her niece's words, and with a sigh of resignation, Henrietta had agreed to tell Susan the whole of her father's history.

"I must say, however," she added peevishly, "that I find it extremely distressing to impart this history to you and not at all kind in you to press me so."

Susan soothed her distraught relative then waited patiently for the older woman to commence.

"Your grandfather had two sons," said Henrietta, thinking that the best place to begin such a story was at the very beginning.

"Yes, yes, I know that," interrupted Susan with a laugh. "My father, David, was the younger and Peter, now Sir Peter, the elder." She fastened her twinkling gaze upon her aunt. "You must not think my mother told me nothing."

Henrietta eyed her niece crossly and, with an effort, continued. "Your father never, as far as I was aware, felt the least regard for your grandfather and, truth to tell, the old gentleman couldn't abide the sight of him either."

"Why ever not, dear ma'am?" asked Susan in amazement.

"Well, it's not for me to say, I'm sure, as I scarcely knew the baronet but I do know that he was a high stickler. He always held himself in the greatest consequence and he absolutely despised weakness and irresponsibility, anyone could tell you that. Actually," continued Henrietta thoughtfully, becoming immersed in her story, "his disgust of his son isn't really to be wondered at for as much as I dislike speaking ill of the departed . . . and you know my views on that subject, Susan . . . your father was a wastrel . . . and worse. Then, too, he refused to take any interest in your grandfather's holdings and estates, which did not help his case." She sighed. "Perhaps if he had hid himself away after some of his scandals or at the very least been a little more discreet, the baronet might have borne it but I regret to say that your father positively flaunted his style of life and that, your grandfather could not endure.

"David used to make wild wagers, betting on anything and everything . . . two flies crawling up a wall, raindrops running down a windowpane, if a young lady would dance more than twice with him, if . . . oh, I don't know all of his silly wagers. Suffice it to say that such action caused your grandfather a deal of mortification."

"I can understand that my grandfather could not have liked such childish behavior above half," Susan said, her brow knit, "but I cannot think that would cause him such disgust as to cut his son off from his family."

"But that was the least of it," Henrietta exclaimed, clasping her hands together. "He played deep, too, you see. Cost your grandfather a fortune."

"But surely that cannot be all, Aunt Henry?"

"Well, no" — Henrietta hesitated — "but I don't think it necessary to continue on the subject of your father's excesses."

"Aunt Henrietta," Susan reproached, "if I'm to understand my grandfather's actions, I must be told the whole."

"Oh, Susan," blushed Henrietta, "I cannot. . . .

truly."

Susan gazed at her aunt in bewilderment, then her troubled brow cleared and she gave a tiny choke of laughter. "Do you mean Women were his downfall?"

"Please," Henrietta begged with a shudder, her cheeks quite pink, "don't make me discuss his . . . his amorous affairs."

"I gather they weren't respectable," Susan querried dryly. Her aunt gave a tiny nod and Susan couldn't suppress a chuckle at the pained expression she observed on the older woman's face. "Were they also of some number?"

Henrietta again indicated that her niece was correct while she looked desperately about for her vinaigrette.

Susan absently handed her the object for which she was searching, a frown once more creasing her forehead.

"That must have been before he married my mother," she said slowly, "for they removed to America soon after, did they not?"

"Yes." Henrietta sighed, replacing the stopper and attempting to regain her composure. "After he had twice killed his man in a duel, your grandfather took action and demanded that David find himself a wife. He hoped, of course, that a bride of good family would serve to settle him down, but alas, he pressed David to marry Shiela and she was sacrificed on the alter of the old man's pride, for David would not give up his pleasures. When the baronet discovered that he had challanged yet another gentleman, and this time the husband of the woman involved, he alerted the constables, then ordered his son to leave the country, never to return. He gave David a deal of money but I venture to say he never forgave him."

Susan attempted, for a moment, to recall her father but her recollections of him were vague and included only tirades against her gentle mother, slammed doors, and then, long absences.

"He must not have found our tiny village to his liking," she mused at last, unable to find much pity in her heart for the man who had caused her mother such great pain.

"No, he did not," her aunt stated indignantly. "He didn't make even the smallest push to become respectable, but was forever traveling to Boston, remaining there for days on end, then returning when his money was gone and positively haranguing poor Shiela for more. She had a small independence, you see, and some jewelry which had been left her by my mother. Well, he went through her money but she absolutely refused to sell her jewelry for she realized that to do so would be folly indeed. She did have a great deal of spirit you know and felt she would need any money she could raise from the sale of the jewels for you children." Henrietta pulled her handkerchief from her sleeve and wiped away a tear. "You remind me so much of her, my dear."

Susan remained silent and after a moment her aunt resolutely blew her nose and straightened her drooping shoulders. "When your father died—"

"Forgive me, Aunt Henry," interrupted Susan gently, "but how did he die? I was only nine at the time, you see, and never really knew."

"A common drunken brawl," declared Henrietta, wrinkling her nose fastidiously. "Extremely vulgar, and it was only your dear mother's credit which kept all of you from being cast off completely after that scandal. She had many friends and her life was happier after that time but I couldn't feel easy about her."

Henrietta had indeed been close to her sister and had, over the years, kept a close correspondence with her. When she learned that even after the death of her husband, Shiela was determined to remain in America, Henrietta sent word immediately that she was joining her sister. She could not feel comfortable, she wrote, knowing her only sister was left with no family about her and, as their parents had died some years before, she had no strong attachments to keep her in England.

Henrietta had been as good as her word and had arrived several months later. She had been welcomed with warmth and affection and the family had settled down to a comfortable life. Their contentment lasted only seven years, for three years ago, in the fall of 1807, Susan's mother had taken a chill, which went immediately to her lungs and she had succumbed several days later.

"Why didn't my mother return to London when my father died?" queried Susan intently, shaking her aunt out of her sad reflections.

"What was that, my dear?" her aunt asked absently. "I'm afraid I was wool gathering."

Susan repeated her question and Henrietta frowned, considering. "Well, she couldn't like living in the same house as your grandfather, you see. He was still alive then and he had shifted the blame for his son's inadequacies from his own to Shiela's shoulders."

"Infamous!" exclaimed Susan indignantly. "How cruel and unjust in him to do so."

"Precisely, but bear in mind, Susan, he was an inflexible man. Pride in his name was all to him. It's fortunate that Peter is not of the same stamp. He had never reconciled himself to losing his brother and begged Shiela any number of times to allow him to help her." She hesitated, then continued softly, "Of course she wouldn't take money from him but I am of the opinion that she had decided to return to England after word came of your grandfather's demise, only she . . . she died before she could carry out her plans. That's why I've taken the liberty of writing to your uncle, my dear. I'm persuaded that Shiela would have done so had she lived."

There was silence for a moment then Henrietta blinked and rose to her feet, shaking out her skirts. "Well, that's all I can tell you, my dear, and I suppose it was time and past that you were made aware of the story, even though," she continued briskly, "there were certain aspects of it which were not at all pleasant."

Susan paused in her stitching, gazing absently at her sister's dark head still bent industriously over her mending. She could only hope that dear Caro wouldn't have to be made aware of her father's history. How very lowering it was, to be sure, to discover that one's parent was a scoundrel.

She set her mending aside and flexed her cramped fingers. Surely it was foolish beyond permission in her to harbor the hope that Sir Peter would invite her to his home, for how could he know that she was not of the same character as her father. And no matter how much she protested to Caro, she mused wistfully, she would have liked above anything the opportunity to travel to England and meet her aunt and uncle.

Susan's reflections, which had at this point become rather dismal, were abruptly interrupted when the door to the parlor was flung open and the youngest of the Phillips children burst into the room.

"You'll never guess!" Robert cried excitedly, the timber of his voice rising from bass to soprano in a manner which normally caused him acute embarrassment.

"Never guess what?" exclaimed Caroline, abandoning her mending and fastening her curious gaze upon her brother. "Come, tell us at once."

Robert, who had received exactly the reaction he had hoped for, strolled casually to the window and leaned his shoulder against the frame. Assuming a great air of nonchalance he stuck his hands in his pockets and gazed out at the garden.

"Come to think of it, you'll most likely not find my news exciting." He hunched a shoulder. "Caro says I could never know anything which would be of the least interest to her."

Susan's blue eyes were alight with amusement as she glanced at her sister, who had risen and was now staring stormily at her brother.

"You're no better than a spoiled little boy, Robert," she cried spitefully, "and I don't want to hear anything you may have to say, so there."

She turned her back on her brother, who had begun to color up at the epithet she had flung at him, then plopped back down on the sofa and poked her fingers in her ears.

A ripple of laughter broke from Susan's lips. "Robert, you're truly infuriating. Just look what you've done."

She went to her sister and, after gently pulling her fingers from her ears, told her kindly not to behave in such a childish manner, that it was exactly what Robert had hoped she would do.

"For you must know," she said, smiling, "he wouldn't tease you so if you didn't give him such satisfaction."

Caro folded her hands in her lap and thrust out her lower lip. "Well, I shall not apologize for calling him a spoiled little boy, for that is what he is, and"—she continued picking up her novel and flicking through the pages, feigning the greatest indifference to her sibling—"I've no wish to hear this news of his, so perhaps he'll have the courtesy to leave."

"This is my house, too, Caro," Robert cried. "Anyway, my news isn't for you, it is for Susan. And she will want to hear it, I promise you."

"Wretch," Susan said. "Now you shall have me calling you a naughty little boy. Tell me at once."

Robert grinned ruefully at his elder sister. "I shall not tease you, Susan. The post has come from Boston and there was a letter in it for Aunt Henry." A mischievous gleam once again entered his eyes. "Can you think who it is from?"

Susan and Caroline exchanged a long look. "It can't be . . ." Caro breathed, her eyes round with wonder as she turned her gaze back to her brother. "Never say it's from Uncle Peter, Robert."

"Oh, isn't it though." Robert laughed as he took

Susan's hands and began to pull her from the room. "Come, goose, Aunt Henry read the letter and sent me to fetch you immediately. You must know what that means."

"Oh, Robert," breathed Susan, gripping his hands tightly. "Do you mean it? You would not tease about such a thing, would you?"

Robert cast his sister a scornful look. "How can you even think such a thing, Susan? But now, you'd better go to my aunt or she'll end up in one of her swoons."

Susan nodded quickly and flitted from the room, her heart hammering so that she felt it would burst. Several moments later she tapped gently upon her aunt's bedroom door and stepped into the room. Henrietta's radiant countenance informed her immediately that she had received the news they had been longing for.

"Dear Susan." She smiled, holding her hand out to her niece. "Your uncle has written at last and his letter contains the most agreeable news imaginable."

Susan sank onto the stool by her aunt's feet. "Do you mean it, ma'am? Am I truly to go to London?"

"Yes, my dear. He says that if you wish . . ." She laughed gaily. "If you wish, he would like you to come immediately. He and dear Lady Sophia are quite anxious that you come for a prolonged visit. He apologizes quite nicely for not having invited you before. He did not wish to force you into dealing with your father's relatives if you found the thought repugnant. Repugnant!" Henrietta repeated with laughing incredulity. "How could he think such a thing?"

"It does show a nice sense of consideration, does it

not, Aunt Henry?"

Henrietta peered at her niece, a smile in her eyes. "Sir Peter's manners are exactly as they should be and I am not afraid that anything you should do would put him to the blush either. You must, however, behave as you have been taught, listen carefully to wiser heads, and try to restrain that abhorrent streak of levity you possess." She hesitated and absently smoothed a wrinkle from her skirt with plump fingers.

"Actually, I am persuaded you shall do quite well, perhaps even be fortunate enough to contract an eligible marriage, but there," she continued briskly, "I shall leave that in Sir Peter's hands."

"Dear Aunt Henry," said Susan with her eyes twinkling, her abhorrent streak of levity making itself known once again, "you cannot mean you are sending me to London for the purpose of accepting the highest bidder for my hand?"

"Now, Susan," exclaimed her aunt sternly, "don't be vulgar. I only hope that you might find someone with whom you could be happy and if he happens to come with a bit of a fortune . . . why, so much the better."

"But Aunt Henry," said Susan, laughing. "I really have no inclination to become anybody's wife."

Henrietta looked truly shocked. "You cannot mean such a thing." She gasped. "Every young lady desires marriage and only think what an advantageous match would do for your brother's and sister's prospects."

Susan clasped her aunt's hand. "Now I see I have upset you and I did not wish to do so, I promise you."

Her eyes twinkled once again. "Shall we say that if a wealthy, titled gentleman were to offer for me, I would not reject his suit without the greatest consideration."

"Now I know you are teasing me, Susan, and I shall not allow you to vex me . . . but your words put me in mind of something . . . what was it?" She rose and began to pace about the room while Susan remained on the footstool, arms clasped about her knees, watching her aunt's preambulations with a fond eye.

"I have it," cried Henrietta, clapping her hands together. "Your uncle has also written to a friend of his who is currently in America, somewhere rather south of us, I believe." She went to her writing table and picked up the letter she had received, hastily perusing it. "Ah, here it is. He is visiting with friends in Virginia and Sir Peter has asked him to visit us before he returns to England and to see to the arrangements for your voyage."

Susan knit her brow. "But how did I put you in mind of him, Aunt Henry?"

"Oh, did I not tell you? T'was all this talk of titles and fortunes."

Susan gazed at her aunt with bewildered eyes. "But Aunt Henry, I still do not understand—"

"He is Lord Carlton, my dear, so naturally when you spoke of a wealthy, titled gentle—"

"Good God," interrupted Susan, collapsing in giggles. "Do not, please dear ma'am, do not say that he is a count. Caro will have the banns read before the poor gentleman arrives."

"Well, I believe he is an earl, actually, Susan," her

aunt replied with a frown, which deepened slightly as she gazed at her niece, who was attempting to choke back her laughter. "Really, my dear, I don't scruple to tell you that I find your behavior sadly lacking. But this is a happy day for us, to be sure. It seems that there is nothing for us to do now but to wait until we hear from Lord Carlton."

Robert and Caroline, when they were put in possession of the facts, were no less excited and thrilled with the news than Susan herself, and for days the three took turns watching at the windows for the friend of their uncle. They discussed the gentleman at some length and could not but wait eagerly for his arrival, convinced as they were of his amiability and good character. Weeks passed, however, without a single line from Lord Carlton, and when two months had gone by, the Phillips began to reverse their good opinion of their uncle's friend, thinking they could have little respect for a man who held his obligations so lightly.

Chapter 2

Lord Carlton did in fact take his obligations quite seriously and it was through no fault of his that he had been kept from discharging the favor Sir Peter had requested. He, like Miss Ashly, had received a letter from Sir Peter in January and that it was now early March and he was still kicking his heels in Virginia instead of concluding his business in the north did not improve a temper already sorely tried.

The fact of the matter was that he had been deathly ill for more than a fortnight from a fever he had first contracted in the Penninsular Campaign and which recurred from time to time with some severity. Recuperation was proving slow and although his host and hostess, dear friends with whom he had spent the last several months, did their utmost to make his recovery easant and painless as possible, he was not a ient.

 d have been content, for Meadowview, the

estate owned by Thomas Waite and his wife, Honor, was the perfect spot in which to recuperate. It was composed of acre upon acre of prime farmland, timbered forests, and rolling meadows. The house itself was a two-story structure, architecturally based upon the classic Greek style of design. Lord Carlton had looked upon it with delight, admiring its simplicity and grace. Even now he found he never tired of the plantation.

When Thomas Waite had sold out of the 3rd Dragoons and had made known his intention to buy property in America and settle there, his comrade had raised a dubious brow. But he had persevered, and Lord Carlton, lying as he was in a four-poster bed located in a sunny chamber at the front of the gracious house, could not but think that Thomas had made a very good life for himself.

The plantation was a full-time business, taking skill and intelligence to operate, but the life was good, gracious, and satisfying. Thomas, who had been something of a rake in his day, displayed none of the boredom and restlessness which had caused his friend such concern and which had often led him into trouble.

"Should get yourself a piece of land here, Carlton," Thomas had murmured one afternoon when the two men rested their horses on the crest of a hill overlooking forest and meadow. "Room to stretch out, you know, and the people ain't half bad. Not up to London standards, to be sure, but good people all the same."

Lord Carlton glanced at his friend then turned his

eyes back to the vista spread in front of him. "I do mean to invest in one or two pieces of land, Thomas, but I must return to London. I'm to be married the end of May, you know."

"What?" ejaculated Mr. Waite, turning in his saddle to stare at his companion. "What sort of bobbery is this? I thought we were old friends, comrades-in-arms, that sort of thing, and here you are, living under my roof for over a month, and just now getting around to telling me that you're about to get leg-shackled."

Lord Carlton looked at his friend, amusement springing to his eyes, "I didn't realize that my announcement would stir such interest."

"That's doing it rather too brown, Carlton," Thomas said, frowning at the tall man beside him. "You might as well tell me the whole. Who's the girl?"

"Elizabeth Wainwright," Carlton replied, picking up his reins and touching his mount with his heel.

"Elizabeth Wainwright?" Thomas repeated faintly as he stared at Lord Carlton's broad-shouldered back.

"Close your mouth, Thomas, and come along." The earl grinned, glancing back.

"You can't mean it, Carlton," stammered Thomas passionately as he, too, urged his horse forward. "Tell me it ain't true. Why, good God, man, you could have your pick of the season's beauties. Mamas are ever willing to parade their daughters out for you . . . could wed any one of them." He shook his head elief. "Elizabeth Wainwright!"

rlton laughed at his friend's consternation.

"Come, Waite, she isn't as bad as all that, I assure you. She's beautiful, well-born, intelligent, and she has a graceful way about her which I find pleasing."

"Stuff!" snapped Thomas. "It's common knowledge the old duke's all to pieces. Elizabeth's his last hope but neither one of them ever found a man wealthy enough for their taste. Everyone's steered clear of that match; besides, she's a cold, calculating sort of female and that's the truth with no bark on it."

"Perhaps she is," Carlton agreed amiably as the horses walked on, "but then, this is no love match. I know very well what I'm getting in to, as does Miss Wainwright. It's my duty to marry. I've realized that for the last several years. Not so much to ensure my comfort and happiness as to ensure the succession of the line."

"Be more comfortable to marry for affection as well."

Lord Carlton raised a brow. "Trying to tell me my business, Thomas?" he inquired gently.

"Good God, no," exclaimed Thomas, putting his mount into a trot. "I can see it would do no good, but you can wager any amount you like that Honor will try to dissuade you."

And indeed, thought Lord Carlton, as he lay in the sun-drenched room, attempting to ignore the nagging headache and aching limbs which persisted to afflict him though the fever had gone, Honor had had much to say upon the matter. Of course, Thomas, eager to enlist her aid in talking him out of the match, had presented his announcement in the worst way possible, exclaiming as he walked into the house that she would never guess what infamous news their guest had just imparted to him. Honor had gazed curiously at Lord Carlton as he laid his whip and hat inside.

"Now what could you have possibly done to put Thomas in such a state?" she asked in her low musical voice.

"Nothing of moment, my dear," replied Carlton calmly. "Merely informed him that I'm to be married soon, but now, I'm certain you can't like us standing about in all our dirt so perhaps," he continued, casting a meaningful look at his host, "Thomas and I should dress for dinner."

Honor, who had made her come-out some years ago and had witnessed the manner in which the young ladies had flocked about her handsome friend, was well aware of the magnitude of Lord Carlton's disclosure and heard the news with rounded eyes.

"My dear friend," she cried, going to him and taking his hand in hers. "Let me wish you happy, but how is it that you have only now apprised us of this news?"

"Well you should ask him, Honor," Thomas grumbled as he, too, laid down his hat and whip upon the table.

Honor looked from her husband back to Lord Carlton. "I don't understand."

Lord Carlton raised her hand to his lips in a gentle salute. "I thank you for felicitating me, Honor, it is more than your cockle-brained husband has done." He released her hand and started for the staircase. "I shall tell you all you wish to hear momentarily, but as

I have no desire to do so in the hallway, I will beg your pardon and go to my room to dress for dinner."

There was a hint of implacability in Lord Carlton's tone and Honor let him go although her curiosity was so aroused that she would not have allowed her husband the same escape had he wished for it.

To her relief, Thomas followed her quite willingly into the small drawing room which opened off the wide entrance hall, and stood by the fireplace, a grim look upon his face.

"Well?" questioned Honor, raising one delicately arched brow in the direction of the scowling man.

"Please, be seated, my dear," he said, waiting until she had done so to tell her his news. When she was comfortable, he began pacing then stopped and stood before her.

"I know you'll not credit it but Carlton has offered for Elizabeth Wainwright."

Honor wrinkled her brow, casting back in her memory to put a face and reputation with the name her husband mentioned. Thomas watched as recognition dawned upon her face.

"Oh no, Thomas," she gasped, one hand going to her throat, "not her."

"My thoughts, exactly," Thomas said angrily as he turned and walked to the fireplace once again, leaning one shoulder against the mantelpiece. "Do you know what Carlton had to say to me? Said she was well born, intelligent, and graceful. As if that's all there is to look for in marriage."

This last was uttered with such spurious disgust that Honor could not help smiling a little. "Indeed?"

She murmured, watching her husband affectionately.

Thomas paused and a smile touched his lips only to disappear as quickly, as he kicked at a log which had threatened to fall out of the fire. "But that is not to the point here. What we must somehow do is persuade Carlton against this marriage. I know that woman and she may now affect to be a pattern card of propriety but she ain't, let me tell you."

"I never quite liked Miss Wainwright but I don't know that she is as terrible as you color her, Thomas."

"Well, she is," her husband responded simply. "You could not have been expected to know of many of her escapades but you may take my word for it, she's a cold creature with a stone where her heart should be." He bowed his head and gazed into the flames. "Carlton would kill her if she brought scandal upon his name and then there would be a pretty mess."

Honor rather doubted that the earl would ever involve himself in anything so vulgar as murdering his wife but she was increasingly curious to discover why her husband thought so little of the lady in question, and indeed, before too many moments had passed, she begged him to explain to her exactly why he held Miss Wainwright in such aversion.

"It was my brother's doing," replied Thomas after a short silence.

"James?"

"No," he answered, grinning ruefully. "One might think so, I'll grant you, for he's wild to a fault, but it was Harry."

"Harry?" exclaimed Honor, taken aback. "But he's

no more than a child . . . and bookish besides."

"Well, he's three and twenty now, Honor, and this happened only three years ago." Thomas sighed. "He never was much in the petticoat line but he met Miss Wainwright when he was down from school, stayed at her father's place in the Cotswolds, her brother invited him. Anyway, to make a long story short, he was dazzled by her and, nodcock that he was, attempted to make her believe that he was wealthy as Golden Ball, or would be as soon as he came into my uncle's estate. A nabob, you know."

"Oh, Thomas, he didn't," gasped Honor, much struck by the inventiveness exhibited by her younger brother-in-law, for as far as she was aware, all her husband's uncles were quite comfortable but nothing more.

"Well, he tried but as it turned out she was too canny to believe such far-a-diddle although she let on to him that she did." Thomas cast his wife a look of disgust. "Harry has more hair than wit when he takes his nose out of those books of his. Could never understand what he saw in her. The girl's a beauty right enough but she's got no warmth, and by God, she was five years older than the lad."

"What happened?" queried Honor, anxious to put her husband back onto the main track of his story.

"She talked him into running off to Gretna."

"Oh, Thomas, no," whispered Honor, quite horror-struck by the disclosure that the daughter of a duke could behave with such impropriety. If the story had ever got out, she must be sunk beneath reproach.

"Oh, she wasn't really going to elope," said

Thomas impatiently. "Just let on to the fool boy that she would. She made all the plans; you know, chaise and four, baggage, time and place they were to meet, and he carried them out meek as you like, too lovestruck to question anything. When the time came, he drove to meet her and she was waiting for him with almost the entire houseparty assembled to witness the joke." Thomas frowned angrily. "Even now I shudder to think how Harry must have felt for they all had a good laugh and the incident was the on dit for weeks."

Honor's brow was knit. "Now that I think for a moment, I do recall some sort of incident which gave my mama such a disgust of Miss Wainwright, but then," she continued with a frown, "it seemed that hardly a week went by when she was in town that her name was not being mentioned."

"Just so." Thomas nodded. "Anyway, the long and the short of Harry's affair was that he was cured of her quicker than the cat can lick her ear and went back to his studies but the damage was done. It took him a long time before he could hold his head up and you can imagine how the mama of any young lady he fancied might receive him." Thomas kicked angrily at the fire once again. "Elizabeth Wainwright's a bad woman and make no mistake about that."

Honor watched the shower of sparks. "I believe you must tell Charles the whole, Thomas."

"Oh, I'm certain he knows of it . . . or did, perhaps he's forgotten, but I'm not going to rake up that sad story again. Pretty figure I'd make. Carlton wouldn't thank me either, I can tell you. Probably just say she was high-spirited." He walked to the door and paused, his hand on the knob. "He'll marry her all right and tight but I wish to God something would happen so he didn't."

Thomas went away to change out of his riding clothes, leaving his wife thinking a number of unladylike thoughts about Miss Wainwright.

Lord Carlton did in fact recall the incident involving his friend's brother, and while he had felt a deal of disgust at the behavior displayed by his betrothed and could not like the resulting notoriety, her escapades had occurred in the past and he did not feel them to be of sufficient import as to cause him to cry off. Indeed, he had given quite a bit of consideration to Miss Wainwright's character and was of the opinion that while she might be spoiled and selfish she was also poised, graceful, accomplished, and of impeccable breeding. And he was determined to curb her wildness so as to be certain she would comport herself with a dignity due his station.

Lord Carlton had never truly been in love although he had, as a very young man, once thought himself so but after that painful episode he had given up any romantic expectations. In his youth he had at one point turned from his studies and sporting pursuits and entered into society with the intention of finding his true love. He had, from the first, attracted a deal of feminine admiration for, in addition to possessing a considerable fortune, his looks were more than pleasing and he carried himself with the lithe grace of an athlete. His gray eyes, heavily fringed with black lashes, proved a startling contrast to his bronzed skin, and his crisply curling dark hair fell boyishly across his forehead in a manner which tempted even the most circumspect of young ladies to brush it back. No fault could be found in his figure either; he was taller than average, several inches above six feet, with broad shoulders which were the delight of his valet for his jackets never required the padding needed by other gentlemen.

In those days he had had easy, frank manners and smiling eyes but in later years while the smile which crossed his face was still charming it could also, at times, become quite cynical, and only with close friends did he ever wear the open, candid look of his youth.

Indeed, as a youth he had not been long in society before he had reached the conclusion that most of the young women of his acquaintance were either insipid or stupid or both and *that* he could not tolerate. His final disillusionment with women occurred when he became thoroughly infatuated with a lady who was betrothed to another. He was totally bewitched by the little golden-haired beauty and the thought that she was soon to marry a wealthy gentleman, old enough to be her father, was not to be borne. She swore in the most pitious way imaginable that she could never care for the gentleman, for her affections had been given totally to her younger lover so it was to be expected that Lord Carlton would make any attempt to save her from such an unwelcome marriage. To this end the couple planned an elopement and for the days preceding the event Carlton had walked about in a haze of love. That he acted out of instincts most chivalrous did not help him in the eyes of society for when the two were apprehended his reputation was quite wrecked. This he might have borne with fortitude had not the damsel he loved, and who had vowed undying love on her part, crushed all his illusions by becoming hysterical when they had begun their journey to the border, sobbing that she was quite terrified and could no longer love a gentleman who so frightened her.

She had been speedily wed to the older gentleman and packed off to the country but Carlton's pride would not allow him to shab off and he had remained in London, shunned by society.

One friend, Sir Peter Phillips, had stood by him, risking the wrath of friend and family alike, and had finally persuaded him into buying his colors, an act which, as Sir Peter logically explained, would see him out of the country until all scandal had quieted and at the same time give him something to occupy his mind.

The scandal had died a quite natural death but Lord Carlton was never again the same carefree, innocent youth who had so idealistically ridden out to save his lady love. Although still warm and open with his comrades in arms, he became quite cynical where the fair sex was concerned and so he now felt that he was making the best match possible, one where both parties were making an unemotional decision.

The simple truth, mused Lord Carlton as he reached from his bed for a book lying upon the table next to it, was that people, like Thomas and Honor, were too susceptible to romantic notions. He felt that he and Elizabeth would deal quite well together. A grim smile touched his lips as he opened the volume, a discourse on farming techniques practiced in America.

Several days later, Lord Carlton felt well enough to join the Waites for dinner and, although he was a trifle shaky, made known his intention to travel the following week. Both Honor and Thomas were appalled at the idea and they attempted to dissuade him, feeling he risked a relapse. When Honor commented that it seemed a foolish chance to take, Lord Carlton replied that he could never let Peter down. She rounded on him, however, exclaiming that he was being foolish beyond permission and that Sir Peter would never have requested such an undertaking had he been aware of the state of his friend's health.

"Seems to me Honor's right, Carlton," Thomas added thoughtfully, pinching his upper lip between thumb and forefinger. "Surely if Sir Peter was here he would tell you himself to send an envoy."

Lord Carlton faced his friend, his mouth tightening a little at the corners. "I daresay he would, Thomas, but the fact remains that he's not here but in London resting quite comfortably in the knowledge that I am carrying out his wishes. You must know from our campaigns together," he continued, with a twinkle in his eyes, "that nothing you can say will stop me so you might just as well save your breath."

Thomas groaned and shook his head despairingly. "How well I do know. No," he said to his wife, who had been about to speak, "it will do no good to tease him. Once he makes up his mind to a thing, there's nothing to be done to turn him from his purpose even if he may be brought home on a hurdle in the process."

Lord Carlton's charming smile flashed. "Doing it rather too brown, Thomas. You'll have Honor thinking any manner of dire thoughts. Believe me, my dear," he said, walking over to her and taking her hand in his, "I run no risk of returning to you in such a manner. Do bear in mind," he continued lightly, "I came through the Penninsular Campaigne without so much as a scratch."

"Yes," said Thomas bluntly, "but no thanks to you for you had more harebrained schemes up your sleeve than any manjack of the company. Not that they wasn't successful," he continued judiciously, "but harebrained all the same. And," he ended triumphantly, "you were one step away from death's doorstep when you had the fever then, too."

"Thomas," said Carlton firmly, "this is not the Penninsula and I have my man to see to my comfort." He turned back to Honor and pressed her hand. "Elliott has been with me forever and he is worse than any nurse would be. Also I shall be stopping in Boston with the Wentworths. I know you have not met them so you will have to take my word that they are very good people and will not allow me to fall ill."

Honor gazed into Lord Carlton's clear gray eyes and answered his irresistible smile with a gurgle of laughter. "Well, I can see you think you have quite bamboozled me but you are wrong, sir."

She withdrew her hand and sat down once again, her attitude all one of determination while Carlton watched with amusement. "Do not laugh at me, Charles," she said with mock severity. "I realize that I cannot hold you if you feel you must go off but at least you shall travel in the comfort of our carriage . . . and by easy stages."

She attempted to pull the corners of her mouth down in a frown but the effect was ruined by the wide grin she perceived on the face of the man towering over her.

"You win, Honor," Carlton said with a laugh. "To tell the truth, I am still a little out of curl and shall not look askance at the offer of your carriage."

That he had given in to Honor's demand with so good a grace could not but cause the Waites even more anxiety on his behalf but there was no more to be said and they had to accept the fact that their guest would be departing the following week.

That day arrived, and when the carriage was brought round, Honor, who had quite often observed both fatigue and pain in Lord Carlton's eyes, insisted that he not drive himself. In this she found she had an ally in Elliott, the earl's batman turned valet. Under his bullying Carlton climbed laughingly into the carriage.

"I surrender." He grinned. "And I promise that I shall not take up the ribbons when we are quit of Meadowview."

Honor, with an air of serene complacency, calmly replied that she had no qualms on that head. "For I believe that Elliott will take better care of you than even I could wish."

"Wretch." Carlton laughed as Elliott grinned and

touched his hat in the lady's direction.

"You may depend on me, madam," he said confidently. "I've been taking care of this fine gentleman since he was in short-coats."

"Elliott," said Carlton good-naturedly, "you positively unman me. Now, drive on before you embarrass me any further."

Elliott gathered up the ribbons, and after one last farewell, the carriage rolled down the long drive.

Elliott spent the next days taking such conscientious care of his master that Lord Carlton was hard-pressed upon many occasions to hold his tongue. But as the travelers neared their destination, it seemed that all his grumblings and dire predictions of relapse were to be fulfilled, for as they reached the outskirts of Boston, Lord Carlton was once again feverish.

"This is a fine fix," muttered Elliott to himself when he had stopped the carriage for the fourth time in an hour to check upon its occupant. "I suppose the only thing for it is to continue to Mr. Wentworth's home," he continued, opening the door of the carriage, "just like you planned."

"Heaven forbid," Carlton said sharply, wincing as the sunlight fell across his eyes. "I can imagine nothing more disgusting than to have a sick friend delivered upon one's doorstep. You may take me to the Albatross." He closed his eyes and slumping into the corner of the carriage. "And shut that damn door."

"But my lord," protested Elliott indignantly, "you need care and nursing of the best sort. Not what you'll find in a common inn, I'm sure."

"Elliott," said Carlton wearily, not opening his eyes, "I shall not impose upon my friends in such a rag-mannered fashion. Now, shut that door and drive on."

Elliott had little recourse but to obey. When the inn (a quite unexceptionable establishment) had been reached, he jealously ushered Lord Carlton in and belligerently ordered the best chamber to be made ready immediately.

"Go easy, friend," murmured Carlton as he freed his arm from his valet's grasp. "That's just the sort of action which would set anyone's hackles up."

He approached the landlord, a good-natured-looking person who seemed more inclined to smile upon Elliott's demands than to take umbrage.

"Ain't no need to apologize, my lord," he said with a smile. "Any noddy could see that your man's that worried over you, and if you don't mind my saying so, looks to me like bed's the best place for you so I'll take you right on up. Sheets and all changed not five minutes ago," he called over his shoulder to Elliott as he started up the staircase, "so there's no need to be sniffing around for damp although I doubt you'll take my word for it."

He reached the chamber and opened the door, standing aside for Lord Carlton to precede him. The room, which was a large and airy apartment with sturdy furniture and a comfortable bed pushed into one corner, met with Carlton's approval and he smiled faintly at the beaming landlord. "This will do quite nicely, and now," he continued, beginning to feel somewhat light-headed, "if you will excuse me, I shall make use of that bed as you suggested."

The landlord eyed him nervously. "Would you like me to send for the doctor?"

"Not at all," murmured Carlton, "my man shall see to me."

The landlord nodded and departed, and Elliott had his master resting comfortably between warm sheets not ten minutes later.

"One thing more, Elliott," Carlton said as he attempted to relax, for from past experience he knew it better to let the pain in his limbs and head wash over him instead of fighting it. "Take a note to Mr. Wentworth advising him of my presence in Boston. I shall call upon him in a day or two."

The valet shook his head in concern over his master's condition and did as he was bade.

Chapter 3

The following day brought no improvement in Lord Carlton's condition but it did, before the morning was far advanced, bring Mr. Wentworth hastening up the staircase of the Albatross. He tapped lightly upon the door and, after being admitted by the valet, drew a chair up to the bed and seated himself.

Mr. Wentworth was an amiable gentleman with rather bluff manners and an abrupt way of speaking which, however, did not hide the compassion and goodwill with which he viewed his fellow man. Lord Carlton had known the gentleman all his life as Mr. Wentworth and Lord Carlton's father had been firm friends since they had gone to Oxford together. After his parent's demise, Carlton had continued the friendship, for he could not help but feel a good deal of affection for the man.

Mr. Wentworth had returned this affection; indeed, he admired and respected his old friend's son so much so that he had fostered the hope that his daughter Alicia might someday made a match with Carlton.

But after numerous visits, even he could see that they regarded each other almost as brother and sister and he had reluctantly put the dream out of his head. After this, Carlton's visits had become even more comfortable, and Mr. Wentworth now felt quite justifiably angry with his friend for not coming immediately to his home.

Mr. Wentworth studied the flushed face of the sleeping man then reached out a hand to touch his forehead. It was burning hot. He turned quickly to the landlady hovering nearby.

"Send for Dr. Brooke at once," he commanded curtly. "Tell him that Mr. Wentworth requires his presence immediately."

The landlady, who had not half liked the responsibility of caring for so ill a gentleman and such an important one at that, hurried from the chamber, thankful to have such a responsibility lifted from her shoulders.

At that moment, Lord Carlton opened his eyes and weakly clasped Mr. Wentworth's hand.

"My good friend," he murmured, attempting a shaky smile. "Infamous of me to be so sadly out of curl but I promise you I shall be better directly. This fever's no stranger to me. I know from experience that the worst of it is of only a few days' duration."

"Hush," Mr. Wentworth responded brusquely, "I'm sadly disappointed in you, Charles, but I shan't be so ramshackle as to comb your hair when you're flat on your back."

"How kind in you, Henry," Carlton murmured faintly, looking amused.

"Well, and much good it will do me when Alicia

gets wind of this," he retorted gruffly, referring to his daughter, who had been watching eagerly for her friend's arrival. He tenderly rearranged the pillows beneath Lord Carlton's head. "You mark my words, that naughty puss will be here quicker than the cat can lick her ear."

"Dear God." Carlton laughed weakly, closing his eyes and drifting back into troubled sleep.

Mr. Wentworth had hoped to move Lord Carlton to his home but he soon saw that that was out of the question while the earl continued so ill, and actually, as Dr. Brooke had brought his own nurse to the Albatross, it was quite unnecessary to do so. Happily in only a few days' time Carlton's health appeared to be somewhat improved, much to the relief of the Wentworths and Elliott, although he was still bound to his bed. The delay his illness had caused chaffed at Lord Carlton and he was becoming slightly alarmed, for if he did not soon set sail for London, he would be late for his own wedding, and he held out little hope that his betrothed could forgive such behavior.

In view of this, he had elected to attempt the journey in three days' time although Elliott grumbled incessantly that he would suffer another relapse sure as anything if he did so.

"I guess I don't need to stand on points with you, my lord, seeing as I've known you as long as I have, so I'll tell you straight out that if you get on that ship without being properly recovered, you'll end up cocking up your toes and Miss Wainwright will like that a deal less than if you was to be late."

Carlton raised a brow. "Perhaps, but I am determined." He raised a hand when his valet made as if to interrupt. "I'm not a clunch, however, Elliott, and I assure you that if, in three days, I'm not feeling more the thing, I will delay a bit longer."

He clasped his hands under his head and gazed pensively at the ceiling. "I still have this business of Peter's to complete but I doubt I'll be riding thirty miles into the countryside very soon."

His gaze shifted once more to his valet. "Perhaps you had better find a solicitor after all, Elliott," he said with resignation. "I cannot like having a hirling take care of business entrusted to me but there's no help for it now. When you have found someone competent, send him to see me. And Elliott . . ."

The valet, who had been about to leave the room, turned and looked inquiringly at his employer.

"I should like to see him no later than ten o'clock tomorrow morning."

Elliott nodded although he was not at all certain if he would have any success in locating a solicitor on such short notice. Happily, he was able to return at a later hour with the pronouncement that he had, by the greatest good fortune, found a man who would be able to act for the earl.

The following morning at a little past ten, Elliott ushered the gentleman in question into Lord Carlton's bedchamber and introduced him as Mr. Simmons.

"You must forgive me for greeting you like this, Mr. Simmons," said Carlton, motioning the man to take a seat near the door. His gray eyes narrowed as he subjected the gentleman to a quick, hard scrutiny.

Mr. Simmons was a young man, whose slight frame was garbed in a tightly fitting coat of vivid green cloth with large silver buttons. Buckram padding did little to disguise his drooping shoulders nor did his thin legs show to advantage in the overly snug breeches he wore. He had scanty hair covering a prematurely balding pate. He had an unhealthy complexion and a habit of licking his lips and fiddling with a crumpled handkerchief, patting his lips with it now and again. He was, in short, the sort of toadeating individual Lord Carlton preferred to avoid when at all possible.

Carlton raised a brow at his valet and motioned him to the bed. "What is this, Elliott?" he inquired in a muted tone.

"I know he's not quite the thing, my lord," whispered Elliott anxiously. "But he's the landlady's nephew and the good woman was very wishful that you employ him."

"Not much business comes in his way, I gather," Carlton remarked dryly. "But how," he continued, regarding his valet steadily, "could you suppose that I should wish to employ such a person?"

Elliott cleared his throat. "I did try to find another solicitor, my lord, but none of the decent ones was available for several days and the landlady assured me that her nephew could do the job for you at a moment's notice. To tell the truth," he continued in his own defense, "I did not make Mr. Simmons's acquaintance yesterday as he could not be located but the landlady is a very good sort of person so I trusted her judgment."

Carlton glanced at the gentleman lounging carelessly in his chair. "Obviously she is a doting aunt."

"Well," retorted the valet, rather miffed, "I offered

my services, if you'll recall."

"My apologies, Elliott," Carlton replied, amusement entering his eyes. "I'd liefer send you now that I've seen Mr. Simmons but I suppose, since he's here, I'll have to have him or risk incurring our landlady's wrath and that," he continued with a rueful twinkle, "is not a thing one in my position should consider lightly."

He nodded dismissal to the valet and, after the door had been gently closed, turned his penetrating gaze back upon Mr. Simmons.

"You'll forgive me," he drawled, watching the man closely, "a small matter which I found necessary to clear up with my valet before I could begin this interview." He frowned thoughtfully at the man, causing him to squirm uncomfortably upon his chair and finally change his careless attitude for one of more respect.

"So, you are Mrs. Goode's nephew, Mr. Simmons?"

"Yes, my lord"—the man smirked unctuously—"but I take care not to tell my acquaintances, I can tell you. Pair of dirty dishes if ever I saw any."

"Are they?" queried Carlton coolly. "Well, your opinion of your relations is of no concern of mine but I find them to be unexceptionable and the fact that I am employing you at all is due solely to the intervention of your aunt on your behalf. I do not scruple to tell you that I do not care for you. The sooner our business arrangement is at an end, the better I shall like it."

"No need to get on your high ropes, I'm sure," Mr. Simmons retorted sullenly. "This is America and you're no better than me over here for all you're a lord."

A long pause followed Mr. Simmons's words, during which time Lord Carlton did not remove his hard gaze from the man's face. When he finally spoke, there was a hint of steel in his tones and his mouth had hardened.

"Let's get one thing straight, Mr. Simmons," he said curtly, "I'm employing you against my better judgment, and while your mission will tax neither your intelligence nor your strength, it will require a certain amount of tact and honesty and," he continued, the threat contained in his cold tone quite plain to the solicitor, who sat dabbing furiously at his wet lips, "if I were to discover that you had played me false, I should not hesitate to show you the full extent of my displeasure." He watched as the man crumpled his handkerchief and stuffed it into his pocket. "Have I made myself quite clear?"

Mr. Simmons, who was not a brave man, mumbled that he had and Lord Carlton indicated a packet and letter atop his dresser. "You are to take those documents to a Miss Phillips. Her direction is on the letter. Both are sealed and are to remain that way until you have put them in the hand of Miss Phillips. Express to her my sincere apologies for my inability to visit her personally and my hope that we shall meet in London upon the completion of her voyage. Have you got all that?"

Mr. Simmons, who had gathered the documents in his hand, nodded. Lord Carlton wearily closed his eyes. "That is all then but be certain you return here directly you are done."

"Yes, my lord," Simmons said, stepping closer to the door. "I shall undertake this task first thing in the morning."

Carlton sighed but did not open his eyes. "You misunderstand, Mr. Simmons," he said silkily. "You are to complete this errand immediately."

"But my lord," the man whined, "if I were to start now, I would not return to Boston until late, and there's no saying but what I wouldn't miss my dinner and I had plans of my own for this evening."

"Spare me these protestations, Mr. Simmons, and simply do as you have been told. I shall expect to see you again late this evening. Now go."

The solicitor muttered a word or two under his breath and slid out the door, his fine feathers ruffled and his temper hot, and he was quite determined to exact some sort of payment for the earl's high-handed treatment.

It was nearing six o'clock when he reached the Phillips's residence and the long ride had had somewhat of a calming effect upon his temper although a crafty look could now be discerned in his beady eyes. Indeed, he was quite determined to stick a spoke in his lordship's wheel.

He was shown into the parlor, and before many minutes had passed, Miss Phillips and Miss Ashly joined him. He rose immediately to his feet and introduced himself then apologized for calling upon them so late.

"My employer is not one to balk at inconveniencing others but I can tell you that I do not like having to complete my business when I can quite easily see that you are about to dine. But there," he continued in a pompous manner, seating himself when the ladies had made themselves comfortable, "let me tell you that I am come from Lord Carlton. He is currently residing in Boston but finds himself too busy to call upon you and so has requested my poor services."

Susan lifted her brows at her aunt, who was frowning deeply, then turned her blue gaze back upon the solicitor. "I am certain your ride from Boston was tedious, Mr. Simmons, and I appreciate your having agreed to do it for I can tell you that we were all becoming a little anxious when we had received no word from Lord Carlton. But now, surely you would like a bit of refreshment . . . some sherry, perhaps?"

Mr. Simmons thanked her and observed that he could indeed do with a glass of wine to settle the dust in his throat. Mary brought the decanter in, and after Susan had poured a glass for him, she resumed her seat.

"I hope that Lord Carlton has not met with an accident or has, perhaps, been ill?"

"No such thing, Miss Phillips," Simmons responded without blinking. "Indeed," he continued self-importantly, "I have come to the conclusion, after an admittedly short time spent in his presence, that he is an extremely unamiable and arrogant man."

Susan stared at the solicitor, her brow knit. "I do not know Lord Carlton so I cannot remark upon his character but he is a friend of my uncle and I should dislike thinking that *his* judgment is not keen."

Mr. Simmons pulled his handkerchief from his pocket and dabbed at his moist lips. "No, no," he said when he had finished, "you misunderstand. I doubt that Carlton would treat such friends as he has in such a rag-mannered fashion but a stranger must be another matter."

Aunt Henrietta, who had, upon Mr. Simmons's addressing her niece, picked up a length of fringe and begun to knot it, now let it fall to her lap.

"I do not understand any of this," she complained with a bewildered air. "Lord Carlton cannot be the sort of person to behave in so uncivil a fashion. Could it not be that he had forgotten this errand and when he remembered it could not make the time to execute it himself? Such an important person . . . so very busy . . ." Her voice trailed off as she once again resumed knotting the fringe. "I must say, however," she concluded faintly, "that I would have liked meeting him, and I know dear Caroline and Robert were so looking forward to it . . ."

Mr. Simmons stared at her, amazement writ on his face. "How can you think that he forgot, ma'am? That would be far worse, I assure you. To hold the trust of a friend so lightly; but then, who's to say, he is altogether so high-handed and egotistical that it would not surprise me."

Susan could not like discussing the character of a man she had never met with one who until moments ago had also been unknown to her, so she turned the discussion to the business at hand. Although such an account of the man her family had been so anxiously awaiting could hardly make her feel complacent, she was too discerning to credit completely the opinions of the solicitor. She had not been favorably impressed by his appearance and could not respect any gentleman who spoke so shabbily of his employer. Thus, she put the matter of Lord Carlton's character from her mind, resolving not to judge him too harshly until she had made his acquaintance.

The solicitor was by this time feeling that he had acquitted himself rather well and that his employer's reputation was completely besmirched in the eyes of the ladies of the Phillips household, though he had to admit Miss Phillips's level blue gaze made him acutely uncomfortable. He concluded his business quickly as both Miss Phillips and her aunt seemed to be less than friendly, and with little further ado mounted his horse once again and made for Boston.

The fact that the ladies, and even the maid when she had shown him the door following the interview, had barely contained their aversion made him wish them all, and in particular Miss Phillips, whose unwavering gaze made him feel as though he had crept from under a rock, to the devil.

The Phillips chit was insolent and too top-lofty by half, he fumed as he jogged along the hard-packed lane which served as a road. One might almost suspect she held herself above him — and she, he sneered, recalling with no little disdain, the shabby gown she had worn, so obviously merely a poor relation. The sly gleam reappeared in his eyes. Miss high and mighty Phillips would have her comeuppance same as Lord Carlton had. Oh, yes, Simmons thought as he put his heels to his mount, he would see to that.

Henrietta, in the meantime, had waited only until the door had closed behind Mr. Simmons before remarking that she had never met such a vulgar little man.

"I could not like him, Susan," she continued indignantly, "no matter how amiable he might like to seem. To talk so of Lord Carlton, why . . . I hardly know what to think on that head."

Susan nodded. "I'm happy to see we shared the same opinion of Mr. Simmons for he seemed quite oily to me. A completely ill-bred sort of person, not at all the kind one would expect a man of Lord Carlton's stature to employ."

"Indeed not," Henrietta said as she put her fringe aside and rose from her chair, shaking out her skirts, "but I think we must afford Lord Carlton the benefit of the doubt in this case, my dear, particularly as he is so good a friend of your uncle. He must have had a good reason for hiring the man."

"Well," Susan replied, "it was not on account of the man's loyalty."

Henrietta smiled and the two ladies adjourned to the dining parlor, Lord Carlton erased from their minds as they began to discuss the preparations for Susan's voyage.

Mr. Simmons returned directly to the Albatross, arriving late but still determined to set his little plot against Miss Phillips in motion. He had decided that what was sauce for the goose was sauce for the gander and could hardly wait to tell Lord Carlton exactly the sort of person he had seen in Miss Phillips.

He threw open the door to the Albatross in the best of spirits and ran up the stairs then rapped stridently upon Lord Carlton's door, but he was so wrought up that he entered the chamber before he had been so bid. Lord Carlton observed him from his bed, his gray eyes the color of gunmetal beneath slightly raised brows.

"If you should ever again chance to beg entry to my chamber, Mr. Simmons," advised Carlton, "I would recommend that you wait for permission to do so before you open the door."

Simmons halted in his tracks, a fleeting look of fear crossing his thin face, but the thought of his scheme gave him a false sort of courage.

"I didn't come here to be threatened," he sneered, curling his lip, and tossing his hat on his employer's dresser.

"Go easy, Simmons," warned Carlton softly. "I find my patience rather shorter than normal." He paused and the expression in his eyes made Mr. Simmons feel somewhat less brave.

After a long moment Lord Carlton motioned to the chair the solicitor had occupied previously and told him to be seated. Simmons did as he was ordered, watching his employer uneasily all the while.

"I've delivered the letters, unopened, I might add, my lord, and now I would like my money."

"A moment, Simmons," Lord Carlton said coolly. "You cannot wish for an end to this any more than I but I desire to know a few of the particulars. Did you see Miss Phillips personally and hand the documents to her?"

"I did," the solicitor said slyly, "and I only wish I had met your friend's . . . ah . . . niece sooner, for a lovelier girl you'd be hard-pressed to find . . . and not at all uppity. Why she was as friendly as my sister Lizzie. Not that I'd ever think of her as a sister." He winked crudely and lounged back in his chair. "I would imagine the young bucks are going to miss her

. . . if you know what I mean."

Lord Carlton had attended this speech with narrowed eyes, a fact which had not escaped the notice of the solicitor, who now felt that it was perhaps time he took himself away.

"If I could but have my fee, my lord, I will leave you to your thoughts," he concluded hastily.

Lord Carlton reached for a purse on the table beside his bed. "I can see that I have not misjudged you, Mr. Simmons. You are vulgar and ill-bred and I doubt very much that you know the word 'honor'. Therefore, I must be more blunt in what I have to say to you." His tone struck a chill in Mr. Simmons' veins. "As you are aware, Miss Phillips is the niece of a dear friend of mine. Therefore, I shall tell you that I will regard any slur upon her character to be a personal affront . . . regardless of its veracity." He paused, keeping his long steady gaze upon his nervous guest then continued softly. "Have I made myself clear, Mr. Simmons?"

The solicitor had become quite pale. He nodded quickly.

"Good," said Lord Carlton with satisfaction. "Then here is your purse and let us hope that we shall not have occasion to converse again."

Simmons took the purse from Lord Carlton's hand and, without stopping to count his money, made good his escape.

After the solicitor had departed, Carlton lay back upon his pillows, deeply troubled by what he had heard. His dark brows drew together. Was it possible that Miss Phillips was no better than a trollop and a jade? Could he allow her to go to Peter? Even as he considered ordering her not to go to England, he realized that he had not the authority to do so. Peter was her uncle and he wished her company. Carlton groaned and called for Elliott to fetch some brandy. The thing was done, for better or worse, and it was now time to turn to his own plans, and damnably complicated they were becoming, too.

Elliott entered the room bearing a tray upon which rested a decanter and glass, and as the valet poured the brandy, Carlton informed him, with some relief, that his business was completed and they might set their sights for London.

Susan also had her sights sets for London and had, with the excitement of the approaching voyage, quite easily put Lord Carlton out of her mind. Only a fortnight after having met with Mr. Simmons, she set out to begin the long journey to London. Sir Peter had requested that she sail under Captain Longsdorf, a gentleman with whom he was personally acquainted, and of course, neither Susan nor her aunt had any desire to go against his wishes. The fact that the captain was preparing to sail in a fortnight's time had set the household in a whirl with Henrietta lamenting the state of her niece's wardrobe and then insisting upon commissioning several more modish grown to be made up, no matter how short the time.

Even after the gowns had been delivered, however, Henrietta still could not feel content.

"You do not know London as I do, Susan," she complained, lifting, what seemed to Susan, a lovely figured muslin from its box and studying it critically.

"I tell you these have not been done right. They are pretty enough, I'll grant you, but so provincial . . . we're years behind the times."

Her voice had risen to a wail. Susan and Caro, who were with her in Susan's chamber, exchanged quick glances, for they had never realized that their plump little aunt could be so aware of fashion. Susan placed her arms about the discomposed woman.

"Dear Aunt Henry," she exclaimed, "these gowns are lovely, and if they are a little countrified, it will not signify, I assure you."

"Now, Susan," exclaimed her aunt impatiently, "you know nothing of the matter. Fashion does signify, and if you're labeled a provincial dowd, it will be all over for you. You shall be regarded as a quiz and I doubt even Peter's credit would be good enough to carry you off."

"But Aunt Henry," interrupted Caro from her perch on the foot of her sister's bed. "Even you must admit these gowns are better than nothing. They'll do very well for the voyage if for nothing else."

Henrietta stared at her niece, much struck. "I daresay Sir Peter and Lady Sophia will want to gift Susan with the wardrobe for her come-out . . . and quite a handsome thing it would be, Susan, which I trust you will remember."

"Oh but Aunt Henry," Susan protested, "I couldn't accept such a gift. Why, these new dresses are all I want — I shan't pretend to be anything but what I am."

Henrietta's hand went to her heart and she sat down quite suddenly in the chair, which had been providentially placed directly behind her. "Oh,

Susan . . ." she wailed, "please . . . you must not be too nice. Recollect, if you will, that you shall certainly put Sir Peter to the blush if you appear as you do now." She looked wildly around her. "Where, oh where, did Mary put my vinaigrette? I always keep it by me."

Caro calmly handed her the vial and stared at her sister, the sparkle of mischief dancing in her eyes belying her thoughtful expression. She studied the simple dove-gray round gown Susan wore, her lips pursed and her brow knit. "Perhaps you are right, Susan," she mused, "and I think even that gown would do were you to don a cap . . . something fetching, of course, with lace perhaps and blue ribbons to match your eyes." She clapped her hands together. ". . . unexceptionable!"

Aunt Henrietta moaned and covered her ears with her plump little hands. "Unnatural children. I shan't listen to any more of this nonsense."

"Oh, Aunt Henry," Susan said, glaring at Caro. "She was only funning. I shall manage somehow. You know how clever I am with a needle. Once I see what the fashions are in London, I daresay I'll be able to improve these gowns with just a touch here and there."

Henrietta offered her niece a rather tremulous smile and turned the conversation to other more important matters which had to be dealt with before Susan sailed.

One of these matters was resolved, to the satisfaction of all, when early the following afternoon, a small, rotund individual presented herself upon the Phillips's doorstep. She, as it was quickly learned, was Mrs. Cummings, the abigail Henrietta had hired, sight unseen, to accompany her niece.

Mrs. Cummings had been recommended to Miss Ashly by a dear friend. As there had been precious little time to be wasted in searching out the perfect person to act as chaperon to Susan, Henrietta had offered her the position by letter, requesting that she join their household a few days before the date they were to sail. Susan could find nothing to object to in the little abigail and in another two days both their trunks were packed and corded, ready to be tied onto the carriage.

The day of departure was at last at hand, and as Henrietta did not feel up to the strain of accompanying her niece to the docks, family farewells were to be said in the privacy of their own yard. Henrietta was disposed to tears, and even Caro had to blink a little rapidly when Susan kissed her good-bye. Susan grasped her shoulders and gave her a little shake.

"Don't you dare weep, Caro. I've half a mind to stay anyway and I can tell you that's all it would take for me to unstrap my trunks myself and carry them back into the house."

Her sister gave her a watery smile. "Goose! How can you speak so? You know you must find a handsome count for yourself and a duke, at least, for me."

Susan laughed and turned affectionately to her brother then climbed into the shabby carriage which was to convey her to the ship. She swallowed hard over something in her throat and fluttered her handkerchief out the window, her eyes sparkling with tears as the equippage rolled out of the yard.

The journey to Boston was long but Mrs. Cummings was a quiet companion, which suited Susan nicely for she was in no mood for pleasant conversation. The carriage pulled up to the docks, and almost before she knew it, Susan had been handed down and was walking carefully up the gangplank, her cloak pulled tightly to her throat in the cool April air.

Her clear blue eyes were now shining with anticipation and her hand, which gripped the railing, trembled with excitement. Once on board she smiled encouragingly at Mrs. Cummings then followed the officer who was to show her to her quarters.

Chapter 4

Lord Carlton had made his way up the same gangplank at a much earlier hour, hoping by that action to avoid meeting any of the other passengers. Much to his disgust, he had been forced to delay sailing although he had allowed his friends to continue in the belief that he had departed a fortnight before. He was now completely recovered from the effects of his fever but hadn't the patience to deal politely with a group of people completely unknown to him.

After a very short conversation with Captain Longsdorf, during which he discovered that they shared a mutual friend in Sir Peter Phillips, Lord Carlton politely requested that his presence remain unknown to the other passengers. The captain raised a shaggy brow at this odd request but, upon meeting Carlton's level gaze, offered no protest. Indeed, he insisted Lord Carlton occupy his cabin, maintaining that that apartment would offer him the most privacy and that he would then be able to enjoy any exercise he might wish to take away from the prying eyes of the other passengers.

Carlton favored the man with his charming smile and thanked him cordially then entered the cabin. He paused to let his eyes adjust to the dim interior, then grinned at his valet, who was occupied in stowing his master's gear.

"I don't know how you manage to make any dwelling, whether it be a tent, a room at an inn, or now the captain's quarters seem so particularly my own, Elliott. If ever I threaten to turn you off, remind me of your ability."

"As if you ever would, my lord," the valet returned, without looking up from his task. "I've been with you too long and been through too much to take any of your crochets to heart."

Carlton raised his brows and regarded his valet with amusement. "Am I so often difficult?"

"Only when you're bored or angry, my lord," replied Elliott, closing the earl's portmanteau with a click. "An' that ain't too often for while you do have a temper you don't often lose it." He frowned a little. "It's just that I see this voyage getting mighty tedious for your lordship but it ain't my place to tell you that you should be with the other passengers."

"No, it isn't, Elliott," Lord Carlton agreed amiably. "I think I shall do much better with the company of the captain and his mate rather than with the passengers."

"Yes, my lord," Elliott muttered.

Lord Carlton pulled a sheaf of papers, which he had been working on the evening before, from a case and seated himself at a table in the middle of the small room. He spread the documents out before him, thrusting his problems from his mind.

Susan, some hours after Lord Carlton had retired to his work, entered the cabin assigned to her and gazed about with curiosity, completely unaware that the man whose character had previously presented such an enigma to her was also on board. He had no place in her mind at present as she looked about her cabin and remarked somewhat doubtfully to Mrs. Cummings, who was engaged in the task of unpacking her things and placing them in the compartments which had been designed for that purpose, that the room seemed very small. The woman commented that she wouldn't, in all likelihood, be spending a great deal of time in the tiny apartment, then stopped quite suddenly and gripped the handle of Susan's portmanteau with great force as the vessel began to move. Anxious for a last glimpse of her homeland, Susan hastened to reassure the frightened woman that they would not sink then hurried back on deck to say her farewells to America.

She was soon joined by another young lady, and after a short time, Susan turned to her companion and gazed candidly at her.

"I know it's not at all the thing to do to introduce oneself to a perfect stranger but as the circumstances are a little unusual, I hope you won't think me terribly forward if I tell you that I am Susan Phillips."

Her companion turned to her with a quick smile and put her hand out. "Do you know I have been standing here wishing Captain Longsdorf would introduce us but I suppose he is very busy at the moment. I am Alicia Wentworth and I'm very happy to make your acquaintance.

The two young women shook hands with pleasure as neither had harbored the hope of discovering another young person among the list of passengers. They soon tired of standing at the rail and gazing at the sea, so they turned to stroll about the deck, each anxious to become better acquainted with the other.

Susan discovered that Miss Wentworth was from Boston and had unexpectedly been invited by her godmother, Lady Phoebe Brandon, to spend a year with her in London. Miss Wentworth commented that she hadn't been abroad before but that her father and step-mama had decided that the trip would afford her the opportunity of meeting her godmother and, she continued to Susan with a mischievious smile, she felt quite certain that her step-mama held out hope that it would serve in aiding her to make a suitable match.

Susan regarded her lively companion with puzzled eyes for she thought Miss Wentworth, with her glossy brown curls and dark, heavily lashed eyes, very beautiful, but began better to understand when that young lady gaily explained that her step-mama was recently come from England and felt that no girl could be thought successful until she had made her come-out. Lady Phoebe, Miss Wentworth continued, had offered to act as her sponsor and her step-mama had thought it an excellent plan.

Susan's eyes twinkled when her companion had finished. "Can you suppose," she inquired, amused, "that every young woman going to London is on the catch for a husband?"

A gurgle of laughter broke from Miss Wentworth's lips. "Never say that's the reason you're traveling to England?"

"Well, so my sister and aunt hope," reflected Susan with a smile.

Miss Wentworth tipped her head to one side. "I shouldn't think you'll have any trouble," she said. "I vow you'll have all the gentlemen tripping over themselves."

Susan flushed a little at this compliment but smiled then turned the conversation to less personal channels, and the afternoon was most agreeably spent in discussions of fashions, the ton, and the various treats which were in store for the two of them.

The progress of their friendship was rapid after that first day, partly because they were indeed the only young people on board the *Mayfair*, if one discounted William Babcock, who was only ten years old, and partly because they found they had many of the same tastes in common. They strolled arm in arm every afternoon and evening unless the day was cold or dirty, and before many days had passed, they were addressing each other by their Christian names. Their friendship, which was quite sincere, had the added effect of easing their homesickness.

The days, which turned easily into weeks, were usually bright and sunny and the evenings mild, and Susan found she was enjoying her adventure immensely. The other passengers were all that was congenial, except perhaps, for Mrs. Turnbull, who was elderly and dyspepsic and prone to rheumatism and could take pleasure in nothing other than conversations cataloging her various pains. It wasn't long before Susan felt she had known them all for any number of years.

These weeks, however quickly they might pass for Susan, secure and happy in her new friendship, were dull and tedious for Lord Carlton. He had completed the whole of his paperwork the first week and after that had written letters to every relative and friend he possessed, and some would be very surprised indeed, to hear from him. He had proceeded to read Captain Longsdorf's rather meager collection of books and had, out of desperation, taken to flirting outrageously with the pretty maid who served him his meals. These various diversions, however, had begun to pale, and after the third week, he found himself anxious and impatient to terminate the voyage.

The frown which had become more and more his normal expression of late lifted slightly as the impertinent little maid, who was clearing away the remains of his dinner, grinned saucily, telling him that it would come on to rain did he glower so and then they would be in the suds.

"For I should be seasick then," she continued pertly, "and that's a thing I can't abide, besides you being served by Grouchy Tom, the cabin boy."

Carlton stretched his long legs under the table and grinned lazily at the mischievous girl. "Perhaps I should do better with a grumpy youth than a chit who giggles and flirts and runs on like a fiddlestick."

"Oh, no, m'lord," giggled the maid, picking up her

tray and moving to the door, "you wouldn't like that above half . . . tetched in his upper works he is and that clumsy." She paused by the door, lifted her chin, and gazed down her straight little nose at Lord Carlton. "That's why I'm to serve yer lordship and the other ladies and gentlemen, don't you see."

"I'm afraid I don't see the connection, my dear."

The maid let an exasperated sigh escape from her lips then shifted the tray in her arms and gazed sadly at Lord Carlton. "It's because I'm a lady, too." Her expression altered and her dimples peeped out of her cheeks as she threw the earl a saucy smile. "Only I ain't really . . . if you take my meaning, m'lord." She turned and slid out the door, leaving Lord Carlton more amused than he had been for many days.

He couldn't miss the invitation in her words and smile, and indeed, she was a beauty, he mused, remembering her vivid little face with its classically straight nose, large pansy eyes, and beguiling pink mouth. She had a charming figure, a fact she did little to hide, and her hair was the color of a new guinea, proving a remarkable contrast to her innocent brown eyes.

But I'll be damned if that little baggage is an innocent, reflected Carlton as he opened a note which he had found by his coffee cup. He read the note and his lips twitched as he refolded it and tucked it in his pocket. Definitely not an innocent, he thought, grinning, as he drank his coffee.

The serving maid, who was indeed quite taken with the handsome nobleman, had unblushingly invited him, in the note, to favor her with a romantic interlude whilst he was on board the *Mayfair*. She had often arranged that sort of thing if she was taken with a gentleman, and if Captain Longsdorf knew of her diversions, he didn't complain as long as she was discreet. She couldn't know, however, that Lord Carlton was on his way to be married, and no matter that it was to a woman for whom he felt little affection, his sense of honor wouldn't allow him to take up with any other woman at that time, no matter how lovely or willing she might be.

After the wedding might be a different story altogether, Carlton thought as he finished the remains of his coffee, a frown once more knitting his brow.

"Er . . . my lord?" Elliott stood by the table obviously uncomfortable and Lord Carlton, whose gray gaze had become rather distant, rubbed his face with one hand then brought the troubled face of his valet into focus.

"What is it, Elliott?"

The man gingerly placed an envelope on the table. "Captain Longsdorf begged me bring this to you," he stammered. "It's from Sir Peter, my lord, and the captain has had it all this time but forgot to give it to you." He hurried on as the earl's dark brows snapped together. "He meant you no harm to be sure . . . says that he has a wretched memory and that Sir Peter knows it well."

"Good God, man," retored Carlton furiously, "what am I to do if Peter has written telling me not to bring Miss Phillips to London? Perhaps he's heard something of her reputation . . ." His jaw hardened and he motioned his valet out then broke the seal of the letter.

By the time he had completed half the missive, the anger in his eyes had been replaced with puzzlement, but when he ended, there was no mistaking the fury in his face.

With an oath he crushed the letter and threw back his chair, knocking the table with his knee as he rose and sending his cup flying. "How dare she . . ." he muttered through clenched teeth as he paced wildly up and down the tiny cabin.

Elliott, who had heard the commotion and didn't lack for courage, slipped quietly into the cabin and stood with his back to the door.

"Bad news, my lord?" he inquired cautiously.

Carlton stopped and stared at the valet then laughed harshly. "I hardly know how to answer you, my friend. Perhaps it is and then again perhaps it isn't." His gray eyes narrowed to slits and his jaw clenched. "It seems my . . . my fiancée"—he spat out the word—"has decided I'm not a large enough fish for her. She cried off without informing me and is even now married to Rockingham."

Elliott's eyes rounded. "Lord Rockingham, my lord?"

"Aye, she caught herself a duke and I wish her the joy of him."

Elliott regarded his master doubtfully. "I've heard—"

"I know, I know," Carlton interrupted, sitting down once again at the table and smoothing the letter. "He has a terrible reputation . . . not an ounce of kindness in the man but he's the wealthiest person in

England, which undoubtedly tipped the scales in his favor. Good God," he sighed, leaning back in his chair and gazing moodily into space, "I'll be the laughingstock of the season . . . again."

"Now, now, my lord," Elliott soothed, "no one remembers your other . . . ah . . . . affair of the heart. You were no more than a lad . . . ."

Carlton sat up abruptly, favoring his valet with a troubled frown. "Have no fear, my friend, those vultures will recall every detail, and for this episode, I haven't even youth to excuse me." He shook his head gloomily. "Women aren't to be trusted, Elliott."

The valet did all he could to lift his master's spirits, but by the end of a depressing half hour, when Lord Carlton requested a bottle of the captain's best brandy, Elliott couldn't see that he had succeeded, for Carlton's eyes were still hard and his brow furrowed.

The valet poured a glass of cognac and placed the bottle near his master's elbow then quietly left the room, hoping that the fine brandy would soothe his anger. And by the time the bottle was empty, Lord Carlton no longer appeared troubled, although the smile on his lips was not pleasant. He curled his fingers around the stem of his glass and, after calling to Elliott to bring another bottle, reached into his pocket to read his fiancée's betrayal one time more. He laid the paper upon the table and attempted to bring the words into focus. They seemed to be blurred. As the earl leaned forward to see them more clearly, he bumped his glass with an elbow and the remains of the cognac ran over the letter. With an oath he blotted the brandy with his handkerchief then looked up with relief when Elliott opened the door, another bottle upon his tray.

"Glad you're here, Elliott," Carlton said with a hazy but still perfectly intelligent glance. "My letter seems to have become soggy and I'm having a little trouble reading it."

Elliott, who knew that his master could carry his wine quite well, took the letter. He began reading what he could of the sopping paper, and Carlton sat up suddenly and raised a hand.

"That's not the one, Elliott," he said, his words slightly slurred. "That's from the woman who loves me. I asked you to read me the letter from the woman who doesn't love me."

"I believe that letter must still be in your pocket, my lord," replied the valet, struggling to keep a smile from his lips.

"Perhaps," murmured Carlton as he poured out another glass of brandy and stared at the amber liquid as he swirled it around in his glass, "but I believe I shall not have you read it after all, I like the one you're reading now much better."

Elliott could not hide his grin, and when Carlton glanced up, the valet saw an answering gleam of amusement in his gray eyes.

"I'm a complete fool, Elliott, but go on now and read to me, perhaps I shall feel better."

Elliott willingly began but stopped after no more than a line, remarking that he could decipher only a few words more.

His brow was wrinkled with effort. "It seems as though the maid has formed a passion for you, my lord, and would like to have you come to her cabin tonight . . . alone." He raised merry eyes to his master's face. "Unless she writes to come to the captain but I cannot think that is what she means."

Carlton, who had finished his brandy, sat regarding his empty glass for a moment. "I'm devilish drunk, Elliott, and I'm sure I would think better of this in the morning but, you know, I'm tempted to take the wench up on her offer."

Elliott gazed complacently at him. "Would do you good to have a little female companionship, if you take my meaning, my lord," he urged. "Would help put Miss Wainwright out of your head, and to my way of thinking, if you don't mind my saying so, you're well rid of that one. She would have led you a merry chase and no use denying it. Quite likely your name would have ended up on the rubbish heap and I know you'd have no mind for that."

"That's enough, Elliott," Lord Carlton ordered as he rose from the table. "I have no desire to hear any more of Miss Wainwright. Instead I believe I shall visit my little charmer."

He peered into the mirror and straightened his cravat then twitched a slight wrinkle from his coat and sauntered to the door. The air on deck was cool, and Carlton, his head swimming a little from the effects of the brandy, began strolling aimlessly in the opposite direction from the maid's cabin.

Elliott called his master's attention to this but said no more when Lord Carlton replied that he knew quite well where he was going.

"It seems to be coming on to storm, Elliott, and I

should think that the freshness of the air might help blow some of the cobwebs out of my head before I go to see my little love."

Just hope it doesn't blow him overboard, thought Elliott with a grin as he moved off at a quick pace in the opposite direction. He hoped to discover the whereabouts of the serving maid so as to inform her that his lordship was coming to visit but his plan met with a momentary diversion when he walked past the entrance to the dining salon and collided with Miss Wentworth, who had at that moment finished dinner and was making her way, together with Miss Phillips, to the rail, where they were to meet a few others of the passengers before taking their evening stroll.

Elliott grasped Alicia's arms to keep her from falling and, after expressing his regret that he may have caused her any undue discomfort, raised his hat and cheerfully wished her a good evening. He continued on his way, unaware that he had left an extremely startled young lady staring after him.

"Whoever was that, Alicia?' inquired Susan.

"I'm not sure, Susan." Her brows drew together in concentration as she looked after the man. "He looks very familiar, but I can't quite place him. I know I've seen him before but it hasn't been on shipboard."

Susan murmured that she would undoubtedly be able to place him sooner or later.

"You're quite right," Alicia said, giving up the puzzle and slipping her arm through Susan's. "The connection will never come to me if I try to think of it."

They strolled about for a few moments, enjoying

the brisk air and remarking upon the captain's comments at dinner, that they might be in for some weather. As the chilly breeze grew stronger, Alicia began to shiver. Susan encouraged her to run down and collect her wrap so they might remain out awhile longer. Alicia was not disinclined to do as her friend desired as she, too, loved the excitement of a storm and, with a promise to return in the twinkling of a bedpost, ran off.

Susan continued her solitary stroll while she waited for Alicia, breathing deeply as the wind whipped the folds of her cloak about her. The breeze grew stronger. As the Mayfair tossed more violently, Susan began to look anxiously for her companion. Turbulent skies had caused the evening to become as dark as night and Susan began to feel distinctly unwell as she continued her walk. After a quarter of an hour thus employed, she began to feel even more uncomfortable and wondered if perhaps some of the rich food she had partaken of at dinner had not agreed with her. Or perhaps it had been the two unaccustomed glasses of wine she had consumed, she reflected uncomfortably as she raised one cold hand to her aching brow, holding on securely to the rail as she did so.

After another strong gust of wind hit the ship, Susan's stomach began to cause her extreme discomfort and she knew that she could no longer wait for Alicia but would have to find a spot out of the weather to rest for a moment before she became quite ill.

With this thought in mind, she entered a dimly lit

companionway, some distance from her own snug cabin, knowing it to be the one which led to the cabin shared by Mrs. Cummings along with Alicia's abigail, Mrs. Lawes, and the ship's serving maid. She scratched upon the proper door and, when no response seemed to be forthcoming, reflected grimly that Mrs. Cummings was, no doubt, comfortably ensconced in her mistress's warm cheery apartment, working happily on her stitchery.

In this, however, she was doing a disservice to her abigail. Mrs. Cummings was, in fact, in Alicia's cabin and was neither comfortable nor happy. She had been quite overset by the approaching storm and so badly frightened by the tossing that Mrs. Lawes had come to her rescue, insisting that the distraught woman join her in Miss Wentworth's cabin until the young ladies returned and that neither woman should stir a foot in the direction of their own apartment until one of the gentlemen or the captain could escort them.

Susan decided, after standing hesitantly outside the cabin, feeling more uncomfortable with each passing moment, that however unseemly it was in her to enter another's room uninvited, she simply had to lie down for a few moments or she would faint on the spot. A wave of nausea washed over her. She hurriedly entered the dark room and stumbled to the bunk, banging her hip painfully against a table in the process but feeling much too ill to bother lighting a candle.

She collapsed on the bed and wrapped her cloak about her trembling form then closed her eyes, hoping that if she could but rest for a few moments, she would feel more the thing and could return to the deck and find Alicia before going to her own cabin.

Before too long her discomfort began to abate and she felt herself slipping into a light slumber and for this reason did not hear the door to the cabin open, quietly admitting the tall form of Lord Carlton. He was still feeling the effects of an overindulgence of brandy, and stood, eyes narrowed, in the doorway.

The interior of the room was pitch black, but as Carlton lit the candle on a nearby table, he observed the huddled form reclining on the bunk and a slight smile quirked the corner of his mouth. He reflected that the chit was no coy lass needing flattery and compliments to get her to bed. He skirted another table in the middle of the room and made his way to the bunk, reeling only slightly as he did so, then quickly disrobed, his gray eyes flashing with sudden passion, and lay down beside the girl. The light from the candle did not reach the bunk and he muttered an oath that he had neglected to bring it with him but decided against going for it; he had seen the pretty little baggage often enough to enjoy the interlude without light. He reached over and took her face gently between his hands, bending his dark head to hers.

Susan surfaced from her dreams feeling that she was suffocating. Her eyes widened in shock as she saw the shadowy figure bending over her and felt the pressure of a mouth pressed gently to hers. She reached to push the figure away, recoiling as if she had been burned when her hands came in contact with the warm smooth flesh of powerful shoulders.

"So, you want to play do you, my dear?" Carlton murmured with a grin when he lifted his mouth from hers.

Confused and frightened, Susan gathered her scattered wits as best she could and attempted to scramble off the bed and escape.

Even in the shadowy darkness of the cabin, Carlton's reactions were amazingly quick and Susan felt herself pulled back and into his hard embrace. Again his lips found hers but instead of the gentle kiss which had wakened her, his mouth was more demanding. He held her to him with one arm about her shoulders, effectively silencing her protests with his mouth while he pushed her cloak away with his other hand. When Susan attempted, in terrified desperation, to break away from the man, he twisted his fingers in the curls at the back of her neck, and at the sudden flash of pain, she held still.

He forced her soft lips apart, his tongue probing gently in her mouth while one hand ripped the bodice of her dress, too impatient to fight the tiny buttons down the back. He finally released her lips and Susan gasped for breath.

"No . . . please, no," she whispered.

"It's too late for that, my girl," Carlton murmured huskily as he pulled her hands over her head, holding her wrists easily in one hand. "You'll learn I'm not a man to tease."

His lips dropped slowly to the hollow at the base of her throat and he kissed the wildly beating pulse as he pressed his body against hers.

"After all," he said caressingly, his lips working

their way to her earlobe, "I didn't send you a note requesting this . . . ah . . . rendezvous."

"Please, you don't understand," begged Susan, twisting her face away from his warm lips.

"Hush . . . hush now, my love," he murmured, ignoring her plea and gently turning her face back to his. He kissed her once again, and as his mouth lingered on hers, nibbling gently at her lips, she trembled a little and her hands, still held in his strong grip, slowly stopped their writhing as a strange warmth spread throughout her body. Once again Carlton pressed soft sensuous kisses along the side of her neck while his hand gently cupped her breast, only the thin chemise she wore remaining between her bare flesh and his. She moaned softly and her blood seemed to turn to fire as his fingers gently teased the peak of her breast. His lips found hers yet again and Susan felt herself responding to the firm but gentle demand. Her lips parted a little in invitation and Carlton, with a harsh moan, deepened the kiss.

Feeling himself moved by the depth of his passion, he raised himself on one elbow and stared down at Susan, trying to make out her features and cursing himself for deciding not to bring a candle. He was oddly shaken and needed to see if she had been affected in the same way.

Susan, however, now that Carlton was no longer touching her or kissing her, had begun to regain her senses. As her blood cooled, her distress at her reaction to her attacker intensified. Now, however, was not the time for recriminations. Feeling that his hold on her wrists had slackened, she surprised

Carlton by lashing out with her hand. She caught him on the side of his head and he grunted, more in surprise than pain, and quickly caught both her wrists once again.

"Truly, truly, you don't understand. If you would but listen to me," begged Susan quickly.

"Later, love," the earl whispered as he bent his head to kiss her again. Her jaw was clamped firmly shut and he chuckled a little. "Come, my dear," he murmured, his lips moving against hers, "you've teased me long enough."

When she continued to keep her mouth resolutely closed, his lips moved to her eyes, then to her ear, nibbling lightly at her lobe and on down the slender column of her neck, bathing the line of it with his warm, moist tongue. His head moved farther down and Susan gasped as his cheek rubbed against the peak of her breast. He turned his head slightly and softly took the rigid crest between his teeth, nibbling with knowing gentleness. Susan felt a wave of pleasure sweep through her and she moaned softly in her throat. He grinned in the darkness, then his mouth traveled to her other breast, gently suckling through the delicate fabric.

His mouth returned to hers, and this time, Susan's lips were parted a little, her mouth soft and sweet-tasting as he dipped his tongue into it. Her heart pounded in her ears and she couldn't stop her traitorous body from responding. His grip had slackened once again and she pulled her wrist from his hand, this time, curling her fingers into his hair and pulling him closer to her. He drew back a little and Susan made a small sound of distress, immediately missing his caresses.

"It's all right, little one," he murmured huskily, as his mouth again trailed searing kisses down her throat. She felt the back of his hand touch the warm sensitive skin of her breast as he deftly unbuttoned her chemise, then gave herself up to the little shocks of pleasure which shot through her as his mouth found her erect nipple. His knee slid between her legs and his hands caressed her body, following the indentation of her waist and the sweet swell of her hips. His breathing grew ragged as his mouth began exploring the silken skin he had touched. He was lost to everything except the taste and petal-like softness of the woman beneath him and his blood thundered in his veins. He knew he could wait no longer and nudged her legs farther apart. His mouth covered hers in a deep, demanding kiss as he entered her with a swift movement. He hesitated when he heard her sharp cry of pain, then made a deep sound in his throat and, again covering her mouth with his, smothering her cries, he plunged deeply into her soft warmth.

When he at last lifted his weight from her, he pulled her into his arms, dropping feather-light kisses on her tear-drenched face.

"I'm sorry to have hurt you," he murmured gently. He hesitated, then added softly, "I was the first, wasn't I."

Susan couldn't speak and he felt her shoulders shake in a deep sob. He held her tightly and kissed her face, tasting the salt of her tears. "Don't cry, little one, the next time will be more pleasurable for you, I promise."

Susan stiffened and pulled away as she heard his words. How could he think there would be another time? He ran a gentle finger down her arm and she shuddered.

"You're cold," he said huskily, experiencing an unaccustomed desire to protect the girl.

He drew her back into his arms and Susan felt a fleeting sense of comfort and security before shame washed over her and she could only pray that he would leave before he discovered her identity.

"P—please," she cried, turning her face to the wall, her voice strained and unfamiliar to her own ears. "Please leave me, I beg of you."

Carlton's brows drew together at the panic in her voice. He was sure she had enjoyed some of the interlude even though she had struggled at first. He felt an odd reluctance to leave her and spoke gently.

"You've nothing to fear, love. When you asked me to meet you here, I assumed you had done this sort of thing before. I never imagined you were an innocent."

A strangled sob escaped Susan's throat. Carlton raised himself on an elbow, attempting to make out her face in the darkness.

"If you're worried about the captain, there's no need," he murmured, stroking her hair with a gentle touch. "I'll make it right with him."

"Please, no," moaned Susan, distraught and anxious only that he would leave her in peace. "Just leave me, please."

Carlton felt his chest tighten at her distress and he

buried his face in her sweetly scented hair then pulled away and rose from the bunk. He found his clothes and, after dressing swiftly in the dark, returned to the bed. He tenderly smoothed her hair from her face then pulled her up into his arms and gently kissed her.

"I don't like to leave you like this, little one," he whispered against her hair. "Are you certain that's what you want?"

Susan nodded into his shoulder, and with a sigh, he lowered her to the bunk. He pulled her cloak about her shoulders then made his way to the door and quietly left.

Susan listened to his departing steps then attempted to get to her feet, stumbling as she did so on trembling legs, which seemed incapable of supporting her weight. She pulled the torn edges of her dress together with shaking fingers, and as her hand brushed the soft skin of her breast, the memory of his caressing hand seared her with shame but also carried with it a bewildering ripple of desire. She covered her face with her hands, overcome by the realization that she was no longer the innocent girl she had been that morning and that the passionate responses she had been unable to control had contributed to her downfall. Standing alone in the shadows, she had to acknowledge the possibility that had she continued to struggle, the man might have listened to her.

Might-have-beens did her no service, however, and guilt and shame scorched her again. Broken sobs caught in her throat and tears coursed down her cheeks as she drew her cloak around her shoulders, clutching it tightly at the throat.

Lord Carlton had quietly entered the companionway, a troubled look in his gray eyes. He walked slowly down the passage, completely unaware of the small figure who had stepped into the deeper shadows at his approach.

Alicia watched the man's departing figure with a bewildered expression in her dark eyes. The man reminded her of Lord Carlton, but that it was he seemed quite impossible. She shook her head, slightly amused that she would allow the flickering shadows in the dim corridor to play such havoc with her senses. Turning, she made her way to the cabin which she had seen the man step out of, knowing it to be occupied by the ship's maid. She scratched lightly on the door, intending to ask the girl about Miss Phillips's whereabouts.

When no one answered the door, Alicia opened it and stepped hesitantly into the room, peering into the deep shadows in the cabin.

She picked up the candle Carlton had left burning on the table by the door. Lifting it, she walked farther into the room, gasping when she saw the huddled form leaning against the wall.

"Who is it?" she asked uncertainly, placing the candle on the center table.

The faint light illuminated the woebegone figure leaning against the wall and when she lifted her head, Alicia saw at once that it was Susan. Her eyes widened, then she went to her friend, drawing her into her arms.

"Susan," she cried with alarm. "What is it? Are you ill?"

She felt her friend's shoulders shaking with sobs and led her to a chair. "Let me help you, my dear."

Susan sat for a moment overcome by shame, before raising tear-drenched eyes to Alicia's.

"What is it?" Alicia demanded again. Suspicion flared in her dark eyes. "Who was the gentleman I saw leaving here?"

"I have no idea. Oh Alicia . . ." she sobbed, and couldn't go on.

Alicia rose, helping Susan to her feet, her mouth set in a grim line. "Let me help you to your cabin, Susan. We can talk there."

She gently removed her friend's hand, which was clutching the neck of her cloak then, after observing that Susan had the garment pulled tightly around her, tied the strings securely.

"Come now," she said firmly, quickly snuffing the candle and taking Susan's arm, propelling her toward the companionway.

The two made their way undetected, to Susan's cabin. Alicia hurriedly opened the door, relieved to see that Mrs. Cummings was not within.

Susan moved like a person walking in her sleep, and Alicia guided her to a chair then knelt beside her and took her friend's cold hands into her own.

"You must tell me," she said urgently, "did he insult you?"

Susan's feelings were in such tumult that she hardly knew whether to laugh or cry. Pain, shock, and fear were still with her but more overpowering were her feelings of shame and guilt. She put her face in her hands, unable to look at her friend. She had been dishonored and that was terrible indeed, but even more mortifying, even more shameful, was the fact that she had enjoyed — yes, *enjoyed* it. Her face flamed as she recalled the depth of passion she had felt.

Alicia gently pulled Susan's hands from her face. "What happened in that cabin, Susan?"

"After you had left me," she said hesitantly, "I began to feel unwell. The cabin Mrs. Cummings uses was nearby, so I went there hoping to rest for a while. I fell asleep, I think . . . and a man . . . a man came into the cabin."

"What did he do?'

After a long moment, Susan said quietly, "He mistook me for another, and he dishonored me."

Alicia stared blankly at Susan. "Do you mean that he . . . he raped you?" she asked faintly.

Susan nodded a little and Alicia felt a flash of rage slice through her shock. Anger blazed in her soft brown eyes.

"Good God, how can such a thing have happened?" She was trembling with fury. "What kind of man would do such a thing? You have no idea who he was?" Susan shook her head and Alicia strode about the cabin, her wrath making it impossible for her to remain calm. "Well, he shan't get away with such an infamous act, Susan. We must go to the captain immediately."

Susan put up her hand in a beseeching gesture. "Wait, Alicia. Perhaps it wasn't rape, exactly. I believe

. . . that I must have encouraged him."

"Oh, my dear," Alicia said, feeling as if her heart would break that such a terrible thing could have happened to one so virtuous as Susan. "You are too kind. What would you know about encouraging a man? You know nothing of such matters."

"I know now," Susan responded with a hint of her old humor.

"Nonsense. We must go to the captain immediately. When we arrive in England, your uncle will take care of matters—"

"Alicia, I won't hear of it," Susan said firmly. "I couldn't bear to bring such scandal upon the family. It is my own burden, which I alone will bear. I don't want you to breathe a word of this, to anyone."

"But what about the man who dishonored you? Suppose he's less than discreet about this unfortunate affair?"

"Strangely I have every confidence in his discretion," Susan replied. "For one thing, he has no more idea who I am than I have who he is. We, neither of us, could see each other in the—uh, dark." She blushed furiously at this revealing statement. "No doubt he still believes I am the maid."

An answering pinkness bloomed in Alicia's cheeks. "And when you marry?" she went on inexorably. "What will your husband think of you?"

Susan's hands tightened on the arms of her chair. "I shall deal with that in my own way when the time comes."

Alicia was full of misgivings, but could see by the obstinate set of Susan's chin that there would be no swaying her. "Very well. I shan't breathe a word."

"Naturally," Susan said steadily, "I would perfectly understand if you no longer wish to associate with me."

A gasp met this brave statement, and a moment later Alicia was beside Susan, hugging her. "Goose," she said, tears stinging her eyes. "As if I would ever abandon you. We are and will ever be the best of friends." She rose and pulled Susan to her feet. "You must get tidied up and into bed. After that we shall think of a plan so that no one will ever guess that anything is amiss."

Susan put herself gratefully into Alicia's hands, and before many minutes had passed, she was sitting in her bed as refreshed and comfortable as was possible under the circumstances. Alicia's mouth had tightened and anger had flared into her eyes again when she helped Susan remove her ruined gown but she had said nothing.

As Alicia seated herself on the edge of the bed, Susan spoke quietly. "What shall I do now?"

Alicia smiled faintly. "Judging from the way the ship is rocking, the storm Captain Longsdorf was cautioning us about is here and that may give you a day or two to regain your composure. No doubt the other passengers will be occupied with the state of their own health and not interested in yours. If anyone inquires, I'll tell them that you're seasick."

Susan heard Alicia's plan with relief, grateful that she would have some time to sort out her disordered emotions. After another half hour of talk, during which time Alicia attempted to put her friend at ease and to divert her mind from the events of the evening, Alicia left, telling Susan that she would inform Mrs. Cummings that she wasn't needed that night.

After Alicia had departed, Susan lay staring at the ceiling for a long time. She prayed that she could find the strength to go on as if nothing had happened but she knew in her heart that she would never be the same again, and that all of dear Aunt Henry's grand plans for a respectable marriage for her niece were out of the question. She could never marry, now. Tears filled her eyes. She might be able to go on as before but nothing could ever bring back her purity and innocence.

She sighed heavily and turned on her side, trying to relax so that sleep would come, but when she did finally slip into slumber, she found no peace, for her dreams were of a man's deep warm voice and gentle touch, and even in sleep, her skin tingled in sweet recall.

Chapter 5

Lord Carlton did not return directly to his cabin as he felt the need for a walk to clear his head even though the breezes had become violent gusts of wind which made strolling on deck a rather hazardous occupation. His thoughts continued to dwell on the girl he had left in the cabin and he could not rid his senses of the light, clean fragrance of her hair and the smooth silky texture of her skin.

He entered his cabin at last, disturbed by the extent to which the incident had affected him. There, sitting on his bed, was the pretty little serving wench smiling coyly at him.

Only the firmest rein upon his emotions kept him from showing his shock. Calling for Elliott to come immediately, he closed the door and leaned his tall frame against the wall, staring at the maid with narrowed eyes while he waited for his man.

Elliott entered the cabin, the look of apprehension

and alarm which showed plainly on his thin face clearing as he took in the picture of his master and the serving maid.

"You called me, my lord?" he inquired with a grin.

"What the devil is she doing in here?" demanded Carlton coldly, his tone of voice telling Elliott more clearly than words that his lordship was in a rare taking.

"Why, my lord," Elliott stammered, his smile of satisfaction replaced by a look of complete bewilderment. "Isn't she here at your request? You had said—"

"I know what I said, Elliott," retorted the earl in a curt voice as he removed his cold gray gaze from the bewildered face of the girl and glared into the puzzled eyes of his servant. "I'll repeat myself only one time more. What is she doing in here?"

"Why, I can't say that I know, my lord, not if you didn't invite her. I thought she was going to be in her cabin like the note said."

"Begging yer pardon, m'lord," the maid interjected timidly, becoming uncomfortably aware that her charms were not exerting quite the same influence over the handsome gentleman as they had earlier.

Carlton shot a hard glance back at the maid. "Well?" he drawled imperiously after looking her over from head to toe. "I'm waiting."

The girl, who had always before been able to use her beauty and powers of persuasion to good effect when dealing with an angry admirer, now made the mistake of overestimating her own charms and underestimating the earl's anger.

"La, sir," she giggled somewhat nervously, gazing

at Lord Carlton from beneath the sweep of her long lashes. "You don't want me to believe that you didn't read my note, do you? Very insulting that would be to a lady." She rose and glided over to the earl, gazing into his face with meltingly soft brown eyes. "I never thought you'd be that overset with the notion of my coming to the captain's cabin or I never would have suggested it, yer lordship."

She smiled archly into his frigid eyes, grasped his hand, and played with his long slender fingers. The maid moistened her full lips with the tip of her pink tongue and gazed provocatively into the earl's eyes. She swayed closer to him. "I thought we could be more . . . um . . . comfortable here, m'lord," she murmured huskily.

Lord Carlton coolly removed his hand from the maid's hot grasp. Any desire he had once felt for the little baggage had long since dissipated, leaving only a bitter taste in his mouth.

"Leave me now," he said softly to the maid, his teeth on edge and a muscle twitching dangerously in his jaw.

"But m'lord," the girl objected, again reaching for the earl's hand.

"Out!" he said grimly, signing for Elliott to open the door.

After the maid had flounced angrily from the cabin, Lord Carlton pulled a chair from the table and sat down heavily, his elbows on the table and his head resting in his hands.

"I don't understand, my lord," a much confused Elliott began. His mouth snapped shut, however, at the glance the earl shot in his direction.

"Leave me, Elliott," Lord Carlton ordered wearily, once more resting his head in his hands.

The valet hurried from the room, not daring to voice any more of the bewilderment he felt by the scene just enacted.

Carlton swore softly under his breath after the door had been pulled to. Who had the girl in the maid's cabin been? He winced as he recalled her pleading entreaties for him to listen to her. He had known from the moment he'd opened the door to his cabin and had seen the smirking wench reclining on his bunk that she could never have been the girl in the cabin.

He rose from the table and stretched out on the bunk and for a moment allowed himself the luxury of recalling the girl's sweet body and passionate responses. He'd felt something . . . something altogether new to him and he dwelt on those tantalizing impressions, attempting to understand the depth of emotion he had experienced. Suddenly he frowned, filled with a sense of self-loathing and disgust. There was little doubt in his mind that the girl or her parents would go to the captain with the tale, but he would face that eventuality when the time came. Tonight, however, the thought that he was capable of so dishonorable and outrageous an act was enough to deal with and it was many hours before sleep overcame his restless thoughts.

The storm which had begun the night before hit the *Mayfair* with no little force, and its fury was enough that Alicia wasn't questioned when she stated, as she and Susan had planned, that Miss Phillips wasn't feeling quite the thing. Indeed, by midafternoon, most of the other passengers had become quite ill, Mrs. Cummings among the worst, and all remained in their cabins, little caring whether they lived or died.

Carlton wasn't numbered among those who were ill, although he more than likely would have welcomed the physical discomfort, and he took to walking the deck even during the worst of the storm, defying the elements to sweep him from the rail, his coat billowing out around him while rain lashed his face.

Elliott watched his troubled master with sympathy and deep concern, for the earl had by now said enough to his valet for the man to make a pretty accurate guess at what had transpired the night before the storm.

When the wind and rain abated, two days later, the passengers quickly regained their health and Susan was also feeling a little better, owning in great part to Alicia's staunch friendship. Indeed, Susan had found her friend's good sense, encouragement, and love invaluable.

Thus it was that she was able, late the morning following the storm, to venture out on deck with Alicia for a short walk in the rain-freshened air. The day was bright, without a cloud to mar the clear blue of the sky, and Susan's spirits lifted even more as she watched the sunlight dancing on the water. When Alicia suggested that they join the others for a light luncheon, Susan was able to agree with a little smile. The two made their way, arm in arm, up the companionway and into the dining salon.

Susan sat down beside Mrs. Williams, who greeted

her with a friendly smile and began clucking over her in a motherly fashion, telling her she had become far too thin and pale.

"Do you not agree that we shall have to see it that Miss Phillips regains her looks before we reach England, Mrs. Turnbull?" the elderly lady called cheerfully to the sour-faced woman speaking with Alicia.

"To be sure, Mrs. Williams, to be sure," agreed Mrs. Turnbull, turning her ferocious dark eyes to stare intently into Susan's. Susan was beginning to feel decidedly uncomfortable with the woman's rude behavior until she heard Mrs. Turnbull's next words.

"Peppermints!" the older woman stated firmly.

"I beg your pardon?" Susan said finally, a smile suddenly tilting the corners of her mouth.

"Peppermints, my dear girl," Mrs. Turnbull said once again. "They are the best thing in the world for keeping one healthy. Good for the stomach and for the disposition. It is too, too unfortunate," she continued, taking a candy from her reticule and popping it into her mouth, "that I have only enough for my own health . . . it is so very unpredictable, you know."

She gave a discreet belch behind her fan as Mrs. Williams leaned over to Susan to whisper into her ear.

"I don't believe there are enough peppermints in the world to sweeten that one's disposition."

Susan gave a quiver of laughter, which she quickly stifled when Mrs. Turnbull gazed at her, an inquiring brow raised.

"Did you say something to me, Miss Phillips?"

"Actually, no," responded Susan hastily, "although I was about to ask Mrs. Williams how she fared during the storm."

"Not too well, my dear," that lady chuckled as she patted Susan's hand, "but it's kind in you to inquire. Poor Mr. Williams was beside himself what with trying to help me. He ain't fond of the sickroom but he did try, bless his heart."

"I can easily understand how he might be overset by your suffering, Mrs. Williams, and I'm extremely happy to see that you're recovered."

Mrs. Williams deftly turned the conversation into other channels as she was of a different disposition than Mrs. Turnbull, who was yet explaining to Alicia, in endless detail, the extent of her suffering, and Susan found herself listening, with amusement, to the gossipy chatter of the older woman.

Indeed, she found, by the end of the afternoon, that she was enjoying the chatter of her friends, and Alicia had cause to hope that Susan wasn't suffering any lasting ill effects as a result of her ordeal.

In fact, Susan had a great deal of pride and had decided before she ventured out to join the others that she wouldn't allow herself to dwell on her troubles. She was made of sterner stuff than that, and if life had dealt unfairly with her, she would have to bear with it privately.

This philosophy along with the calm weather and idyllic days which followed offered Susan the perfect opportunity for recovery. The days were warm and gentle and she began to find delight in the golden sunshine and soft clouds trailing across the blue sky. As the *Mayfair* neared the end of her voyage, the violence done to Susan, along with her overwhelming guilt and shame, had faded as much as was possible and she firmly thrust from her mind all memory of the night in the cabin. This was more easily accomplished during the day, however, than at night, when there were still dreams of a stranger's kiss which set her pulse hammering and left her with a strange longing when she woke.

At last, one bright spring day, the small craft reached England. The wind had freshened behind her, causing Susan's spirits to rise as she stood by the rail. Alicia joined her and then Mr. and Mrs. Williams who delighted in pointing out the tidy green fields and toylike villages perched on the coastline. Here and there, sunlight glinted on a fresh bubbling streamlet making its way down to the sea.

The *Mayfair* docked in Portsmouth after eight weeks at sea and Susan waited on deck hoping that it would not be overly long before her uncle arrived. She felt exhilarated by the hurly-burly going on about her and both excited and nervous with the thought of making her uncle's acquaintance at long last.

Alicia had departed a short time past after taking a hasty leave of her friend, giving Susan a hug and thrusting a crumpled slip of paper into her hand.

"My direction," she said with a smile, her brown eyes warm. She held Susan's hand for a moment. "I hate to leave you." The smile faded and she was suddenly serious. "Are . . . are you all right now, Susan?" she asked hesitantly.

Susan met her gaze squarely. "Yes, I feel quite recovered from my little bout with seasickness," she said with a faint smile.

Alicia considered her for a moment then nodded slightly. "You have my direction if you need me." She gave Susan another quick hug. "I must go now or my godmama's coachman will leave without me."

"What would I have done without you, Alicia," Susan said softly as she returned the embrace. She smiled and tucked the slip of paper into her pocket. "Go now . . . only think what Lady Brandon would have to say if her coachman returned with an empty carriage."

"He doesn't look at all patient." Alicia laughed, glancing at the man, who was walking his horses up and down the dock.

With one last kiss and one last promise to call in Grovesnor Square at the first possible moment, Alicia turned and hurried down the gangplank to join her abigail, who was waiting patiently in the chaise.

Susan continued to wait by the rail, enthralled with the activity taking place around her, but after an hour thus employed, she began to become aware of the intense heat and elected to repair to her cabin to wait in its relatively cool interior for the arrival of her uncle.

Lord Carlton, who was also waiting to depart the ship, had passed the previous weeks in daily expectation of hearing that one of the young female passengers had met with an accident. As this had not occurred, he had subtly questioned both Captain Longsdorf and the ship's doctor the previous evening, as to the likelihood of any violence occurring during one of their crossings and both men had laughed, exclaiming that theirs was the most peaceful occupation imaginable, storms notwithstanding, the doctor adding that if it weren't for seasickness, from which most of the passengers suffered at one time or another, there would really be nothing at all for him to do.

"Surely you exaggerate." Carlton smiled, lifting one brow. "I cannot believe all your crossings are so tame. You must become quite bored."

The doctor thought for a moment, pinching his upper lip between slender fingers then shook his head and laughed. "No, I'm afraid I must disappoint you, my lord. We're no swashbucklers, Captain Longsdorf and I." He leaned closer to the earl and continued in a husky whisper, "The truth of the matter is that we both are addicted to chess and these quiet crossings offer us not only peace but long evenings in which to play."

Carlton glanced at the captain, who smilingly nodded his agreement, and the earl turned the conversation to another topic. He was relieved to think that perhaps the girl he had mistaken for the maid hadn't been the innocent he had thought or she surely would have raised a hue and cry and he would by now have been forced to marry her.

Captain Longsdorf now knocked upon the door of his cabin and Lord Carlton bade him enter, deciding at last that he would no longer dwell upon the mystery, and that whoever the lady was, she had enjoyed the interlude as much as he.

He greeted the captain and invited him to take a glass of wine in celebration of the end of the voyage.

"Afraid I'll have to decline, my lord," replied the captain, apologetically. "Duty calls, you know. But you may use my cabin for as long as you like."

Carlton offered his hand to the man. "Thank you, Captain Longsdorf, but I'll be off as soon as my valet has everything in order."

The two men shook hands and Captain Longsdorf returned to the deck. A short time later he went down to Susan's cabin to inform her that Sir Peter had arrived and was presently waiting to meet her.

Susan murmured that he could bring her uncle down immediately and, after quickly washing her hands and tidying her hair, sat down to wait, her hands suddenly cold and trembling.

Well now, my girl, she told herself sternly as her knees also began to shake, this is no way to behave. She caught her lower lip between her teeth and squeezed her eyes shut, willing her body to stop quivering. Whatever would Caro think of such behavior, she mused as she opened her eyes and sat up a little straighter. Susan's eyes began to dance as she pictured her sister's reaction . . . she would surely say that any sister of hers who could behave in such a manner was a cow-hearted, insipid, milk and water miss who didn't deserve such good fortune . . . and what's more to the point, Caro would be right, she decided. She rose and squared her shoulders then jumped slightly as a knock sounded upon her door.

She smoothed her skirts and bade the gentlemen enter. As the two men joined her, Susan gazed somewhat anxiously at the tall man standing beside the captain and found herself responding to the warm smile which crinkled the corners of his blue eyes.

After Captain Longsdorf departed, leaving the two alone, Sir Peter took Susan's hands in his, holding them as if he were afraid she might suddenly disappear.

"My dear niece," he murmured huskily, "you can't

know how I've longed for this day."

"As have I, Uncle Peter," replied Susan gravely, a shy smile touching her lips. "And Aunt Henry would never forgive me if I did not immediately offer you my thanks for this opportunity."

"Pooh, nonsense," laughed Peter, taking her hand and tucking it under his arm. "I won't hear of any thanks. Indeed, I should be thanking you. But there," he continued, patting her hand, "I can see that I'm embarrassing you so why don't you tell me of your family?" He escorted her from the cabin. "First, however, I must apologize for arriving so late." He shook his head. "Can't blame you if you had given up on me. Broke a wheel not ten miles on the other side of Portsmouth but all is in order now, although I don't doubt but what we'll have to break our journey at an inn, a delay which I'm certain your Aunt Sophy will have something to say to me about."

He winked at her, and his blue eyes, so much the color of her own, twinkled with amusement. They walked to the gangplank and Susan bade Captain Longsdorf farewell, then allowed her uncle to hand her into his carriage.

Sir Peter's carriage was well sprung and Susan rested comfortably against the plum-colored, velvet squabs as the journey to London commenced. She felt her initial shyness ebb as her uncle chatted with her, breaking his conversation from time to time to indicate any point of interest they passed. She was soon put completely at ease by her companion and her naturally lively curiosity began to assert itself. She observed the passing countryside with great interest and attended her uncle's comments with attention and concentration, adding a few of her own, which quickly showed Sir Peter her dry wit.

Questioned about herself and her family, she responded enthusiastically by bringing her uncle completely up to date on the activities and personalities of Aunt Henry, Caro, and Robert and it wasn't long before Sir Peter began to feel that he would recognize them all at first glance.

He leaned back into the corner of the carriage, observing the animated face of his niece as he listened with enjoyment to her recital of her voyage. His eyes narrowed, however, when she broke off in midsentence, a flush in her cheeks and her eyes averted.

"What is it, Susan?"

"Nothing, Uncle Peter." She forced her eyes to meet his and smiled although her lip trembled ever so slightly. She clenched her hands together. She would have to be more careful. How she hated to have to watch her words with her own uncle but the desire to confide in him had been almost more than she could bear.

She had been telling him of her friendship with Miss Wentworth and had then begun explaining Mrs. Turnbull's cure for seasickness when she had suddenly been reminded of the storm and the laughter in her eyes had faded as quickly as had the color in her cheeks. She felt an overwhelming urge to lean her head against her uncle's comfortable shoulder and weep until she had no more tears. But that would never do. What good could come from giving pain to such a fine person, particularly when the damage had been done and there could be no way to repair it?

Susan forced her hands to relax and gazed into her

uncle's questioning face. "Truly, it is nothing," she exclaimed with a slightly forced laugh. "It is only that I seem to be running on like a fiddlestick, which is not at all my usual style, I assure you."

Peter took her hand in his, subjecting her to an intense gaze. "Are you quite certain there is nothing else?"

Susan felt tears pricking at her eyelids but she opened her eyes wide and pressed her uncle's hand. "Of course not. I suppose I am tired. Will we reach the inn soon, do you think?"

Peter politely changed the subject as his niece so obviously desired, but he was troubled by the pain he had seen so fleetingly in the dark blue of her eyes. Perhaps he was wrong though, he mused as he answered Susan's questions concerning the inn. Perhaps the child was merely tired, as she had every right to be.

By the time the carriage pulled into the cobbled courtyard of the Holly Tree Inn, Susan was indeed fatigued and quite aware of the shortcomings of even the most comfortable of vehicles. Her uncle had not again brought up the subject of her voyage and she had by now completely recovered her composure although she was not certain she could retain it if questioned more closely about the passage aboard the *Mayfair*.

She was, however, too exhausted to dwell upon the problem, for the emotional turmoil she had been through together with the jarring she had received as a result of traveling over deeply rutted roads had rendered her almost incapable of remaining alert even for the simple meal her uncle requested.

Indeed, she was hard put to refrain from yawning when Sir Peter pulled out a chair for her in the private parlor he had bespoken. He took note of the dark circles beneath her eyes and could not repress a grin as she finally surrendered to a prodigious yawn.

"I trust it is the circumstances and not your companion which you obviously find tedious, my dear," he said with a twinkle in his eye as he seated himself and poured a glass of wine for Susan.

She cast an apologetic glance at him. "You were not supposed to see that, Uncle Peter. Aunt Henry would say I was quite sunk beneath reproach."

A second yawn unexpectedly followed the first and Susan blushed in earnest, glancing surreptitiously at her uncle, who was carefully placing a breast of chicken upon her plate.

He smiled at her. "Now that one I did not see and so shall not comment upon, my dear. Now, will you have some of these delightful green peas?"

A ripple of laughter broke from Susan's lips. "You are a complete hand, Uncle Peter."

He grinned and placed her plate in front of her, encouraging her to eat. When they had finished, he rose and helped his niece from her chair.

"I believe it's now time for you to avail yourself of your bed, Susan."

She voiced no protest to this welcome suggestion. Her uncle led her from the room and up the stairs, handing her over to Mrs. Cummings, who had arrived at the Holly Tree some time ago in a second carriage as she was to continue as Susan's abigail until they had reached London.

That good lady needed only one glance at her

mistress's drooping eyelids to know that it was time and past she was abed and so quickly helped her into her nightclothes, offering little in the way of conversation. Susan retired, sinking gratefully into the soft bed, and was sound asleep before Mrs. Cummings had snuffed the candle on the table beside her.

As the journey the following day was to be of short duration, Sir Peter gave Mrs. Cummings orders that his niece was not to be disturbed. Susan woke quite late feeling much refreshed and eager to continue.

The small party arrived at Sir Peter's London residence, Spencer House, shortly before dark. Susan stepped down from the carriage quite taken aback by the splendor of the imposing brick structure before her.

Her uncle chuckled at her amazement. "It really is quite comfortable," he whispered as he led her up the steps. "Don't let the exterior put you off."

"Well, I must say that Caro would be quite, quite impressed," Susan murmured.

The massive front door was opened, and the butler, a tall, thin man with graying hair and an unflappable manner, stood just inside welcoming them. Reaching out an immaculate, white-gloved hand, he took Sir Peter's hat while Susan gazed about her in appreciation.

"This is my niece, Miss Phillips, Woods," Sir Peter said, pulling Susan's wandering attention to the man. She gave the butler a smile.

"Lady Phillips did receive the message I sent from Portsmouth, did she not?" her uncle asked Woods.

Woods inclined his head and spoke in his precise fashion. "She did, Sir Peter, and is presently waiting your return in the yellow saloon."

Peter turned to offer Susan his arm. She, however, had remained on the threshold and was gazing with delight at the graceful sweep of staircase which rose from the large black and white marbled foyer and at the huge crystal chandelier which hung from the ceiling. He observed her wide-eyed gaze with amusement.

"Well, what do you think? Do you approve?"
"Most certainly, sir," Susan responded. "Your home is lovely but I must ask you to forgive me. I am sure I have quite put you to the blush by staring at everything like a country mouse."

"Come, come, Susan. You in no way bear the least resemblance to any country mouse of my acquaintance, I assure you, but now . . . let me tell you that I certainly shan't forgive you if I am to be addressed as 'sir.' "

"Yes, Uncle Peter," Susan said demurely.

Peter drew her arm through his and escorted her up the staircase to the yellow saloon.

"Hah!" Peter responded with a grin, halting before a closed door. "I think it's I that is the mouse, not you, my girl. You're pluck all the way though, I can tell, but that won't help me any with Sophy." He winked at her and with a wry grin turned the handle of the door.

Susan, who was by this time quite anxious to make her aunt's acquaintance, not believing for one moment that a gentleman like her uncle would live under the cat's paw, glanced quickly about the room as the entered. She found Lady Sophy seated on a small yellow damask sofa, near a window which looked out upon the garden and which had been opened to admit the fragrant evening breeze. Susan was struck by the air of quiet elegance and serenity which was so much a part of the tall, fair-haired woman. She was leafing aimlessly through the pages of a book but she quickly set it aside and rose at the sight of Sir Peter and Susan.

She approached Susan and took both hands in her own. "Welcome to Spencer House, my dear," she said gently, her gray eyes reflecting the welcome of her words. She led Susan to the small sofa. "I trust that your journey from Portsmouth was comfortable?"

"Yes, quite comfortable, thank you. Truth to tell, though, I was a bit tired last night, and more than happy when Uncle Peter suggested we stop at the Holly Tree."

Peter stood behind his wife, placing one hand fondly upon her shoulder.

"I appreciate the help, Susan," he said. "But I'm afraid it will do no good. You can see what a termagant I married. No doubt she will have my head for arriving so late."

Lady Sophy covered his hand with one of hers. "Idiot," she murmured fondly. He seated himself in the chair by the open window. She slanted a teasing glance in his direction then turned once again to her niece. "I must admit, however, Susan, that I had begun to despair of ever meeting you."

"You are much too kind, Lady Sophy."

Lady Sophy laughed merrily. "I was not feeling at all kind last evening when I realized that I would be forced to wait another day to see you, I do assure you. But before we speak further, my dear, I must tell you that both your uncle and I deeply regret the death of your mother." Sympathy was apparent in her calm gaze. "I know it's been several years now, but the death of one's mother is never easy to recover from. You all must have gone through a terrible time."

"Well, it wasn't easy," replied Susan candidly, "but with Aunt Henry's help and kindness we've done quite well."

Lady Sophy nodded. "Yes, I can see that you have."

The conversation continued for some moments with Lady Sophy inquiring after the health and welfare of Susan's brother and sister. Then she rose and offered Susan her hand.

"Come," she urged, "you are beginning to look a little fatigued. Wouldn't you like to go to your chamber and rest a bit before dinner?"

Susan agreed with alacrity, grateful for the opportunity to rest and change into fresh clothing.

Later, after Sophy had seen Susan comfortably reclining upon the chaise in her room, she returned to the saloon and gazed happily at her husband, who was waiting patiently to talk further with her.

"Well, Sophy," he said after he had seen her seated. "What do you think?"

"She's charming, Peter. Witty, intelligent, lovely . . . she'll become an Incomparable, see if she doesn't."

Peter raised a brow. "Spoken like the doting aunt that you are," he teased.

"Pooh," retorted Sophy, "we'll be tripping over all the young men in London once our niece has made her come-out, Peter, mark my words."

"Oh dear, dear," Peter said. "Perhaps I'd better practice looking appropriately stern and—er, avuncular. Put the fear of God into those young dandies, eh?"

Sophy took one look at her amiable, good-natured husband and burst into delighted laughter.

Chapter 6

The following morning, Susan woke late feeling much refreshed. She rolled over and snuggled back down under the light quilt, listening with delight to the birds singing in the branches beyond her window.

Dinner the night before had been a private affair. Susan had become better acquainted with her aunt and uncle, finding them both to be as amiable and warmhearted as ever she could have hoped. Her uncle might be wealthy and well born, Susan mused as she contentedly watched the sunlight cast flickering shadows on the wall by her bed, but neither he nor her aunt had shown any more sign of arrogance or consequence than they had displayed earlier, and she had felt completely at ease with them.

A light scratching sounded on her door, bringing her out of her reverie and her voice was gay as she responded.

"Good morning, Susan," smiled Lady Sophy as she closed the door gently behind her. "I trust you slept well?"

"Quite well, thank you," Susan replied cheerfully, sitting up.

"I don't mean to intrude but there is much we need to talk of this morning. Would you join me in the yellow saloon after you have breakfasted?"

"Certainly, Aunt Sophy. I'll be with you just as soon as I can get washed up and dressed."

Susan threw back the covers after her aunt had left and stretched luxuriously. Then the door opened once again. She watched curiously as a young woman not much older than herself peeked about the door. She was a pretty creature with large dark eyes, which at that moment expressed her agitation, dusky curls, all but covered by a large mob cap, and a neat figure.

"May I enter, my lady?"

"Well, I'm not your lady," observed Susan with a friendly smile, "but you may certainly enter." She hopped out of bed and walked over to the door. "Here," she offered kindly, "let me help you with the door."

She held the door open and the girl entered, carrying a pot of chocolate and a dish of warm rolls. "Oh, you mustn't help me like that, my . . . I mean, ma'am," she said, flustered, as she put the tray on the table. "I'm to be your new maid, you see, only as this is my first day and"—she drew herself up proudly—"I might add, my first position, I'm not quite sure how to go on."

"First you must tell me your name." Susan smiled as she sat down once again on the edge of her bed.

"Sarah Stubbens," the girl replied primly, dropping a small curtsy.

"How do you do? I am Susan Phillips, Sir Peter's

niece."

Sarah smiled shyly. "Yes, I know, my . . . er . . . ma'am."

"Why don't you call me Miss Phillips?" suggested Susan. "That way we'll go on quite comfortably, don't you think?"

The maid nodded. When she had left, Susan concentrated on her breakfast, then dressed quickly and made her way to the yellow saloon.

She found Lady Sophy seated at a small desk, looking through a sizable stack of cards and invitations. She glanced up as her niece entered the room.

"I daresay Spencer House is going to be very popular the remainder of the season if I am to judge from the number of people who have already called. And all because of you, my dear."

"You cannot mean they wish to become acquainted with me?" Susan asked in astonishment as she seated herself in the chair her aunt had signed for her to take.

"Most assuredly." Sophy smiled, turning in her chair to face Susan. "But you shan't be required to meet all of our friends at once. Peter and I are making plans for your come-out ball, but until that time you will not be thought to have been launched into society. Which brings me to the point." She replaced the stack of cards on her desk. "Your uncle and I have decided to give a very small rout party in your honor this Wednesday. We are inviting only our closest friends."

"Oh how kind of you, Aunt Sophy," declared Susan. "I should like, above anything, to meet your friends."

"Good," Sophy cried, clapping her hands together, "and the first thing we must do is to go shopping." Her delicately arched brows drew together as she regarded the morning gown her niece was wearing. "I am the last person who would criticize, my love, but I'm afraid your gown is sadly outmoded."

Susan glanced down at her gown, fingering the folds of the figured muslin, which seemed to her more than a little shabby when seen beside the confection her aunt had donned.

"Yes, Aunt Henry did mention that our seamstress was not exactly *au courant* in her designs," Susan said, blushing.

"Henrietta, as always, was correct," replied Sophy with a light laugh, "but not to worry, my love. You cannot imagine what pleasure it will afford Peter to outfit you for the season, and as for me, why I shall adore having such a good reason for spending his money."

Susan began to protest but her aunt was having none of it. "Now I won't let you spoil my fun," Sophy said. "I have been so looking forward to shopping with you."

At last Susan gave in graciously and they spent the remainder of the day on Bond Street. Susan quickly got into the spirit of the expedition and by the time the two were ready to return to Spencer House, the chaise was loaded with packages and bandboxes and its two occupants were exhausted.

The following afternoon Sophy was engaged in penning a final list of preparations for her rout when Lady Brandon and her goddaughter were announced and ushered into the saloon. Lady Sophy rose to greet them.

"Dear Lady Brandon, how good of you to call. It's been some time since we last saw you."

She led her guests to the sofa and gave orders to the footman to inform her niece, who was engaged in what to Susan seemed interminable fittings, of their visitors, then turned back to her guests.

"Will you take some refreshment, Lady Brandon?"

"No, thank you, my dear. We have only come for a moment. This chit"—a smile softened her words as she glanced at her young guest—"was at sixes and sevens until I promised that we would call today, and she should have the opportunity of renewing her acquaintance with Miss Phillips."

At that moment, Susan rushed into the room, her hands outstretched and a happy smile making her face glow.

"Dear Alicia, how good it is to see you again. It can never be but two days since we parted. Oh, but forgive me," she continued with dismay when she had caught sight of Alicia's godmother.

Lady Sophy introduced her to that diminutive lady, and after Susan had dropped her a curtsy, the four women chatted for a few moments. Alicia and Susan then drifted over to the pianoforte, where they seated themselves on the bench and Alicia began to pick out a few notes.

"I simply couldn't wait another moment to discover how you are going on, Susan," she exclaimed, giving up the pretense of music and turning excitedly to Susan. "Do you find Lady Phillips pleasant? I vow Lady Phoebe is all kindness, although her manner may seem somewhat abrupt at first. Did you know that she is quite a good friend of your aunt and uncle?"

Susan hadn't. Alicia happily rattled on. "Aunt Phoebe went into a kind of retirement after her daughter married some fifteen years ago and now feels launching me by herself may be too much so she has come to inquire if we may not have our come-out together. Is that not the very best of news?" Her laughter caused Sophy to glance up and smile warmly at the two young women.

"I had not realized a young lady would be joining your household, Lady Phoebe," Sophy murmured, turning back her attention to the elderly woman seated beside her.

Lady Phoebe quickly took the opportunity her companion's words afford her and explained her plight.

"Please do not worry, Lady Phoebe. I should be delighted to bring Susan and Miss Wentworth out together. They seem to be such particular friends. Perhaps you and your niece would care to join us tomorrow night. We have a small rout party planned, nothing elaborate, I do assure you, but it will afford the girls a chance to meet some of our friends."

Lady Phoebe happily agreed to this idea.

A quarter of an hour later, Lady Phoebe rose, signing to Alicia that their visit was at an end and the two ladies departed.

The morning of Lady Sophy's rout dawned fine and clear, the weather seemingly in perfect accord with her plans. The sun shone from a cloudless sky and a soft breeze kept the day from becoming too warm. Apart from Susan, however, no one inside

Spencer House had even noticed the beauty of the day.

The house was alive with feverish activity. The housekeeper, a Mrs. Bartlemay, seemed to be everywhere at once, supervising the cleaning of the great chandelier, ordering tradesmen about, watching with an eagle eye as vases of flowers were properly placed, and taking charge of numerous other chores.

Lady Sophy was likewise employed with last-minute details. Susan helped her until Sophy declared that Susan had done quite enough and must now repair to her chamber to rest. Susan obediently returned to her bedchamber. After Sarah had helped her remove her gown she lay down upon the chaise and closed her eyes.

After a moment or two however, her eyes snapped open, and with an abrupt gesture, she swung her legs off the chaise and sat up.

"It's no use, Sarah," she lamented with a wry smile, as the pretty maid folded her gown. "I cannot possibly rest."

"But you must, Miss Phillips. Everybody knows Lady Phillips's parties last until all hours. You'll be needing this rest and that's the truth."

"No," Susan responded cheerfully, taking her old muslin out of the abigail's hands and pulling it over her head. "I'm far too excited to rest. I shall go into the garden for a bit."

Susan turned and held her hair off her shoulders so Sarah could fasten the tiny buttons. She then drew her brush through her thick curls and threaded a pink ribbon round her head to keep them back.

She turned to the maid, whose lovely dark eyes and

trembling lip plainly showed her distress. "You'll ruin your dress, Miss," Sarah objected.

"Oh, for goodness sake, Sarah," Susan began in exasperation. "I'm only taking a stroll in the garden." She saw a tear sparkling on the maid's dark lashes and took a deep breath, wishing she had not spoken quite so hastily. "It's all right, Sarah, truly it is," she promised, "but if it will make you happier, I will take one of Cook's pinafores. That way there will be no opportunity for my dress to get soiled . . . the apron shall quite probably go round me three times, though."

Sarah agreed with relief and went to fetch the pinafore.

The sash was quickly tied, and Susan gratefully escaped into the peaceful garden.

She walked up a finely raked gravel path and happened upon a small garden, hidden in a corner and shaded by an ancient yew. Roses rambled along a tumbled rock wall and small wildflowers bloomed among ferns.

Delighted, Susan knelt along the border of the garden, unmindful of the soil clinging to her dress. She began to hum softly to herself, feeling quite content to be out of the confusion which reigned within the house.

A portion of the excitement she was experiencing, as she well knew, came as a result of learning that Lord Carlton was numbered among her aunt's guests. Her curiosity about the man had increased considerably and she reflected upon the enigma he presented as she picked one of the roses and held it to her face, breathing in its delicate fragrance.

Unbeknownst to her, the object of her musings, Lord Carlton, had come that afternoon, albeit somewhat tardily and somewhat against his better judgment, to pay his respects to Sir Peter's niece. Actually, he was concerned for his friend and could not wait another day to discover what Peter had made of his niece's character. He happened, at this most opportune moment, to stroll out of the house as he had been erroneously informed that Sir Peter was taking a breath of air in the garden. Looking about for his friend, he caught a glimpse of Susan, whom he mistook for the lovely new serving girl he had heard talk of. He approached her, thinking to inquire as to the direction Sir Peter might have taken.

Lord Carlton was actually quite curious to meet the newest member of the Phillips staff for he had heard quite a bit of juicy gossip about the chit — one morsel being that Peter had stolen her from under the noses of several gentlemen who had certainly not wished to employ her as maid. She would, without a doubt, be better off with Peter, Carlton mused as he neared the kneeling figure, and he applauded his friend's convictions.

Susan, who had tucked the rose in her hair, glanced up and discovered that she was being scrutinized by a tall gentleman who was approaching her with long easy strides. He was clad in a superbly cut blue coat of Bath superfine which fitted across his powerful shoulders without a wrinkle. Cream-colored pantaloons and gleaming, gold-tasseled Hessians shod his long legs. Though she was impressed with the simple elegance of his attire, it was his countenance that arrested her attention. He was the undoubtedly most handsome gentleman Susan had ever encountered — the perfect image of Caro's count. Oh, if only her sister could see her now. Susan's blue eyes danced with amusement as she pictured Caro's reaction.

Her candid regard of the stranger offered him the opportunity to study her enchanting face and laughing eyes. His brow rose in appreciation. A grin lit his face as he reached her side.

"Playing the truant, are you, my girl?"

Susan began to rise, suddenly realizing he must think her one of the maids.

"No," he ordered abruptly, "don't get up. I don't wish to spoil your fun." He leaned casually against the trunk of an apple tree, thrust his hands in the pockets of his pantaloons, and regarded Susan with his delightful smile.

"Truth to tell," he continued, "I was happy to escape myself."

Susan settled back, enjoying the stranger's light, teasing companionship, yet fully aware that he would revert to behaving as a well-mannered, proper gentleman were she to reveal her identity. As she settled back, a spark of mischief danced in her eyes and the temptation to continue to play the role of the maid was too great to resist.

Lord Carlton gazed with appreciation at her dusky curls and enchanting blue eyes, thinking that she was much better placed in the garden among the wildflowers than in a hot kitchen.

More and more amused by the gentleman's lingering scrutiny, Susan could not repress the smile which tilted the corners of her mouth. She rose and dusted off her grimy pinafore, then imitated the soft lilt of one of the housemaids as she informed the earl that she truly must return to the house.

Carlton's eyes widened slightly as she rose. "You aren't quite the child you looked, are you, my girl?" he remarked lightly, his eyes dropping and running lazily over her body.

Susan turned pink and decided that the little game had proceeded quite far enough. She started for the house but Lord Carlton caught playfully at her hand.

"Come," he teased, "there must be some reward before you take to your heels if you wish me to remain silent about your truancy."

Susan drew herself up and opened her mouth to let him know, in no uncertain terms, who she was and that this silly game was done with, but before she could do so, he had taken her hands and pulled them behind her back, gathering her in a strong embrace. Startled, she twisted in his arms, her eyes blazing with indignation as she gasped an angry protest, but his arms tightened and his face drew closer.

"Hush, my girl," he murmured huskily, and before Susan could offer any further protest, he claimed her mouth in a gentle kiss.

Susan, who was too astonished to react as she knew she should, found she could not have moved away in any event for her legs seemed suddenly to have turned to water. Carlton felt the unmistakable response from her soft lips and immediately deepened the kiss hungrily. At last Susan wrenched her head aside and stepped back, her cheeks flushed and her eyes wide with confusion.

"Good God . . . what am I doing?" she whispered, her voice catching in her throat.

Carlton reached a hand to her, his breathing ragged and his brows drawn together in a dark frown.

"My dear—"

"No!" Susan cried as she put up a trembling hand to keep him from drawing her into his hard embrace once again.

She stared at him for a moment longer, amazement and confusion apparent in her wide blue eyes then turned quickly and ran down the path and into the safety of the house.

Lord Carlton remained by the tree, a troubled look clouding his eyes. What the devil had come over him of late? First the girl on the ship and now this little kitchen maid. He could not understand his reaction to the girl. What bothered him more than anything was that he, who had prided himself on his ability to remain removed from the passions which often caused his friends to behave like idiots, had been reduced to a trembling schoolboy by the touch of that warm sweet mouth.

He picked up the rose which had fallen from Susan's hair and studied it thoughtfully, toying with the idea of offering the maid his protection. No, dammit! he decided with narrowed eyes. He was far better off keeping the lady bird he had rather that give the ton such a tantalizing on dit. There was already quite enough talk about him, particularly since Lady Rockingham had seen fit not to remove from London. He had not seen her as yet but the time would come and the meeting would no doubt be eagerly observed.

Damn Elizabeth, he thought again, crushing the flower in his hand. Crying off, as she had, and in such a manner, had brought him just the sort of notoriety he abhorred. No, he would not add fuel to the fire. The pretty little maid would have to do without his protection. Besides, he reflected with a cynical twist to his mouth, he seemed to have become just the sort of "gentleman" Peter was attempting to protect the little maid from. Turning on his heel, he walked quickly down the path and entered the house.

Some moments later he gathered his hat from Woods, instructing the butler to inform Sir Peter that he had called, then climbed into his waiting phaeton and drove away.

Susan watched his tall figure from her bedroom window, her cheeks still flushed as she thought again of the stranger's unexpected embrace. She gently touched her lips with her fingertips, then colored even more, deeply embarrassed as she recalled her reactions. She had neither cried out nor swooned, either of which a young lady of good breeding should have done had she found herself in such a compromising situation, which would have been unlikely in any event. Instead, she had found herself enjoying his embrace and it had taken all of her willpower to pull away.

She drifted over to her wardrobe and fingered the soft stuff of her new gown, wondering dreamily if the gentleman would be attending her aunt's rout. Surely he was quite a good friend of the family to call the day of the party and to use the garden so freely. Suddenly the blood drained from her cheeks and the fabric fell from cold fingers.

How could she had been so caper-witted, she wondered in horror. The stranger would surely recognize her at the party, and how was she to explain her behavior in a satisfactory manner? He would certainly think her fast . . . a tease and a flirt. Susan turned and walked to the chaise, sitting down abruptly. Perhaps she could brazen it out, pretending it a case of mistaken identity when he recognized her, which he would, of course.

After pursuing this line of thought quite hopefully for a few moments, she gave a tiny shake of her head and squared her shoulders. If the man did, indeed, attend the rout, she would simply have to show him by her behavior that she was not as forthcoming as she had appeared in the garden. Hopefully he would say nothing to damage her reputation.

A light scratching on her door interrupted these unpleasant and unprofitable ruminations, and upon her direction, Sarah entered to assist her in preparing for the rout.

When the abigail's ministrations were finally complete, Susan gazed into the pier glass and stared in amazement at the reflection of the fashionable young lady mirrored there. Her gown was of pale blue gauze over a white satin slip and it clung gracefully to her slim figure. Blue ribbons of the same hue were threaded through her dark hair, which the maid had brushed into artful disarray and the now unwelcome anticipation of meeting the handsome stranger had put pink color into her creamy skin.

As she joined her aunt and uncle at the top of the staircase to welcome the guests, Susan felt decidedly nervous, uncertain whether to hope the stranger would be early, arriving before many other guests were about to witness their meeting, or if she would rather he be late, when noise might serve to cover his words. Fortunately her state of agitation began to lessen as it became evident that he was going to be late if, indeed, he put in an appearance at all.

Susan had relaxed so much so that she was able, after a half hour of greeting Lady Sophy's guests, to smile with genuine pleasure when she caught sight of Alicia, her dark eyes and glossy brown hair shown off to perfection by her blossom pink gown.

"How lovely you look, Alicia." Susan smiled after her friend had made her curtsey to Lady Sophy. "I shall be able to join you in a moment or two. I believe almost all of my aunt's guests have arrived."

Alicia took Susan's hand, pulling her away from the other guests with a barely concealed excitement. "Has Carlton arrived then? I vow I shan't talk to him if he has, though. Do you know that I have been a week in London and he has not yet been to call?"

Susan pressed her friend's hand and smiled sympathetically. "I'm afraid he has not arrived yet, Alicia, but I know my aunt expects him. Perhaps he will come soon."

Alicia made a small moue of disappointment as she released Susan's hand then shrugged and turned aside, smoothing her long white gloves with the greatest show of indifference.

"Well, I don't care then if he has so little regard for friendship. I don't know that I want to see him if he does arrive."

Susan, whose back was now to the receiving line, turned to respond to her friend's statement, much the same as she would have to a similar thought expressed by her sister, when her action was arrested by the sound of a familiar, yet unwelcome voice.

It was that of the stranger who had kissed her, and from the teasing manner in which he greeted Alicia, Susan was left in no doubt as to his identity. The desire to run directly to her chamber was extremely strong but Susan knew there was nothing for it but to turn and greet the earl. She drew a deep breath and raised her chin then turned and faced the gentleman with the haughtiest look she could manage.

Carlton stared at Susan in blazing recognition as she greeted him and a flicker of something undefinable appeared briefly in his gray eyes before they were shuttered, leaving his face a cold, forbidding mask.

A pregnant silence ensued, for Susan was too nervous to utter another word and Carlton's anger was perilously close to surfacing.

Completely bewildered by Susan's obvious discomfort and by Lord Carlton's equally obvious rage, Alicia spoke brightly, hoping to quiet the troubled social waters she found herself in.

"I'm completely out of charity with Carlton, Susan, but I do hope the two of you will become friends. You have not met before, have you?" she queried with a hesitant smile when neither Susan nor the earl responded to her introduction.

"Of course not," responded Susan uneasily, attempting, with little success to remove her gaze from the earl's inflexible countenance.

Lord Carlton stared at her in cold scrutiny. "Forgive me, Miss Phillips, but you bear an amazing resemblance to a young woman I met only this afternoon." A barely concealed edge of sarcasm underscored his words. "I recollect, however, that she appeared to be . . . ah . . . shall we say, somewhat differently attired."

Alicia, who was completely at sea over the actions of her friends, attempted to keep the conversation on a conventional level by lightly informing the earl that Miss Phillips had only recently arrived in London and he could not possibly have made her acquaintance.

"Yes, I did know that . . . stupid of me to have thought that I had met her," Carlton drawled at last, releasing Susan from his cold gaze.

"If you will forgive me," he continued, speaking to Alicia, "I believe I see a friend I must greet."

Susan watched the earl's retreating form in some distress. She could not feel that she had handled the situation at all well and, after resolving to talk of it with Alicia at a later date, turned to rejoin her friend, who was speaking to Lady Phoebe.

Lord Carlton had meanwhile made his way to a group of four persons standing in the very center of the room.

Sir William Swithin, standing at the edge of the foursome, was a stout gentleman of the variety who is more at ease riding to hounds then conversing in a London drawing room. He tugged at his ill-fitting jacket as he attended his wife. Lady Caroline, a plain but kindly lady and the aforementioned gentleman's spouse, was a bosom bow of Lady Sophy and was anticipating, with great pleasure, the opportunity to help launch her friend's niece upon a successful season.

"Not that I should wish to presume too much, dearest Sophy," Lady Caroline had sighed when she had helped her friend prepare for the arrival of her niece, "but it would be so lovely to have a charming, prettily behaved young lady in one's charge. Frederick," she continued, referring to her husband's son and heir by a previous marriage, "well, Sophy, you know what Frederick is. There's no use wrapping it up in clean linen . . . he's totally unmanageable and . . . and churlish."

"Now, Caroline," Sophy soothed, "no doubt he is going through a stage. You know what young men are like."

While Sophy deftly led her friend away from the painful topic of her stepson, she could not but reflect privately that Caroline had indeed nicked the nick. The boy was a lout and the silliest puppy in London.

Freddie's main ambition in life seemed to be to gain the title of Tulip of the Ton and to this end he aped, as did many other young men, the dress and manner of Beau Brummell without ever quite matching the superb fit of the Beau's jackets or even coming near his wit and style. His face, unfortunately, was round and pasty, topped by thin ginger-colored locks, which he tried, with little success, to arrange à la Byron. His close-set green eyes were small and protruberant.

Freddie had, of course, accompanied his father and step-mama to the Phillips's rout and he had been much impressed with the beautiful Miss Phillips. He would have liked to approach the young lady but did not like to be too much around Carlton, a man who, oddly enough, made him feel foolish. So he had waited impatiently until their conversation ended. When he saw the earl walking away, he minced hurriedly over to Susan and her friend, Miss Wentworth. Actually, he mused as he ogled the young women, either one was a prize. How would he ever choose between them?

Carlton, meanwhile had made his way over to Amabel Mawson.

Mrs. Mawson, a widow and Sir William's sister's child, was a tall, slender creature with thick blue-black hair dressed high, thus showing her graceful neck and alabaster skin to the best advantage. She wore what would have been a demure gown of lilac muslin if it weren't for the dampened petticoats beneath, a fashion which risked censure—and pneumonia—in order to display a young woman's charms.

Mrs. Mawson had come to the Swithin residence only the evening before, unexpected and not wholly welcome since she had recently been embroiled in a rather distasteful scandal involving two married gentlemen. Everyone had hoped that she would show the good sense to remove from London until things had cooled but . . . here she was, as Caroline had sighed to her friend when she had begged Sophy's pardon in bringing an uninvited guest to the rout.

As Lord Carlton conversed with this slightly disreputable young woman, it was quite obvious to Susan that he did not, in any way, find her company distasteful. The uncomfortable twinge she felt in her breast at this thought she did her best to ignore. After all, she scolded herself, the man and his friends meant nothing to her.

When dinner was announced, the earl escorted Mrs. Mawson to the table, where he found, to his displeasure, that he had been seated beside Miss Phillips by Lady Sophy.

Susan had by now recovered her composure. She

felt rather at fault for the incident in the garden, and she embraced this opportunity to set all to rights between them. In this, however, she was to be thwarted. Lord Carlton's excellent manners prohibited making his displeasure to be in Susan's company obvious but he managed to make it felt by Susan just the same.

Her every attempt to converse with him provided only scrupulously polite monosyllabic replies, after which he turned his attention back to the dashing Mrs. Mawson. In exasperation, Susan turned to Freddie Swithin, who was more than happy to monopolize her attention.

Freddie was congratulating himself on the success of his plan to be seated beside Miss Phillips. He had sneaked into the dining parlor some moments before dinner had been announced and taken his namecard from its place beside that of his stepmama's, exchanging it for the one next to Miss Phillips. He would have liked to have removed Lord Carlton from his place on Miss Phillips's other side but did not have time and so had to be content with only a part of the young woman's attention.

As it turned out, however, Freddie found Miss Phillips turning quite often to him for conversation, which he put down to his skill at the art of polite flirtation. By the end of the dinner, Freddie was quite sure that he had dazzled Miss Phillips with his wit and charm.

After dinner the drawing room had been cleared for dancing and the young people quickly began to form couples for the first set. Susan watched Lord Carlton from the tail of her eye as the musicians warmed up, hoping that he might ask to lead her out. When she saw him bow over the hand of the daringly dressed Mrs. Mawson, however, she quickly turned her attention to Lady Sophy, surprised once again by the slight twinge of disappointment she experienced.

Sophy frowned as she, too, caught sight of the couple. "Oh dear," she murmured.

"Is something wrong, Aunt Sophy?" questioned Susan.

Lady Sophy turned to Susan, a frown creasing her smooth brow. "I'm sorry, my dear, I didn't realize I had spoken aloud. I was only wishing that Lord Carlton would not take up with Mrs. Mawson. There's been scandal enough on both sides. This is all the fault of Elizabeth Wainwright, but I shall say no more on that head." She pressed her lips together. "Mrs. Mawson has obviously set her cap for him and if he isn't careful she'll catch him, too. She's a ruthless scheming . . ." She turned to her niece and smiled ruefully. "There now, that's enough of that. You shall think me a spiteful old biddy. This is your party . . . you must go off with one of these young men and join the set that's forming."

At that moment Freddie Swithin stepped up to beg Lady Sophy's permission to dance with her niece. This Sophy was forced to grant, though she could see Susan did not look any too happy.

Susan accompanied Freddie out on the floor, grateful that there was to be no waltzing since neither she nor Alicia had yet been received at Almacks and, as Lady Sophy had explained, no young woman of good breeding would dare the dance until she had won the approval of Lady Jersey and the other patronesses.

She did not think she could bear the sensation of Freddie's arms about her although, curiously enough, as she reminded herself while she and Freddie joined the others, she had not minded Lord Carlton's strong embrace in the least.

She quite unconsciously touched her mouth with her white-gloved fingertips as she thought of his kiss, and she glanced at him. He was staring at her, one dark eyebrow quirked and a look of sardonic amusement on his handsome features, and Susan immediately dropped her hand to her side as though her fingers had been scorched. Tearing her gaze from his face, she turned nervously to Freddie, startling him with a dazzling smile and quite missing the dark scowl which flashed across the earl's face when she did so.

By the end of the set, Susan felt as disturbed by Lord Carlton's enigmatic stares as she did by Freddie's heavy-handed flirtation and she desired nothing more than to sit alone for a few moments and attempt to compose her disordered thoughts. To this end she begged Freddie to bring her a glass of lemonade. As soon as he had departed, she escaped to a small alcove at one side of the room. The draperies were half open. Susan gratefully sank into a small sofa hidden from view.

To her dismay, she heard the sound of a masculine footstep only moments after she had made herself comfortable. Freddie must have seen where she had gone. Snapping her fan against the cushion of the sofa in irritation, she turned to face him. The angry words died in her throat and her heart gave a curious, although not altogether unpleasant, flutter when she saw that her visitor was Lord Carlton.

The early stared coldly at her. "I trust I'm not intruding? If you're waiting for Mr. Swithin, however, I'm afraid you'll be disappointed. I saw him searching for you, and as I know well that Peter and Sophy would wish to avoid a scandal, I informed him that you had retired with the headache."

Susan's lips tightened and she felt a cold chill course through her body at the insult handed her. "I daresay you're the one who must be disappointed, my lord. I certainly was not waiting for Mr. Swithin. I merely wished to be alone."

Blandly ignoring her words, Lord Carlton leaned against the paneling, his arms crossed.

"Indeed," he said incredulously. His inscrutable gray gaze was fixed on her angry face. "It's time we had a talk."

"I do not see that we have anything to discuss," Susan said coolly, unaccountably hurt that he thought she had arranged a tête-à-tête with a sapskull like Freddie Swithin.

"I can understand that one would not wish to discuss a botched scheme," the earl drawled softly, toying with the black ribbon of his quizzing glass while he studied her face.

Susan shot him a bewildered glance. "I confess you have me at a loss, my lord."

"You won't gammon me, my girl, with that innocent air." His voice was suddenly taut with anger as he pushed himself away from the wall and towered over her. "You understand quite well, but if you wish to play games, why then I shall spell it out for you." His lips twisted cynically. "You are nothing but a scheming flirt hanging out for a wealthy husband and are using Peter's hospitality to that end. You forget, my dear, that I alone of all of Peter's friends know of your straitened circumstances . . . and of your reputation in your own village." He ignored Susan's cry of outrage and continued. "No doubt you were well aware of my identity this afternoon and of the fact that I am both wealthy and eligible now that I'm no longer affianced to Miss Wainwright . . . Lady Rockingham. Do you perhaps anticipate a proposal of marriage, Miss Phillips?"

He stopped in front of her and leaned down, catching her chin in his hand, forcing her to look at him. "None shall be forthcoming, my dear."

Susan twisted away from him and jumped to her feet, brushing tears of rage from her eyes.

"I assure you, my lord, that marriage to you is the last thing I wish." Her voice trembled as she attempted to control her anger at his insulting words. "I see now that you are as rag-mannered as your man, Mr. Simmons, intimated. My mistake lay in discrediting his words. You are arrogant, condescending—" She halted abruptly and breathed deeply, feeling choked by the insults she wished to heap upon his head. "I wish you would leave me, my lord," she said in a quiet but deadly voice after she had regained a portion of her composure.

Lord Carlton glared at her, his fists clenched and a muscle twitched in his jaw. "Just so we understand one another, Miss Phillips." He began to walk from the alcove then turned on his heel to face Susan once again.

"One thing more before I leave you to your musings." His eyes were as stormy and cold as the sea on a winter's night and Susan shuddered as she looked into them. "I don't wish to have my name bandied about so you will refrain from speaking of our . . . shall we say, indiscretion? I shall do the same and perhaps you'll have better luck with Mr. Swithin. One last word of warning, however, Miss Phillips. I urge you to be more discreet from this time forward, for if I should hear that you have caused Peter any disgrace, make no mistake: I shall not hesitate to make you pay for it."

Susan flinched at his harsh words and averted her head. Carlton gazed at her finely chiseled profile for a moment, then turned and stalked away, furious with the girl and furious with himself for the unaccountable desire he felt to take her in his arms and punish her in a way he might enjoy.

After he had gone, Susan took out her handkerchief and dried her eyes. Shock and anger and something more . . . a flicker of doubt in her own mind overcame her and she sank down upon the sofa. Perhaps Carlton was in some way correct, not in his accusations that she expected an offer from him but in his all too obvious opinion of her character.

The memory of the night she had been seduced crept into her mind and she covered her eyes, attempting to push it back into the corner she had relegated it to. Her sense of justice would not allow her to do so, however, and a tiny voice reminded her that there had been moments when she had experienced a feeling of passion and had responded quite wantonly to her attacker's embrace. Then again in the garden she had felt the same warmth in her veins when Carlton had kissed her. Shame engulfed her. . . . it was becoming clear to her that a part, at least, of the earl's low opinion of her might be justified.

She sighed a little, rose, and smoothed her dress. This wasn't the time for such lowering reflections. Straightening her shoulders, she made her way back to the dancing, astonished that the party was still going on and that no one seemed aware of the scene just played out in the alcove. She tilted her chin defiantly as she caught sight of Lord Carlton dancing with Mrs. Mawson and smiled shakily at Alicia, who had joined her.

Chapter 7

Lady Sophy's rout was considered a huge success. For several days following, Susan was besieged with invitations and flowers. She had, in truth, made something of a hit, despite the fact that from her standpoint the evening had been a disastrous one.

After the humiliating interview she had endured with Lord Carlton, Susan had determined that he should not discern how his words had hurt her. To that end she had spent the remainder of the evening dancing and flirting with a gaiety and sophistication she had been unaware of possessing. If her laughter had seemed a bit brittle and her eyes too brilliant, none of the party had taken notice, with the exception of Lady Sophy, whose worried glance had followed her niece's graceful form from time to time.

Sophy tried to put her anxiety aside, reflecting that Susan's strained behavior at the rout had of course been due to nervousness. But over the next few days, she continued to observe a lack of laughter in her niece's blue eyes and a lack of spirit in her graceful walk.

"Not that she is moped, precisely," Sophy hastened when she talked of her feelings with her husband. "But she does seem a bit blue-deviled of late."

"Has she said anything?" ventured Peter calmly as he stood beside his wife's desk, absentmindedly admiring her fine hand while she wrote out the invitations for Susan's come-out ball.

"Of course not, Peter," murmured Sophy, a frown creasing her forehead. "I — I see something in her eyes, though . . ." She returned her pen to the standish and focused all of her attention upon her husband. "I know you will think me twitty, Peter, but I have a suspicion that something occurred the night of the rout which has caused Susan some discomfort. No doubt it's my woman's intuition — now do not smile at me in that odious way, I am quite serious — but it is not like our niece to be so — so" — she waved her hand in a broad gesture — "Oh, I don't know . . . so dispirited."

"Come, come, Sophy." Peter laughed, attempting to tease his wife out of the morass of depressing thoughts she seemed to have sunk into. "Do not refine upon it. It is quite possible this quiet manner we are observing is Susan's true character. We do not know her very well, after all."

"Fudge," said Sophy crisply, "Don't be such a slowtop, Peter. You know as well as I that Susan is hardly a quiet, docile little mouse."

Peter sighed. "I dare say she's suffering from homesickness. Perhaps," he mused, "Charles would have an idea about how to bring her back into spirits once again."

"Pray don't bring Lord Carlton into this!" Sophy exclaimed. "I already have a word or two for that gentleman."

Peter's brows shot up and he looked questioningly at Sophy, for it was quite unlike his wife to ring a peal over Carlton's head.

"What has Charles to do with all this, my dear?"

"Nothing, really," she returned crossly, "except that I would have thought he would show the good manners to call upon Susan after the rout but not a word have we heard from him. I must own that I don't like his actions above half. It's almost as though he were avoiding us and that's not at all like him."

"Us, my love, or Susan?" Peter's eyes twinkled. "Not trying your hand at matchmaking, are you, Sophy?"

Sophy's eyes clouded. "You may laugh if you like Peter, but they would suit quite well. I've had it in mind right from the beginning. but Charles is deliberately being contrary—I dare say he's seen through my plans. The man is too sharp for his own good," she concluded crossly.

"Now don't get on your ropes, Sophy," Peter said. "I happen to know that Charles left the day after your rout for Fairfields. You know he hasn't been home for some months so it's completely natural that he should want to check his lands. Besides," he continued, "it would not be at all well done in us to meddle about in Charles's affairs in such a fashion. You shall simply have to allow things to fall out as they will."

"Oh, I know you are right, Peter." Sophy sighed, pulling a handkerchief from the pocket cunningly concealed in her morning dress and dabbing at her eyes, which were suddenly damp.

"You must know how close Charles's happiness is to my heart, though. I've watched him harden ever since that first scandal with Miss Bently, and now to have his affair with Miss Wainwright end in such a way has turned him into a veritable cynic."

She paused and glanced at her husband, her eyes blazing. "You may be certain of one thing, Peter. Lady Rockingham shall never be welcome in any home of mine. Why, I've never heard of such ill-bred behavior."

Peter gently removed the now crumpled handkerchief from her hand. He tilted her face up and wiped away the tears. "I assure you I feel as badly for Charles as you do, Sophy. I had hoped that he would marry and settle down but that's over now and you know as well as I that the scandal will die down."

"Yes, but will Charles allow any woman close to him again?"

Peter sighed. "I can't answer that, my love. I do know, however, that Charles is quite capable of handling his own affairs, and that his patience would be stretched were he to hear this conversation. No, Sophy," he continued calmly when his wife made as if to interrupt, "you know as well as I that he will brook no interference in his affairs. Rest assured that if he forms an attachment for Susan, he will tell us of it. Now then," he went on, changing the subject to a more congenial one, "tell me of your plans for decorating the ballroom."

Sophy realized when she was beaten and gracefully acquiesed, although she remained troubled by both

Lord Carlton's continued and rather pointed absence from their home and by the despondency she sensed beneath Susan's calm, gentle manner.

The come-out ball, which was held on the appointed evening, went as well as Lady Sophy and Lady Phoebe could have desired. Everyone agreed that it had been a positive squeeze, one of the most successful balls of the season.

Lady Cowper herself remarked upon the fresh beauty of the young American girls. And their season was assured of success when Brummell mentioned to his hostess that he was of the opinion that Miss Phillips and Miss Wentworth would "take." Raising his quizzing glass, he surveyed the girls from head to foot as they danced with two of their dozens of eager young suitors. "Depend upon it," he drawled to Sophy, "your niece and her friend will provide a delightful diversion from what had promised to be a dull season indeed."

His voice faded as his attention shifted to a tall, immaculately dressed figure. "The only gentleman who remains immune to your niece's charms is Carlton. I wonder . . ." A lively curiosity flared up in his brown eyes as he watched the earl, who was currently employed in glowering at the lovely Miss Phillips as he had been all evening. Brummell felt certain that an interesting story lurked somewhere.

Carlton had attended the ball against his better judgment although courtesy and his affection for Peter and Sophy dictated that he do so. He now felt, after observing Peter's niece flirting carelessly all evening with a gaggle of young men barely out of short coats, that his assessment of her character had been too merciful and that it was his responsibility to protect the good name of his friend from her machinations. He also felt that her gown was shockingly immodest for a girl of her tender years, though he had to acknowledge that she looked remarkably enticing in it—a fact which served only to irritate him further.

Lady Sophy would have been hard-pressed to understand the earl's extreme reaction to her niece's apparel. She herself had begged that Susan select the filmy gown of ivory sarsenet over rich ivory satin, which now clung enticingly to the young woman's slender form, and had not thought that the fashionably low bodice should offend anyone's sensibilities. Indeed, there were any number of other women, young and old, who were more immodestly attired.

Sophy's gaze now lingered appreciatively upon her niece as she watched the dancing figures before responding to Brummell's query. "Yes, I rather think that there isn't a woman alive who would please Carlton at this juncture," she said, more sharply than she had intended. "And I assure you, Susan has far too much sense to be put in awe of any man's arrogance."

Oddly enough, Brummell found his curiosity even more piqued by this rather cryptic statement. He thought perhaps he'd remain in London for a week or two instead of removing to Brighton as he had originally intended.

As the days passed, Susan found herself much in demand and she attempted, without success, to keep thoughts of Lord Carlton from her mind. She was forced to admit to herself that as absurd as it might seem, she was in danger of becoming infatuated with the man even though it was quite obvious, from his behavior, that her feelings were not reciprocated.

He had been to visit her aunt and uncle several times since the ball. While always coolly polite to her, Susan felt certain he was still of the opinion that Sir Peter and Lady Sophy needed to be protected from her. She had spent several sleepless nights after her come-out examining those aspects of her character which so surprised and alarmed her and she had at last been forced to conclude that she had inherited her father's unstable characteristics — in particular, his passionate nature. She had also decided, however, that her emotions would be held in check at all costs and that even Carlton, if he unbent at all in his dealings with her, would find her unexceptionable. For the moment this was not to be, for any conversation she held with him was guarded and stilted and she felt extremely frustrated that he wouldn't allow her the opportunity to show him that he was in error in his judgment of her character.

Unbeknownst to her, Susan had two champions who were busily attempting to change his view. Alicia, who had ridden with the earl several times, talking of her family and reminiscing over times past, had finally dared broach the subject of his strange aversion to her friend. She had pursed her lips and cast a speculative glance at the tall gentleman beside her and then had plunged in, remarking in her frank way that she couldn't understand how he could be so cool and unfriendly toward Miss Phillips.

"It's almost as though you hold her in contempt, Charles, but I can't feel that you know her well enough to do so." Her dimples flashed. "She is a loving, amiable sort of girl, you know, and I do wish the two of you could become friends."

Carlton looked amused as he dropped his hands and let his fretful pair of bays out a bit. "Minx! Don't try to use your wiles on me." He knit his brow as he cast a quick glance at his companion. "I respect your opinion, you know, Alicia, but I can't let you sway my judgment. Obviously you and I have formed completely differing opinions as to Miss Phillips's character. Perhaps she appears differently to those of her own sex but I find her singularly lacking in integrity and principle."

Alicia stared at the earl, her eyes round with amazement. "Susan?" she managed at last. "Lacking in principle? I can't imagine how you arrived at such an assessment but I shall tell you, my friend, that there is no one I'd rather have by my side if I were in a fix than Susan."

"Your loyalty does you justice, little friend," was Carlton's only response and Alicia could but hope that he would think about what she had said.

Not so with Brummell. He visited Lord Carlton several days after Alicia had spoken to the earl, for much the same reason, but he wasn't content to sit back and let his friend meditate privately. He called quite early in the morning and found Carlton being helped into a well-fitted coat of dark green superfine.

Brummell paused upon the threshold until Elliott

had completed the procedure then strolled into the room.

"Sorry to disturb you, Carlton," he drawled as he took a chair near the window and gracefully crossed one leg over the other. "Appalling thing—to intrude upon a man's toilette."

Carlton grinned at his friend. "Ah, yes, I suppose it is if one takes one's appearance so seriously that it requires hours of concentration to complete the job. Fortunately I am not such a stickler. But tell me what calamity has caused you to leave your house at this hour. Thought you were in Brighton, actually."

"And so I shall be just as soon as I get this business cleared up. I'm come to protect a lady's name, you see."

Lord Carlton gazed at his friend, a flicker of surprise in his eyes. "Never knew you to bestir yourself for a female before, George. She must be quite a charmer."

Brummell raised his quizzing glass and stared coolly at the earl. "Come, come now, Charles, you must know whom I mean."

Carlton sighed. "It seems the lovely Miss Phillips has bamboozled the whole of London—even you. I must remember to congratulate her. Before you comb my hair, however, I beg for the solace of a cup of coffee."

He held the door open for Brummell to precede him. "Let's go down and you may chastize me while I have my breakfast."

The two men entered the breakfast room moments later, and after Carlton had poured two cups of coffee, he seated himself and, with a look of resignation, motioned to his companion.

"You are at liberty to begin, George."

"You're taking this too lightly by half, Charles." Brummell frowned. "Talk is going about that you know of something in Miss Phillips's past of a scandalous nature." He stirred his coffee. "I like the girl, Charles, and what's more, I like Peter and Sophy. My credit is good enough to carry her off when I'm here, even in the face of your dislike, but I venture to guess that she'll be shunned when I leave unless you take matters in hand."

He placed his spoon on his saucer. "The chit's much more interesting than the usual variety of schoolroom misses we see, Charles. Actually, I've grown quite fond of her."

"You sound positively avuncular, George," Carlton remarked with a frown. His gray eyes were grave. "I value your friendship, George, and your opinion." He rose and offered Brummell his hand. "You have my word on it that I shall not malign Miss Phillips's character while you are gone . . . that is, not unless she does something to warrant it."

Brummell clapsed the hand offered him. "I guess I can't expect more than that Charles, but I think you'll be pleasantly surprised when you get to know Miss Phillips."

This opportunity presented itself the following day, an especially fine afternoon, when Susan and Alicia decided upon a drive in the park to revive spirits which had begun to flag just a little from the rounds of parties and entertainments they had been attending.

The two young women attracted a great deal of

attention whenever they chose to drive in the park. This day was no exception, although there were fewer admirers as many of their acquaintances had departed for their favorite watering places.

The women did, however, to their mutual chagrin, encounter Freddie Swithin, dressed in a yellow coat with huge buttons, a hideous waistcoat, apple green breeches, and brilliantly polished Hessians. As he was headed in their direction on a nervous bay, there was nothing for it but to direct the coachman to pull up the horses.

Freddie drew alongside the carriage and bowed to the two ladies, a heavy hand on the reins causing his horse to sidle dangerously near the vehicle.

"How do you do, Miss Phillips, Miss Wentworth," he drawled affectedly. "I had hoped I might have the good fortune to run into you today. You're both looking excessively beautiful this morning. My dear Miss Phillips, I must tell you I was positively crushed that you did not attend the opera with your aunt last evening." He shook his finger teasingly in her direction. "If you had only known what heartache would result from your absence, I'm certain you could not have stayed away. Your presence, dear lady, was sorely missed."

With these words Freddie removed one hand from his reins and, with an amorous look, reached for Susan's hand. At this movement his mount began to dance skittishly about, nearly unseating him. In a fit of temper he pulled too hard on the animal's tender mouth. The horse responded by rearing and bolting down the path, taking the hapless Freddie with him.

"Oh dear," Susan said in some bewilderment.

Those two words were all that was necessary to send Alicia into a fit of laughter.

"People will see you," Susan said, elbowing her companion. But the sight of Alicia trying to suppress her laughter by pressing her gloves against her lips soon had Susan in whoops of laughter herself.

"Oh, Alicia," she gasped, trying to control herself. "What a quiz Freddie is."

Susan's laughter bubbled out again and both girls were once more reduced to helpless giggling. Because of their hilarity, they did not observe the two gentlemen who had seen the incident and had ridden over.

Lord Carlton cleared his throat and attempted to hide his smile as he interrupted their laughter.

"Miss Phillips? Please excuse me but I saw that Mr. Swithin was experiencing some, er, difficulty and thought I should inquire if all was well."

Susan glanced quickly at the earl, who was mounted on a superb gray and was holding it next to the carriage with all the ease of an accomplished horseman.

"All is quite well here, thank you, my lord," Susan replied, her eyes still alight with laughter. "Freddie's horse was merely giving him a bit of trouble."

Carlton, who was discovering that it was not so terribly difficult to be pleasant to Susan, found his lips twitching with amusement. "Just so, Miss Phillips. I have always considered the horse to be a very intelligent creature."

Lord Carlton's companion had been holding himself aloof from this converstation, although a wide grin on his face showed that he shared their amusement and he now urged his horse forward.

"Do you think you might introduce me to these lovely ladies, Charles?"

"Forgive me, Oliver. I should have done so at once. Allow me to present Sir Oliver Seaton, ladies. Oliver," he continued easily, "these are the young Americans who have taken London by storm, Miss Phillips and Miss Wentworth. Until now I had presumed them the most sober and high-minded of young ladies."

"Now that's doing it a bit brown!" Susan protested to Carlton, as Sir Oliver and Alicia struck up a conversation. "And here I had become rather fond of being thought a—how was it that you so charmingly put it?—a *scheming flirt*."

Carlton leaned forward in his saddle, resting his forearm on the pommel and holding his restive mount easily, as he gazed thoughtfully into Susan's upturned face. As their glances caught and held, Susan observed, with astonishment, that his gray eyes were warm and smiling.

"I apologize, Miss Phillips. We are none of us perfect and it seems that I've erred in forming a too hasty judgment." The corners of his mouth turned up in the delightful smile that few but his closest friends were ever priviledged to see, and Susan wondered how she could ever have thought him a proud, disagreeable man.

An undefinable change came over Carlton's face as he continued to gaze into Susan's frank blue eyes. A change which did not escape the notice of Sir Oliver and Alicia, who each observed privately with a good deal of satisfaction that their two friends were displaying all the signs of the blossoming of deeper affection for each other.

"And do you plan to remain in London for the summer?" Oliver was asking.

"No, I'm to accompany Susan when she goes to Bath," Alicia replied. "My godmother, Lady Brandon, will be departing this week but has permitted me to remain with her cousins, the Stanleys, for Susan's birthday dance and then travel down with the Phillipses. We shall be leaving in two weeks, is that not so, Susan?"

Susan responded somewhat breathlessly that Alicia was quite right.

The four talked quietly for a few moments longer until the horses became too restive for easy conversation, at which time the gentlemen bid their adieux, Sir Oliver promising to pay his respects to Sir Peter and Lady Sophy and shyly inquiring of Alicia if he might one day call upon her.

Alicia, whose day had brightened considerably, told the coachman to drive on, then turned to her friend and smiled. "You know, Susan, I'm of the opinion that you would do quite poorly in cards."

"Whatever do you mean, Alicia?" queried Susan, flashing a startled glance in her friend's direction.

"Simply that you are positively radiant, my dear," she said lightly, nodding to a young gentleman in a high-perch phaeton who was attempting to attract their attention. "And only a nodcock would fail to surmise that Carlton had much to do with it."

Susan flushed and smiled but said nothing, and the carriage turned toward Spencer House.

Only a week later Susan was hard-pressed to recall that sense of contentment and happy expectation as she attempted to fight off the queasiness in her stomach which she had been experiencing every day for the last ten. Upon rising that morning she had been violently ill and the likely reason for this illness could no longer be ignored. It was quite possible that she was increasing.

Her mind balked at the thought, but as she pressed a cool cloth to her mouth and sank thankfully back onto her bed, she forced herself to examine the possibility. She had experienced none of her regular signs and knew full well that many expectant mothers were taken with violent illness for several months. But what was she to do?

She rose and walked slowly to her window, gazing with unseeing eyes into the garden. Her fists clenched at her sides. After what she had been through, to suffer this, too. What would her uncle say? Would he turn her from his home, returning her to Aunt Henry in disgrace? Poor Caro . . . her bright hopes for her sister, not to mention her own prospects, would be quite smashed.

With an effort, Susan turned her mind from her problem as Sarah entered the chamber to help her dress. She wondered briefly what the abigail thought, for she no longer brought anything more than tea and toast for her mistress's breakfast, but Susan felt too miserable to inquire after the girl's thoughts.

The maid had, indeed, guessed the cause of Susan's illness, but as she had told her mother when she had visited her a week past, wild horses couldn't tear the knowledge from her. Oh, yes, she was one who knew how to keep her tongue between her teeth, for her Miss Phillips was a good girl, make no mistake about that, and if there wasn't some reasonable explanation for all this, then her name wasn't Sarah Stubbens.

Indeed, all the servants felt a deep affection for Susan. They had responded immediately to her gentle, open ways and her polite, yet considerate and always perfectly proper treatment of them.

Sarah in particular had fallen under her spell and would never have said or done anything to hurt the young American. She had, in fact, told Mrs. Bartlemay in no uncertain terms that she knew Quality when she saw it and that it didn't depend upon a lady being an Englishwoman born and bred to achieve it, whatever some people thought.

"Sir Peter and Lady Sophy's Quality, which I daresay you won't deny," Sarah declared, glaring at the housekeeper as if daring her to argue the point. "So it would stand to reason that their niece is too, and so she is."

Mrs. Bartlemay could only agree, and as Sarah helped her mistress dress for the day, she was reminded again of the strength of character Miss Phillips was displaying and thought her very romantic and noble.

She couldn't know how Susan was struggling that morning with her sense of injustice, through which the first fingers of panic were beginning to make themselves known. For a few moments of weakness, to suffer a lifetime of disgrace. The effect of all the inner turmoil Susan was experiencing was to cause her at last to burst into tears and to spend the remainder of the day in bed even though she and Lady Sophy had an appointment for the final fitting of the gown she was to wear on her birthday.

When Sophy entered her room later in the afternoon, she felt immediate concern for her niece. The girl looked spent and had dark circles beneath her eyes.

"Why, my dear," she murmured, going to her niece and chafing her icy hands between her own warm ones. "I had no idea you were ill. Sarah said you were tired, but nothing more. Perhaps I should call Dr. Heathcote."

"Please do not bother, Aunt Sophy," exclaimed Susan with forced lightness. "I shall be right as a trivet by tomorrow."

"I knew I should never have allowed you to ride out with Charles and Oliver yesterday, not as overcast as the day was."

The memory of the ride she and Alicia had taken in the company of Lord Carlton and Sir Oliver to see the sights of London flashed through Susan's mind. They had all enjoyed the outing, and although Lord Carlton had initially seemed reluctant to join in their merriment, he had finally thawed. The time had passed so comfortably, as if they had known each other for years, that Susan was tempted to think that the earl was beginning to warm to her. She broke off these musings as she hastened to reassure her aunt that the previous day's adventure had nothing to do with her current malaise. She explained her fatigue by casting blame on the taxing and unaccustomed round of social affairs in which she had been taking part.

Sophy gazed at her niece for a long moment, her eyes keen and questioning, but after issuing a stern injunction that she remain in bed for the remainder of the day, she said nothing more.

The following morning Susan attempted to ignore

the nausea which continued to plague her and dressed quickly in a becoming rose-colored muslin walking dress trimmed with a double row of ribbons of a deeper hue. She placed a little straw hat with ribbons of the same deep shade at a fetching angle on her dark curls then picked up her pelisse and departed for the home of Lady Brandon.

A stern-faced butler, whose countenance softened immediately upon recognizing Susan, answered Lady Phoebe's door and, after sending the carriage round back, ushered her up to Alicia's small drawing room as he had many times in the past weeks. Alicia, who was seated at a dainty escritoire busily engaged in penning a letter to her father, rose and came to her friend when she saw the look of concern on Susan's face.

"Why, Susan, whatever is the matter?" she asked, taking her friend's hand and leading her to a small sofa.

Susan waited until the butler had closed the door firmly behind himself then sighed and grasped Alicia's hands tighter still, her eyes filled with anxiety.

"I vow I'm all about in my head this morning, Alicia," she said, pausing as her friend gazed at her intently. She then took a deep breath, straightened her shoulders, and looked squarely into Alicia's troubled eyes. "I need to talk to you, dear friend. I'm afraid I don't have very pleasant news."

"Susan," breathed Alicia in exasperation, "you are behaving like a want-wit. Don't keep me in suspense another moment."

Susan gently removed her hands from Alicia's grasp, clasped them tightly together in her lap, then tilted her chin. "I believe I am to have a child."

The silence in the room was absolute as Alicia paled, eyes wide and shocked. She paused for a moment to compose herself then darted a quick glance at the closed door.

"Does anyone know of this?" she whispered.

Susan shook her head. "I shall have to tell Uncle Peter soon."

"I'm certain he'll handle things admirably," Alicia responded quickly although doubt edged her tone. She paused, then spoke in a hesitant voice. "Perhaps your wisest course would be to tell your aunt, Susan. I'm sure a woman would understand a thing of this nature far better than a man."

Alicia thought of how her own dear father might react to such a piece of news and fairly shuddered at the vision it brought to mind.

Susan shook her head decidedly. "I could never do that, Alicia. She had been all that is kind and good, and this is certain to cause her great pain."

"Whatever shall you do, Susan?" Alicia burst out, tears filling her eyes.

Susan pressed Alicia's hands then turned aside. "Of course the ton will never forgive me when the news of my condition gets about. I can't play the ostrich, Alicia." She sighed. "I don't even know quite why I've burdened you with this knowledge, unless it's that you were such a comfort to me on board the *Mayfair*."

"And you must know that I'll do anything I'm capable of to help you now," interrupted Alicia fervently, "Perhaps I'll have an idea when I've had a chance to think things through. I'm afraid my brain is sadly muddled now."

Susan smiled wryly. "Yes, it does take a bit of doing to become accustomed to, doesn't it?"

She rose, gathered her reticule and pelisse, then smiled warmly into her friend's steady brown eyes. "You see, Alicia, I'm feeling more the thing already, but I must go now. . . . Aunt Sophy is anxious that Madame Chenier complete her work on the gown for my birthday."

She read the question in her friend's eyes. "I won't tell my uncle until after my birthday ball. I doubt I'll take much pleasure from it but Aunt Sophy is so looking forward to giving it for me, I can't disappoint her."

She bid her friend adieu, then turned and walked rapidly out the door, leaving Alicia gazing after her, a worried expression on her face.

Chapter 8

Sophy had planned the ball which was to celebrate her niece's twentieth birthday for the first week of July, and it was to be on the smallish side as many of their friends had already removed from London, but as responses to her invitations were received, Sophy could not help boasting a little to her husband.

"Everyone who has been invited has accepted the invitation!" she bubbled happily when her husband joined her for tea, several days before the ball. "Not that it shall be a squeeze precisely, but it will be quite a respectable crowd, I daresay."

Peter watched fondly as she poured the fragrant liquid into fragile cups. "But of course, my dear. You are a most accomplished hostess. Everyone delights in being included in one of your do's."

"Fiddle-dee-dee, Peter." She took a small sip from her cup. "You know as well as I that it's Susan all these young men wish to see."

She picked up the list of guests, running a slim finger thoughtfully down the page.

"I vow I've never heard of so many young men remaining in the city after the season has ended. Look at this" — she tapped her nail against the paper— "even George Brummell has accepted and I know he has already taken up residence in Brighton."

Raising her head, she looked thoughtfully at her husband. "Surely George has never before gone so out of his way to show his approval of a young woman."

Peter replaced his cup in its saucer and reached for the list. After glancing at it, he handed it back to his wife and smiled, saying that perhaps the Beau had formed a tendre for their niece.

"Come now, Peter, that's doing it a bit brown, as you would say. Why, sometimes I think that George doesn't give tuppence for the fair sex." She paused for a moment at the thought of the great Brummell returning to London for her niece's ball then looked at her husband, whose eyes were sparkling with suppressed amusement.

"Laugh if you like, Peter," she said agreeably, rising and taking his arm, "but I'll wager that we shall not have Susan living with us for too much longer. I only wish . . ."

Peter grinned sympathetically. "So your matchmaking has come to naught, has it, Sophy?"

Lady Sophy knit her brow. "Well, Charles seems to be fond of Susan but then he seems just as fond of Alicia . . . oh, I don't know."

"Well, don't trouble yourself about it," advised her husband. "I'm not at all anxious for her to leave us anyway."

Sophy could only agree with this thought.

The following morning, the day before her birthday, Susan awoke feeling so poorly that Sarah would not listen to her murmured objections but informed Lady Sophy that her niece was ill. Sophy came to the chamber at once and, upon observing the startling pallor of Susan's face and the dark smudges beneath her eyes, drew Sarah from the room intent upon asking the maid a few questions. After she learned from a stubborn Sarah of the nausea her niece had been experiencing, she sent immediately for Dr. Heathcote. That gentleman arrived at Spencer House within the hour and insisted, over her vigerous protests, that she be given a complete examination. When that task had been completed, he pulled a chair up to her bed and sat down heavily, his kindly face intent and anxious.

"Don't be concerned about sparing my sensibilities, doctor," said Susan sympathetically after several deep sighs had come from the rotund little man. "I assure you that I'm already acquainted with my condition, and so, will not swoon."

The doctor's white eyebrows rose slightly. "It's too early to be absolutely certain, you understand, my dear," he said, observing his patient carefully, "but you do bear all the signs of being with child."

Susan nodded, feeling at least some measure of relief that events were coming to a head and that she wouldn't have to keep her despicable secret much longer.

Dr. Heathcote patted her hand kindly. "I shan't inform anyone of this, if you'd rather I didn't, Miss Phillips, but I would advise that you make your uncle aware of the situation. I assume you haven't already done so?"

Susan shook her head. The doctor gave her a list of instructions and assured her that the morning sickness would soon pass. He then took his leave, telling Sophy, who was waiting anxiously in the yellow saloon, that her niece had been suffering from a very slight case of influenza besides burning the candle at both ends and that she needed to rest.

Later that same day, against her aunt's better judgment, Susan dressed and descended to the library, hoping to find her uncle there. She was anxious to have done with the interview for she knew she could no longer, in good conscience, postpone it.

Her uncle, however, wasn't within, and Susan proceeded to make herself comfortable, determined to wait however long as was necessary. She was leafing aimlessly through the pages of *The Ladies' Home Companion* when Woods interrupted, announcing that Lord Carlton was come to call.

"My uncle isn't at home at present, Woods," Susan said quickly.

Woods cleared his throat. Susan looked up to see that Lord Carlton stood at the butler's elbow. He stepped around Woods and into the room, his eyes warm with concern as he strode over to Susan, one hand outstretched.

"You must forgive me, Miss Phillips." He smiled, taking her hand and holding it firmly. "I dislike bursting in on you like this, but I had come hoping for news of you, and when I heard your voice, I could not resist talking to you in person."

Susan gazed speechlessly at the tall gentleman. could he have heard of her condition from Alicia?

... no ... impossible. If that were the case, he would hardly have been so pleasantly concerned.

Carlton, who was watching her face, carefully noticed the bewilderment which flickered in her eyes. "I had heard you were ill," he remarked gently, releasing her hand and glancing about the room. "May I sit down?"

Susan nodded politely, and much to her surprise, he took the seat next to her on the little sofa, turning slightly to face her.

"I must say," he said lightly, attempting to put her at her ease, "it's gratifying to discover that reports of your illness were exaggerated."

Susan gazed impassively at the earl, trying to regain her composure, which had been sadly shattered. She prayed that she could keep him from seeing the effect of his presence so close beside her.

"I'm touched by your concern, my lord," she teased as she inched away from him, finding she could not think when he was so near. "I had thought you, of all persons, wouldn't have been overly concerned that I might be feeling out of countenance. Or perhaps the truth is that you rushed here to confirm the report of my illness? It is rather difficult to be fortune-hunting when one is out of curl."

Carlton grinned appreciatively. "I deserved that, Miss Phillips." He paused and his face became grave. "I'm afraid I made a cake of myself the night of Sophy's rout. I was distressed by the event in the garden, more so because of the scandal I have been enduring . . ." He scanned her face intently. "No doubt you've heard of my, er, engagement?"

Susan nodded. "Well," he said, rising and beginning to stride about the room. "I'll not bore on with my feelings in either matter . . . suffice it to say that I'm sincerely sorry for my actions." He grinned down at her. "I'm not much used to eating humble pie, Miss Phillips, so please do bear with me."

He sat down beside her once again. Susan's pulse leaped at the look of gentle concern, mixed with another undefined emotion, which he bestowed upon her.

Carlton searched her face intently. "Elliott, my valet, informed me that you had not been feeling well since the night of the rout party." He broke off at this point and smiled at the startled question in her eyes. "I believe your maid, Sarah, is a particular friend of his although I have told him any number of times he is much too old for such nonsense. He swears he is only taking the place of the father she lost but I have the impression her feelings run a little deeper. Anyway, to continue . . . as I have furthered our acquaintance, I've come to the conclusion that I did you a grave disservice the night of Sophy's party, and may have, by some of the shocking things I said, sent you into a decline." He reached for her hand and held it with both of his. "Please accept my apologies, it's very important to me that you do."

Susan stared at the earl in dismay. She could not think that he spoke to many young women in so unconventional and personal a manner. It could mean only one thing. She had dreamed of receiving an offer from him and even now her heart leaped joyously at the thought although she knew that he would despise her when he learned of her condition. She gently removed her hand from his grasp, anxious only to have the now painful interview done with before more was said.

"Of course, I forgive you, my lord," she asserted gaily, attempting desperately to lighten the tone of the conversation. "Actually, my so-called decline is merely exhaustion resulting from an overindulgence in pleasure, or so Dr. Heathcote assures. Pray set your mind at ease. The fault is mine alone."

She began to rise, the smile which she had pasted so firmly on her lips trembling ever so slightly, when Carlton gently pulled her back down beside him. She felt the hard length of his leg burning through the thin muslin of her gown and prayed that he could not feel how her leg trembled at the intimacy.

He retained her hand and gazed gravely into her eyes. "I have one thing more to discuss, Miss Phillips, before you escape, although I fear I may be somewhat premature."

Susan pulled her hand from his hard grasp and jumped to her feet. "I beg you will say no more," she cried in agitation.

Tears filled her eyes and, to her fury, began to run down her cheeks. She averted her head, hoping he would not see how deeply she cared . . . oh, if only she could allow him to continue . . .

Carlton rose and reached for her chin, turning her face to his, he then removed a handkerchief from his pocket and tenderly wiped her cheeks.

"I certainly hadn't intended to make you weep," he murmured huskily, his throat suddenly too tight to swallow.

At that moment Peter cleared his throat several times to announce his presence.

"Not at all the thing, Charles," he chided good-naturedly as he closed the door behind him. "You're alone for five minutes with my niece, teasing her no doubt, and she's reduced to tears."

"I wasn't teasing Miss Phillips, Peter," Carlton objected curtly, wishing his friend to the devil. "On the contrary, I was quite serious."

"Dear me," prodded Peter, unable to resist a little teasing of his own. "This sounds rather interesting."

"Peter," warned the earl grimly, "if you continue in this ridiculous fashion, I shall take myself elsewhere."

"Then by all means." Peter grinned, standing away from the door. "Perhaps your absence will bring a smile back to my niece's face."

Carlton drew a deep breath then gave a crack of laughter. "Perhaps you're right, Peter." His laughter died and he glanced tenderly at Susan. "As a matter of fact, I wished to say something of a private nature to your niece but I should by rights discuss it with you first."

Peter's brows rose. "By all means, Charles, come round tomorrow . . . now wait, tomorrow's the ball, better make it the day after."

Carlton nodded and took Susan's hand, a smile playing about the corners of his mouth. "I wish I could say more, Miss Phillips, but you've asked me not to, so I'll wait until I've spoken with Peter." One dark brow quirked enticingly and Susan longed to smooth it with her fingertip. "That's what you wanted, isn't it, my dear?"

Susan nodded, feeling that events were hurtling past her much too swiftly. She forced a wan smile, a lump in her throat and the possibility of more tears making talking a very precarious business. Lord Carlton seemed satisfied, however, and after bowing to Susan, he bade Peter farewell and took his leave.

Peter turned to his niece with a smile. "It sounds as though we may soon have some good news for your aunt."

"I—I wish you wouldn't say anything to her just yet, Uncle Peter."

"As you wish, my dear." He looked keenly at her. "What is it, Susan? Is anything wrong?"

This was the opportunity Susan had been waiting for, but after the preceding events, she needed time to put her thoughts in order. She smiled brightly at her uncle and replied that she was a little blue-deviled.

"Well, well, there's nothing in that," comforted her uncle, patting her hand. "No doubt your birthday party will chase away the megrims. Never saw anything like a ball to bring the sunshine into a young lady's face."

Susan attempted a cheerful response then excused herself and fled to her chamber.

Her birthday had taken on an added significance as she felt that the ball would probably be the last one she would be attending in London. As she prepared for it the following evening, she felt in alt one moment and depressed the next.

Sarah was worried about her mistress but kept her tongue between her teeth, except to suggest that Susan allow her to apply a bit of rouge to her pale cheeks. After she had done so, she nodded and smiled at the reflection Susan presented in the pier glass, saying that her charge now looked fine as a fivepence, and even Susan herself was inclined to agree.

She was dressed in a lace gown of her favorite color of pale blue over an underskirt of deeper blue and wore matching kid slippers. The slim, high-waisted dress emphasized her slender figure to perfection and her only jewelry was a string of matched lustrous pearls given to her that morning by her aunt and uncle.

She departed her chamber and turned her steps toward the large drawing room, where her aunt and uncle were greeting the few special guests who had been invited to dine with the family before the ball. Her uncle rose and went to her at once as she entered the room.

"You look enchanting, my dear," he remarked, tucking her hand under his arm and drawing her into the room. Before very many minutes had passed, most of their guests had arrived and stood scattered about in congenial groups.

Sir William and Lady Caroline, along with Freddie, had been invited to take dinner with the family as had Sir Oliver and Lord Carlton, and Susan watched eagerly for those two gentlemen while she attempted to keep Freddie from pressing his attentions upon her as he seemed determined to do.

The gentlemen arrived at last and Susan felt her spirits rise although she attempted to hold them in check, warning herself quite firmly that it would be very ill advised in her to allow her feelings for Lord Carlton to make themselves known to any of the others.

When dinner was announced, the earl, who was

offering his apologies to his host and hostess for his tardiness, took the opportunity which had presented itself and offered Susan his arm, begging that she allow him the privilege of escorting her into dinner.

She quickly accepted, ignoring the peeved look which Freddie flashed in her direction. Upon reaching the dining room she made the happy discovery that Sophy had placed the earl on her left hand.

Dinner was superb although Susan tasted very little of it. Instead she conversed eagerly with Lord Carlton, who seemed intent upon monopolizing her attention.

Sophy slanted a glance in the direction of her niece from time to time and was well satisfied with the direction the evening was taking. She herself was enjoying her chat with Lady Caroline immensely.

When the final removes had been dispensed with, Lady Sophy and Susan along with Sir Peter greeted their other guests as they arrived, and judging from the number of people they greeted, the ball was assured of success.

Susan was finally given leave by her aunt to join the others and she walked quickly over to Alicia, who was chatting gaily with Sir Oliver. Lord Carlton approached the group and addressed himself to Susan as the first strains of a waltz came from the musicians.

"Shall we attempt the waltz, Miss Phillips?" he queried lightly. "Now that you've won the accolades of Lady Jersey, it wouldn't be unseemly to do so."

As much as she desired to dance with him, Susan couldn't feel that it was proper, in her present predicament, to encourage the advances of any gentleman, particularly one who seemed to need little further encouragement. She stood silent, casting anxiously about for a reasonable excuse.

The earl's lips tightened as he waited for her response. Did she truly not care for him or was she still angry at the error he had made in his evaluation of her character?

"Come, Miss Phillips," he commanded at last, taking her hand in his firm grip and leading her out onto the floor.

"I think you must return me to my chair, my lord," she ordered breathlessly. "I had really not intended to dance this evening."

Carlton tightened his grip on her hand and placed his arm about her, swinging her into the waltz, and showing not the least inclination to bend to her wishes. He smiled down into her face, one eyebrow arched with disbelief.

"Come now, Miss Phillips. You cannot think me caper-witted enough to believe that you are going to sit out every dance on your own birthday. That's stretching it too far by half. Now, Miss Phillips, you mustn't frown so." Lord Carlton laughed as he drew her a fraction closer to him than was quite proper. "People are certain to think that you hold me in excessive dislike," he teased, "and then I shall be forced to abandon you to the arms of another swain. Mr. Swithin, I am sure, would be more than happy to oblige."

The earl glanced about, looking for that resplendent young man and, upon observing him, bent his dark head closer to Susan's and whispered conspiratorially in her ear. "See how he stands in wait, Miss

Phillips," he breathed. "Not for one moment would I feel comfortable with him hovering so. You do see now, do you not, that you must be pleasant to me so I will not cast you off?"

Susan had to chuckle despite herself.

The earl was a superb dancer and Susan finally relaxed in his arms, giving up her attitude of reluctance and allowing the strains of the lovely music to carry her away. For those few moments she forgot her uncertain future, giving herself over to the swirling music and Carlton's strong embrace.

When the music ended, Lord Carlton returned her to Alicia and, after the smallest of bows, departed.

A myriad of feelings had overwhelmed him as he had danced, the most urgent being tenderness and the desire to protect the girl in his arms. He had allowed himself to recall for an instant the sweet sensation of her lips pressed to his, and the memory had set his pulses hammering. He had nearly offered for her the day before and still meant to, for he could not get her out of his head.

Susan seated herself calmly beside Alicia although she did not feel at all relaxed. Doubts assailed her and she feared she had seemed overly coming during their waltz. Oliver joined her, claiming a dance, and she attempted to put her troubles to rout as she once again whirled down the floor.

During the waltz she looked about and noticed Alicia in the arms of a handsome young officer in his regimentals but she could find no sign of Lord Carlton. Oliver regarded her searching gaze with amusement.

"Gone to the card room," he said teasingly, giving a

quick laugh at the indignant look which flashed from Susan's expressive eyes when she icily informed him that she was quite certain she had not been looking for anyone in particular.

"And definitely not for Swithin," Oliver remarked drily. A frown crossed his face as his thoughts dwelt on Freddie.

"Should warn you that I overheard him making a wager with one of his cohorts that he'd dance at least four waltzes with you tonight, Miss Phillips," he said to Susan in a troubled voice.

"Why that insufferable little . . . little toad," exploded Susan, forgetting entirely that she had been on the verge of reading Sir Oliver a very good scold on the virtue of minding one's own business. "If it were not such terribly bad ton, and quite certain to be remarked upon, I would not allow him even one dance. That, it seems, I must do, but no more."

"Not a man to take refusal well, Miss Phillips," Oliver added hesitantly. "Fact is, acts like a spoilt child. Only a warning, though," he concluded rather hastily when he noticed that his words had caused the militant sparkle in her eyes to be turned upon him once again.

The dance ended with Susan stating quite wrathfully that she was in no doubt as to her ability to handle Freddie Swithin, and Oliver left her, determined nevertheless, to find Carlton and inform him that, in his opinion at least, Swithin might prove troublesome.

The evening continued to be one of enchantment for Susan, who had soon realized that her behavior would be more certain of occasioning remark if she were not to dance than if she did, regardless of how she felt in the matter. She had thus far danced every dance, managing rather adroitly at the same time to avoid Freddie Swithin. She now stood by the French windows leading to the garden, quietly sipping champagne. She had in truth imbibed the golden wine too freely as everyone insisted upon drinking a toast to her birthday.

As she remained quietly waiting for Alicia, who had gone to repair a slight tear in the hem of her gown, she sniffed appreciatively of the warm, flower-scented air coming from the garden. The breeze caressed her shoulders and she decided that nothing could be quite so lovely as to step out for a breath of fresh air.

She swayed slightly as she moved away from the door and entering the garden seemed suddenly more difficult than she had first supposed. Objects began to appear a bit fuzzy and she turned from the entrance, deciding that perhaps she should lie down for a few moments. Before she could take a step in the direction of her chamber, however, a hand was laid upon her arm. Startled, she glanced at the gentleman who had appeared at her side.

"At last I have you to myself, Miss Phillips," Freddie Swithin mouthed after executing an arrogant bow. "I must own that I have been waiting impatiently all evening to dance with you and had at last begun to think you were attempting to avoid me."

"Not at all, Mr. Swithin," Susan said coolly, forcing a tight smile for the rude young man. "I cannot think how you came by such an idea. Indeed, I should be glad to dance now except that I'm feeling rather tired."

"Perhaps then," he said, gazing boldly at her as he retained his tight grip on her arm and led her toward the French windows, "you would honor me with a walk instead. I vow you are looking quite flushed with the heat and are in need of a stroll." He raised his thin eyebrows. "Can it be that you were hoping I would come over and suggest this very thing, Miss Phillips? Was that your reason for lingering so at the doors?"

Susan attempted to remove her arm from his grasp but found that she could not do so without causing a scene so she simply murmured that she had entertained no such idea and that in fact she did not at all care for a stroll but she might step into the garden for a moment. She was seething with indignation but Freddie, who was convinced that she had been hoping for just such a flirtation, did not notice her reluctance as he pulled her out of doors, where they were soon beyond the line of vision of the dancers within.

"I should like you to release my arm, Mr. Swithin," Susan exclaimed sharply, wishing desperately that she had not drunk so much wine.

"I shall do no such thing, my dear," replied Freddie. "I've cooled my heels all evening, enduring this boring party as best I could whilst I waited to find the opportunity to be alone with you, and I'll not give it up now."

As he spoke, he pulled her out into the garden, and when Susan fell against him after stumbling on the stones, his arms were instantly about her, smothering her face against his coat.

"I should have known you'd not be able to resist me," Freddie muttered, his hands beginning to move over her back as he pressed wet kisses on her neck.

Susan was at first too stunned by the young man's ridiculous words to respond and, when she was able to protest, could only beat futilely upon his back. An observer paused for a moment at the open door, then strolled casually into the garden.

"Very interesting scene," Carlton drawled. "Perhaps, however, Mr. Swithin, I should suggest that this is neither the time nor the place for such activities."

Freddie glared at the speaker. "I don't think Miss Phillips finds my caresses distasteful, my lord. It was she, in fact, who initiated them." As Freddie spoke, he did not release Susan.

"Release her instantly and get out of this house before I thrash you within an inch of your life," Carlton snapped, rage mounting in his voice.

Freddie flashed the earl a look of pure hatred, before abruptly releasing Susan and retreating into the house. Lord Carlton caught Susan's arm and moved with her into the moonlight, away from the light streaming from a window.

"Did that sapskull hurt you?" he asked angrily, a muscle working in his jaw. He received no answer and took her shoulders in his hands, looking worriedly into her face.

"Susan . . ." he began anxiously, his look of anxiety changing as he stared intently at her. "Good God," he murmured, lips twitching with barely suppressed amusement. "I think you're foxed."

Susan heard him and drew herself up in the attempt to deny his accusations.

"I—I'm most certainly not foxed, my lord," she stammered angrily. "Merely tired. And now, I think I should like you to help me to my bed. I have an a—abominable headache."

As she finished, her words were slightly slurred and she gazed at the earl, attempting to regain her poise but managing only to look adorably confused.

Carlton grinned hugely. "I should think you do have a headache, my dear, and escorting you to your chamber is hardly an invitation I can refuse. Alas, I find I'm forced by honor to remember that you're a member of my friend's family and not take advantage of the situation."

What was the man rambling on so about? Susan wondered, as she stared up at him, her brow knit.

"You know," she mused finally while she regarded him through the haze in which he floated, "you're quite a handsome gentleman. Just like Caro's count."

Carlton grinned once again, his smile fading as he gazed for a long moment into the dark blue of her eyes. He then slowly gathered her into his arms and smoothed the hair back from her brow. "It seems I have no honor left when you look at me like that, my love," he murmured.

"N—nor I, my lord . . ." Susan whispered shakily, feeling as though she were drowning in his intense gaze.

With a softly murmured oath, Carlton lowered his mouth to hers in a gentle kiss, then drew back startled at the response he felt.

Susan put her arms around his neck, feeling wonderfully safe and secure. "It's quite all right for you to . . . kiss me, my lord," she whispered, a shy smile tilting the corners of her mouth as she swayed slightly. "You see, I . . . rather like it."

"Damnation," Carlton muttered, lowering his mouth once again to hers, knowing full well that he was taking advantage of her slightly tipsy state but unable to help himself.

This time his kiss was hard and demanding, and Susan felt like the bubbles from the champagne she had drunk were exploding in her veins. She tightened her grip around his neck and pressed herself to him, her soft mouth responding urgently to his demands. He groaned as he felt her lips part and his kiss became deeper, more passionate.

Suddenly he backed away from her and pulled her arms from around his neck, staring into her bewildered eyes, his own dark with passion.

"My God," he muttered huskily, "I'm no better than Swithin." His stare hardened a little as he thought of the scene he had interrupted. "Although," he continued bitterly, "if this is how you responded to him, I believe I owe him an apology."

Susan felt as though he had slapped her, and all the lingering warmth she had felt from his kiss turned to ice. "How can you even think such a thing?" she gasped, wishing she could think a little more clearly.

"Quite easily, my love," he responded harshly. "He did mention that you enticed him into the garden."

Susan pulled away from him, her head clearing rapidly and her sense of shame at her behavior growing as rapidly. "Then it must be as you thought, my lord," she said hotly, "and I'm merely after a husband."

Carlton gazed at her for a long moment. "I no

longer know what to think, my love."

"I wish you will stop calling me your love in that odious fashion and return me to my aunt," Susan responded icily, feeling she couldn't tolerate another moment in his presence after her wanton behavior. Why was it that the man always seemed to bring out the worst in her?

"Certainly," he replied, a glint of mischief suddenly sparkling in his eyes. "I only hope you'll not be embarrassed tomorrow morning by your, er, behavior tonight."

A hot blush stained her cheeks as she turned on her heel and stumbled past him and back into the ball room, where she found her aunt searching anxiously for her.

Carlton stepped forward and offered her a rather hurried explanation of the earlier events in the garden and Sophy quickly took her niece to her chamber, tut-tutting her concern as she went.

"What is it, Charles?" Peter queried, concerned about the picture Susan had presented as she had entered the room, her face flushed and her bosom heaving. "Has Susan met with an accident?"

Carlton's lips twitched. "I'm afraid she had a bit too much wine, Peter." He paused and his eyes grew cold. "Also, there was a small problem fending off an unwanted admirer."

At least one hopes he was unwanted, Carlton reflected angrily.

"Which young pup would dare such a thing in my own house?" Peter demanded.

"Don't become overly alarmed, Peter," Carlton replied soothingly. "I've sent Mr. Swithin home with the promise of a sound thrashing should he ever attempt such a thing again."

Peter looked relieved, and he remarked that although he had never had two good thoughts to rub together about Freddie Swithin, he hardly struck him as a villainous cad.

Carlton nodded, his face carefully controlled and his tone curiously flat. "I agree with you, Peter, but I'll kill him if he every lays a finger upon Susan again."

Sir Peter and Lord Carlton exchanged a speaking look, after which the older man smiled. "Just so . . . you may call on me at your convenience."

Carlton agreed but, as people were departing, said nothing more and took his leave with Oliver.

Susan filled his thoughts as he listened, with little concentration, to Oliver's conversation after he had climbed into his phaeton and gathered the reins into his hands. She was an enchanting girl. The niece of his dearest friend and so lovely . . . his blood warmed as he remembered her ardent response to his kiss, then his eyes narrowed . . . could he trust her? He had found no woman, with the exception of Sophy, worthy of trust. They were selfish, silly, and deceitful but it pained him, more than he cared to admit, to think of Susan in that fashion. And yet, he mused, he had been involved with her in what would be construed, by some of his friends, as very real flirtation on two occasions.

She must have known he was going to offer for her and still she had gone with Swithin into the garden. Perhaps she had even led him there and had encouraged his advances . . . his mind balked at continuing in that line of thought and he suddenly shook his head, attempting to drive such disagreeable, but all too possible, ideas from his mind.

As his horses stopped in front of his residence, he forced himself to give up on the problem of Miss Phillips's character. He had decided to offer for her and would do so at the first opportunity on the morrow.

Chapter 9

Susan did not appear at the breakfast table the following morning until quite late, for she had awakened with a terrible headache. That, combined with a bad case of self-loathing as regards her actions of the evening before, caused her, after emitting a groan of remorse, to give in to temptation and to return for several hours to the cacoon-like safety of her bed.

When she did appear, neat as a pin in a sober gray morning gown, relieved only by a white collar at the neck and bands of lace at the cuffs, she discovered from her uncle, who was still at the table reading his newspaper, that her aunt had not yet arisen.

"Such a charming surprise, however, to have you join me, Susan," he said with a quick smile, folding the journal and pouring out a cup of coffee for her. "I was quite afraid I should be forced to endure a solitary meal. Sophy rarely makes an appearance before early afternoon after one of her parties."

"I don't wish to interrupt you, uncle," returned Susan with a little smile, thinking that she could hardly blame him if he preferred reading to her company that morning.

Peter gallantly assured her that she was in no way intruding. After filling her plate with kidneys and eggs from the sideboard, he resumed his seat, remarking that if she desired, he would have more of the York ham sliced and sent up.

Susan refused and attempted to eat what had been placed before her but soon gave up and sipped her coffee as she stared pensively before her.

Peter laid his fork aside and peered at her. "You seem unusually quiet this morning, Susan. Would you care to tell me what's troubling you?"

Susan drew in a deep breath and folded her hands in her lap. "I'm afraid I disgraced you and Aunt Sophy quite terribly last night, sir," she said, looking squarely into his warm eyes.

"Fol-de-rol," objected Peter, waving his hand as if to put a halt to her apology. "If that's all that's amiss, you must put it from your mind. It's of no consequence, I assure you. That sort of thing happens now and again to everyone and is nothing to be in a pelter about. Why, I remember a time when your Aunt Sophy . . ." He grinned at Susan and one eyelid flickered. "Ah, well, no matter. The point is that very few people know of your, um, shall we say, indisposition? Only myself, Sophy, and Carlton. All the others were told that you had to retire with a sick headache brought on by all the excitement. So you see, all is right and tight."

He withdrew his watch and glanced at it. "You must excuse me now, my dear. I have some business to take care of in the city but I shan't be gone long."

Susan rose and walked with him to the door. He collected his hat and walking stick from Woods then turned once again to his niece. "Bye the bye, if Carlton should come before I've returned, beg pardon and ask him to wait. Not likely to happen, though," he mused with a quick grin. "Takes these young men all morning to dress."

Susan continued to stand as she was after Woods had softly closed the door behind her uncle's retreating back.

"Is there something I can do for you, Miss Phillips?" he inquired anxiously, noting the frown creasing her brow.

"What . . . oh, no, thank you, Woods," she replied, with a slight shake of her head. "I was merely thinking of something." She turned and made her way back to the breakfast room suddenly feeling an icy calm.

She knew that Lord Carlton was coming to offer for her and she knew that she must turn him down. A shiver went down her back at the thought of his reaction, then she tilted her chin bravely and clenched her fists. She must find the courage to face him, but oh, how terribly hard it was going to be.

She picked up a cup of coffee at the sideboard and walked with it to the table, absently setting it down and staring at a reflection of herself in the large gilt-edged mirror hanging over the fireplace. What would it have been like to be able to marry Lord Carlton, to become his countess? She frowned at her image then started and gasped as another figure was reflected in the mirror.

Lord Carlton smiled and took her hand. "Forgive me," he said apologetically. "I didn't mean to frighten you. Woods let me know where to find you."

Susan quickly withdrew her hand from his and moved nervously to the door. "Shall we remove to my uncle's library, where we may be more comfortable?"

Carlton smiled again. "I had certainly meant to use Peter's library this morning but I had rather hoped he would be in it."

Susan didn't respond to the light humor in his tone, and as they reached the library, Carlton softly closed the door and took her shoulders in his hands.

"I apologize for my behavior last night," he said.

"My lord, please," she said, pulling away.

He took her chin in his hand, turning her face up to his and forcing her to look at him. "Never say you're embarrassed to see me now." He gazed warmly into her eyes, and his voice was suddenly a little husky. "I have only the fondest memories of last night."

"Oh, don't . . . you mustn't say anymore," Susan cried fiercely, jerking her chin from his grasp and moving quickly to the French doors.

Carlton stood as he was for a moment, an odd light in his eyes. "Surely you understand why I've come this morning, don't you, Susan?" he asked quietly.

"Yes, I believe I do."

Carlton frowned. He crossed the room in quick strides and once again pulled her around to face him, this time rather more roughly. "I take it you mean to refuse me."

She gazed at him for a long moment and then gave an almost imperceptible nod. "I'm sorry," she whispered. "I hadn't meant to make such a sorry botch of the job."

Carlton stared at her, his fingers digging into her shoulders. "There is someone else, perhaps." His voice was flat, emotionless.

Susan found herself at a loss for words.

"Well, is there?" Carlton demanded, barely resisting the urge to shake her.

"No . . . yes . . . not exactly."

Carlton released her. He strode over to the fireplace, thrusting his hands into his pockets, and stared into the flames. "A rather ambiguous response," he commented drily.

Never had Susan imagined that turning down his offer would be quite so difficult. "My lord," she said in a stifled voice, "I cannot marry you nor anyone."

"I was under the impression that you felt something for me," Carlton said calmly. "Was I wrong?"

Susan took a deep breath. "Yes, you were wrong."

Carlton turned to look at her.

"No, you weren't wrong," she said. She sunk into a sofa, as if her legs could no longer support her. "My lord, I cannot lie to you. I do care for you. And there is no one else . . . in the sense that you mean."

In an instant, Carlton was at her side, gathering her hands in his. "Then why, for God's sake, will you not marry me?"

"I cannot."

"Why?"

"My lord, do not ask me."

"I am asking you."

"I cannot tell you."

For once, Susan could not blame Lord Carlton for the look of complete exasperation that came over his face.

"My dear, I shall make you tell me," he said softly.

Then she was in his arms and he lowered warm open lips to cover hers. He tightened his hold around her tense shoulders and his mouth became more insistent. With a soft cry of anguish Susan yielded to the hunger within her that had burst into flames at the touch of his mouth. Her arms went about his neck and her lips parted, allowing him freedom to explore her mouth.

Carlton's pulse raced as he felt her body press against his. He forced her soft lips further apart, greedily deepening the kiss, savoring the sweet taste of her mouth. Responding to her needs, Susan timidly imitated his actions, her tongue slipping into his mouth, becoming bolder as the pleasure mounted.

With a slight groan, Carlton cradled her head in his hands, and his lips touched her eyes, her cheekbones, and the fine line of her jaw before returning to her mouth. Susan felt as though her body were made of spun sugar and that it was melting under the heat of his mouth as she eagerly returned the kiss, matching his passion with her own.

At last Carlton lifted his head, but was unable to let her go. Susan leaned against him, her heart hammering in her ears. "Please, my lord," she said faintly, knowing that for both their sakes she had to make them stop. "You must let me go."

"Why won't you marry me?"

"Because—"

"Why?" he said, his lips at her throat.

"Because I am with child." Susan shut her eyes; she couldn't bear to see the expression on Lord Carlton's face.

There was a long moment of terrible silence.

"Indeed," he said at last in an icy voice.

She opened her eyes but immediately looked away from Carlton's face, which had gone white, and the ugly light in his eyes.

"Whose child?"

She stared mutely at her hands clasped in her lap. How could she tell him that she didn't know.

"Ah yes," Carlton said, rising to his feet. "The lady refused to name the father. How commendable. How noble. How trite. My dear, isn't it a bit late for discretion!"

Susan's eyes blazed at his withering sarcasm. How dare he speak to her so!

"My lord, you have made your point sufficiently, I think. I am a dishonored woman for whom you can have nothing but disgust. At least give me credit for having turned down your offer of marriage, which you must admit would have been an easy solution for me. And now I must ask you to leave me."

"I guarantee you, my dear, it would not have been an easy solution for you," Carlton replied. "But perhaps you're right. I should thank you for admitting this before we were married. But tell me, is it because you have a bigger fish on the line?" He saw her back stiffen slightly. "Oh, don't worry, your sordid little secret is safe with me. Indeed, I'm most anxious to follow your progress. I admit I'm curious to see the price you set for your undeniable beauty and, er, good breeding."

Susan continued to sit for quite a while after he had left the house. Although she was very pale and shaking a little in reaction to the ugly accusations he had flung at her head, she did not blame him, for she knew that he had been very badly hurt. Instead she blamed only herself.

As Lord Carlton left the house, his groom could easily see from his thinned lips and angry scowl that his employer was in a rage and he wisely refrained from comment when he was tersely informed that he would have to find his own way home. In spite of his wrath, however, Carlton easily and efficiently threaded his phaeton through the press of traffic until he had left the city behind. At that time he allowed his feelings some release and lowered his hands, giving his team office to run. His hands were steady and his driving faultless but an observer would have been chilled by the fury in the hardened eyes. It wasn't until he had feather-edged a blind corner, narrowly missing a chaise and four, that the earl slowed his team. Still enraged, he turned his lathered horses and made his way back to the city.

When he arrived at his house, he threw his hat and gloves down upon a side table and entered his book room, calling for Elliott to bring him a bottle of brandy.

His butler entered somewhat warily moments later, having been informed of the earl's mood by the footweary groom, who had returned before his master.

Carlton looked coldly at the man as he placed the bottle and one glass on the desk. "I called for Elliott, not you, Brixton."

"Begging your pardon, my lord," the butler said stonily, "Mr. Elliott left the house above an hour ago, on personal business."

"I am not to be disturbed," Carlton said in a dangerously soft voice. "And if I find that you cannot protect me from visitors, I shall find someone who can. Have I made myself clear?"

Brixton murmured that he had and quickly made his escape. He paused for a deep breath of relief after he had closed the door behind himself then made his way to the kitchen to warn the rest of the earl's staff that the groom had been in the right of it and Lord Carlton's mood was nasty indeed.

The earl spent some moments sunk in his chair, brandy glass in hand, experiencing the most turbulent and confusing emotions of his life. He was furious with Miss Phillips but no less was he angry with himself for having been taken in by her wiles. Unaccountably, however, a great deal of his rage was directed at the unknown father in the case. He felt it was fortunate that he didn't know the man, for his hands itched to feel his throat between them.

He leapt to his feet, no longer able to remain inactive, and began to pace about the room telling himself that Miss Phillips was a jade . . . a totally unprincipled baggage, and that he was better off without her. At last he sank back in his chair with his only companion, the hollow satisfaction that he had been right not to trust her.

Susan, on the other hand, had not been allowed any respite in which to attempt to regain control of her disordered emotions for after Carlton had departed, Woods had ushered Miss Wentworth into the library.

"I'm sorry, Alicia," Susan said, frowning slightly. "I have the headache, so I'm afraid you'll have to hold me excused from a visit."

Alicia gazed at her consideringly for a moment then removed her gloves and bonnet. "I'm sorry you're not feeling well, but I think you had better hear what I've discovered."

Susan sighed and pressed two fingers lightly to her temple. "Well, if we must talk, at least let us go to my sitting room, where we may be more comfortable."

She asked Woods to have tea brought up. After she and Alicia were seated, and the tea poured, Susan turned to her friend.

"I'm afraid you've found me in low spirits, Alicia."

Alicia frowned for a moment then said enigmatically, "Well, perhaps alls well that ends well."

"Whatever do you mean?"

"I shall begin at the beginning. Lady Brandon and I were involved in a slight carriage accident . . . no . . . no, Susan," she said quickly, seeing that Susan was about to interrupt, "we're fine. But our accident occurred near Lord Carlton's residence, so quite naturally Lady Phoebe and I elected to solicit his aid." Alicia paused for a moment. "Do you remember the man I couldn't place when we were on the *Mayfair*?"

Susan frowned then slowly nodded her head. "I vaguely remember something of the kind, Alicia, but why?"

"Because he came out of Lord Carlton's house to help us. He is the earl's valet . . ."

Susan looked bewildered. "But what has that to say to anything?"

Alicia looked earnestly at her friend. "The night I found you in the maid's cabin I had seen a man in the companionway. I couldn't make him out, but he was dressed like a gentleman and something about him reminded me so much of Lord Carlton. Of course I was under the impression that Carlton had sailed before we did so I put the resemblence down to my imagination."

Susan was gazing at Alicia in horror. "What are you saying?"

"That Charles was the man who seduced you."

Susan's eyes were wide with shock. "I don't believe it. It's not possible."

"Well, it is, Susan," Alicia continued ruthlessly. "I told Elliot that I recognized him from the *Mayfair* and he remembered me too. I quite naturally asked him if Lord Carlton had also been aboard. He admitted that Charles was indeed on board but had demanded complete privacy." Alicia stirred a little uncomfortably. "The remainder of the conversation was a trifle embarrassing but Elliott was aware that something untoward had taken place. Actually, he had pieced most of the puzzel together."

"But . . . but how can you be so certain it was he . . . and . . . and me?"

"Oh, Susan, unless two young ladies were mistaken for maids and ravished on the voyage, it was indeed Lord Carlton."

Susan looked stunned. "What shall I do?"

"Do?" repeated Alicia. "I should think that the first thing you should do is acquaint the earl with this information. Elliott came with me and he can go back with us to face Charles."

Susan was aghast. "I could never . . . would never tell him about this, Alicia."

"Well, you must," replied her friend tartly. "He is the father of the child you carry, my dear."

The initial shock Susan had felt upon hearing Alicia's tale had begun to ebby only to be replaced with the dawning of anger. She got up from her chair and began to pace.

"When I think of the humiliation I had to suffer this morning . . . the agony I've been through. Oh, no, my friend. I shall never tell him . . . I despise him!"

"That's all very well," pronounced Alicia prosaically, "but your child will need a name and I'm of the opinion that he deserves the one that is rightfully his. In fact," she continued firmly, "if you feel unable to see him today, we'll send Charles a note asking him to call tomorrow and you can tell him then."

"He'll refuse to come," Susan flashed, "and if he did come, I wouldn't receive him."

Alicia stood up and smoothed her skirt. "Well, I can see that you need some time to reflect upon this, so I shall take a turn around the garden, then perhaps we can discuss rationally what is to be done."

Susan made herself sit down and pour out a fresh cup of tea but her hand was trembling a little as she did so, and she knew that it would take some time to restore a semblance of order to her mind. For the moment, however, the thought of Lord Carlton enraged her. The things he had said about her character ... she shuddered, remembering the scene that morning. That he had accused and condemned her so ruthlessly ... when he was the author of all her misfortune. She found herself trembling once again as rage engulfed her. She knew that Alicia was right and she should inform him of the truth. She also was aware that the solution to all her problems lay in marrying him, but she felt she could not. A rush of tears came to her eyes and she angrily dashed them away. Her sense of the injustice of the situation and her own ill usage increased as did the determination that she would never marry him.

When Alicia returned to the sitting room, she found that Susan's emotions were enough under control, to give a semblance of composure. To Alicia's dismay, however, she discovered also that her friend was stubbornly refusing to marry the earl, although she had agreed he must be informed of the whole unfortunate matter. With that, Alicia had to be content.

A note was quickly penned, requesting that the earl visit Susan the following morning, and handed to Elliott to take to his employer.

"Don't let him ignore it," Alicia said urgently when she handed him the note.

"That he shall not do," Elliott replied grimly,

touching his hat. "But don't you worry, Miss Wentworth," he continued, correctly reading the anxiety in her soft eyes. "We both know that his lordship would be the first to want to make all right."

Alicia smiled gratefully, but thought, as she watched the man make his way hurriedly down the street, that Susan might prove more of an obstacle than Carlton.

As she was returning to join Susan in her sitting room, she met Sir Peter on the stair.

"Well, Miss Wentworth," he said jovially, "has Carlton accompanied you today?"

"Why, no, Sir Peter," she replied, stammering a little.

"Hmm . . . can't imagine what ails the man. He requested an interview." He smiled down at her. "I daresay you know the reason. Sophy and I couldn't be happier. Well, no matter," he continued. "You go on up to Susan. No doubt Charles will get here before too long."

Alicia continued on her way, thinking wryly that the affair was becoming more and more tangled, what with Sir Peter ready to fire a notice of the betrothal off to the *Times*.

She visited with Susan for the remainder of the afternoon but finally had to take her leave with no word from Lord Carlton in response to their note. Susan had by this time completely regained her composure although Alicia hadn't been able to shake her decision.

"But what will you do, Susan, if you don't marry Charles?" she had asked anxiously.

There was a stricken look in Susan's eyes but she had replied firmly that she would return to America. "I know Aunt Henry won't turn me from her door," she smiled faintly. "And you know I've always said that I didn't really wish to marry."

Alicia shuddered but said nothing more, wisely deciding to leave it to Lord Carlton to change Susan's mind.

The following morning Susan dressed carefully then went down to the breakfast room. Her aunt was just finishing a light repast although there was no sign of her uncle.

"He had to go out, Susan," Sophy said, responding to her niece's inquiry. "He'll be gone for the better part of the day. Did you have something in particular you wished to discuss with him?"

"No, Aunt Sophy," said Susan politely. "I'm expecting Lord Carlton sometime today, however." She paused, blushing a little. "Would you mind if I met with him alone?"

Her aunt raised her brows at this unusual request. But having heard from Peter that there could be a betrothal in the wind and gathering from the fact that Charles hadn't paid the expected call upon Peter that there might be a lover's quarrel to be patched up, she smiled and agreed to the plan.

"When he calls, I will have Woods show him to the library. You may be private there,"

Susan smiled her thanks and finished her coffee, grateful that her aunt hadn't requested an explanation. She didn't like deceiving her relatives, for they had shown her nothing but kindness. If only she could endure the interview with Lord Carlton, then leave England forever, they would never have to know of her disgrace. She knew that they didn't deserve such shabby behavior from her but she could think of no other way to protect them.

Damn the man, she thought as she made her way to the library, if only he would come so she could have done with this. Her mouth hardened a little as she reaffirmed her decision against marrying him, ruthlessly silencing that part of her which would, in spite of all she had learned, like nothing more than to be carried off in his arms.

Fortunately, she didn't have long to wait before Woods announced Lord Carlton.

"I understand from your letter that you particularly wished to speak with me," Lord Carlton coldly said.

Susan invited the earl to sit down.

"This interview wasn't my idea, my lord," she said angrily. "Indeed, it was Alicia and your man, Elliott, who made me see that I must talk to you, distasteful as I find it."

"Pray go on," Carlton said. "This promises to be most edifying."

Susan's eyes snapped with fury. "You shall hear me out, my lord, for I've discovered that your role in this . . . this farce is not insignificant."

The earl's attention was arrested. "Farce is an apt word, Miss Phillips. But I fail to see your point."

"My point," Susan said acidly, "is that you are the father of the child I carry."

The earl sat in silence for a moment then the corner

of his mouth twitched a little with the beginnings of a smile.

"Well, that's a leveler to be sure, Miss Phillips, although I'm sure you must see how absurd such an accusation is. But how does it come about that you have only now chosen me to play the part of father? And how can you think I would agree when we both know better? That has me in a bit of a puzzle, my dear."

"I didn't choose you," began Susan scathingly. "Indeed, I had little choice in the matter. It happened on board the *Mayfair*."

Carlton's eyes narrowed and he stiffened a little.

"Yes, my lord," continued Susan relentlessly, "we were on board at the same time, worse luck for me."

"Good Lord, can this be true?" the earl exclaimed. "Why didn't you tell me before?"

Susan looked at him with contempt. "Can you think that I would have had anything to do with you if I had known? No, I never knew who it was in that cabin . . . it was too dark and I was too confused to know anything. I didn't know who you were, that is, until yesterday. It was Alicia and Elliott. They had seen each other on board although Alicia didn't know who he was until yesterday. They talked and came to me with their findings."

"So that was why Elliott was away yesterday," mused Carlton, watching Susan through narrowed eyes. "It appears that my past comes back to haunt me." He paused and regarded the toe of his boot with interest. "Is it indelicate in me, I wonder, to remind you that you didn't find me altogether repulsive?"

Susan blushed rosily and Carlton looked at her, laughing a little. "Yes, I can see that it is. You know, I was really rather sorry not to have been able to pursue our relationship."

"I must say, you are taking this in remarkably good spirit, my lord," Susan snapped.

"I assure you I am not," Carlton replied, his mouth twitching once again. "In fact, I am excessively shocked. I only wish I had had the good fortune to be present at the interview Alicia carried on with Elliott . . . priceless."

"I'm sure it was extremely uncomfortable for both parties," Susan replied, refusing to be drawn into banter.

"I daresay. However, it looks as though we need to address a certain issue once again."

"I have no desire to address any more issues with you, Lord Carlton, for I have quite made up my mind as to what course I shall pursue."

Carlton studied her countenance. "And what is it you have taken into your head to do, my dear?"

"I'm not 'your dear,' my lord," said Susan, "and my plans are my own."

Carlton leaned comfortably back in his chair once again. "Could it be that you have decided to return to America? Yes, I can see that it is but let me tell you that it won't answer," he continued, his calm, almost avuncular manner quite setting Susan's teeth on edge. "No, decidedly not . . . only consider, you'll be making a hazardous voyage, quite alone, in a rather advanced state of pregnancy. Unless, of course, you mean to shab off immediately?" He raised a brow and read his answer in the determined set of her chin. He rose and strode to the window then glanced back at her. "It won't do, my dear," he said softly. "I'm afraid circumstances force us to marry."

"I'm afraid not," Susan said stubbornly.

"Don't misunderstand me, Susan," Carlton said softly. "If I have to drag you to the altar, you shall marry me."

"My lord," Susan began, struggling to hold a rein on her wrath. "I'm sensible of the honor you do to me." She put her hand to her forehead. "But it is not a marriage either of us could wish."

"Good God," flung out Carlton as he began to stride about the room. "Of course it's not the marriage we could wish, but I'll not tolerate another scandal attaching to my name."

"Is this solution then to save my name or yours, my lord?" asked Susan as she watched him.

He stopped in front of her. "Both," he snapped impatiently. He stood regarding her for a moment. "Can you possibly believe that there would be no talk if you suddenly returned to your aunt? Already several people know of your plight and two at least know of the role I played."

Susan gasped. "You can't think that either Alicia or Elliott would speak of this."

"My dear child," Carlton said cynically, "I've little faith in human nature. Besides surely your doctor and your maid have some knowledge of the affair. No," he continued, bending over her and placing his hands on the arms of her chair, gazing steadily into her eyes, "there is no other solution to this coil. Even a hasty marriage won't silence all the gossips but I prefer that to the story which would certainly circulate were you to flee so mysteriously."

Susan bowed her head and gazed at her hands, then raised her eyes and looked into the face so close to her own. "I fear I'll need some time before I can think clearly."

"You know what your answer must be, my dear," Carlton said. "You go with your aunt and uncle to Lady Bessborough's party tonight, don't you?"

She nodded. "I'd thought to cry off, however."

"Don't. I'll look in there tonight, and perhaps if you'll give me a dance, we can have a word. I'll wait no longer, however. If you've not made up your mind by that time, I'll seek an interview with Peter and lay the whole before him. He at least will understand that a speedy marriage is all that can be done to rectify the matter."

"You couldn't be so cruel," whispered Susan anxiously. "He and my aunt must know nothing of this." Tears came to her eyes. "They have been so kind . . ."

Carlton took her arms and pulled her up, holding her close to him and looking steadily into her eyes. "I don't want to hurt you, Susan, but you must agree to this. If you don't, you have my word that Peter will know the whole."

Susan broke out of his hold. "I've said that I'll think on the matter." She went to the door, feeling that she could endure no more. "If you will please leave me now," she said in a stifled voice, struggling to hold back a sudden rush of tears.

Carlton walked to the door and put a hand on her

shoulder. "Until tonight then, my dear."

Susan gently closed the door behind him. She knew that she must sort out her thoughts and decide what she would do, but the scene she had just gone through had taxed her severely and nothing coherent emerged from the whirl of thoughts in her brain. At last the headache which had been nagging her all afternoon forced her to put her problem from her mind and retire to her room. She knew she must appear at Lady Bessborough's party that evening but she was no closer to a decision than she had been before Carlton had left.

She woke, somewhat refreshed, to find Sarah lighting her candles and pouring hot water into the bowl by her bed.

"Lady Sophia said to let you sleep until the last possible moment, Miss Phillips," the abigail said with a smile. "And so I have, but now you'll have to hurry some. Your aunt and uncle are nearly ready."

Susan felt less than ever like attending a party but she thanked Sarah and quickly dressed, then joined her aunt and uncle.

She had not a chance to converse with her aunt and could see the curiosity evident in both Sophy's and Peter's eyes, but her aunt only smiled and pressed her hand saying that there was no time for a cose but that she was admittedly curious as to her niece's interview with Lord Carlton that afternoon.

"Can't understand all the mystery, Susan," said her uncle as he climbed into the carriage after his niece and wife. "We all know . . . at least I think we know . . . that Carlton's going to make you an offer."

"Peter," remonstrated Sophy gently, seeing a faint blush come into Susan's cheeks. "This is neither the time nor the place to harangue Susan." She leaned comfortably back against the cushions. "I have no fear but that everything will come out in the end."

Susan gazed intently at her aunt. "Would my marriage to Lord Carlton please you then, ma'am?"

"Should say it would," Peter chuckled, answering for his wife. "Sophy's had the thing planned since the day you arrived."

"Peter!" cried Sophy, aghast. "How can you say such a thing? It's true that I thought you would suit," she said, turning to her niece, "but if you cannot like a proposal from Charles, why, I daresay the right man will come along in time." She again pressed Susan's hand. "We aren't eager to give you up, you know."

Susan returned a trembling smile, and then as Peter and Sophy began to talk together, she was left to her thoughts, bleak as they were. Her resolution never to marry the earl was weakening. Obviously, from her conversation with her aunt and uncle, such a marriage was not only approved of, but sought. She shrank back a little in her seat. They must never know what transpired aboard the *Mayfair*. Such news would only hurt them both terribly. She gazed drearily out the window. There was really no other course but marriage open to her. What a fool she had been to think she could slip quietly back to Boston. No doubt they would have to know were she to attempt such a thing.

When they arrived, Susan looked about the room

after she and Sophy had laid aside their wraps, but she did not see the tall form of Lord Carlton. Instead her eyes lit upon Alicia, who quickly joined her.

"I rather thought you wouldn't be here tonight, Susan," Alicia said anxiously, "but I'm so glad to see you. Did you speak to Lord Carlton?"

Before Susan could confide in her friend, the two were surrounded by gentlemen eager to claim their hands for the country dance, and Susan reluctantly let herself be swept away.

Susan's partner was a dashing young man in regimentals with a ready wit and good-natured smile and he soon had Susan feeling quite at ease. When he returned her to her aunt, however, Freddie Swithin was hovering nearby, and Susan couldn't think how to turn him down. She shivered a little as she looked into his face. His smile seemed a little cruel, and a greedy glitter shone from his eyes. He tightened his grip on her hand and swung her into the waltz.

"I had not known you and your father and stepmama were attending this party, Mr. Swithin," Susan said politely.

"Nor are they. M'father had to return to the country but I remained on purpose to attend." His gaze swept the room and his lip curled in a sneer. "I don't see your self-appointed protector here tonight, Miss Phillips. Perhaps he has bowed out?"

"I prefer not to discuss my affairs with you, Mr. Swithin, and if you persist, I shall have to ask you to return me to my aunt."

"This time you shall listen to me!" Freddie hissed. "I shall not be fobbed off again."

"Very well, Mr. Swithin, I shan't fob you off. Say what you will."

After a moment of surprise, Freddie proceeded to pour out his feelings for Susan. When he had done, she gazed at him curiously, a little repulsed but curious nevertheless as to why he had chosen her to fix his ardor upon.

"Mr. Swithin," she began, as calmly as possible, "I can't think what I have said or done to offer you the least encouragement but you must believe me when I say that I have no affection for you."

Freddie stared at her in consternation, then as the dance ended, his brow cleared and he smiled. "It's all the same with you women. You must needs be begged and pleaded with. I won't give up, my dear, you can be certain of that."

With these words, he returned her to her aunt, and as Susan stood gazing after him in disgust, she heard Lord Carlton's voice in her ear.

"So, he is still pursuing you, my dear. The question is . . . are you encouraging him?"

Susan whirled around, fire flashing from her eyes. "I will not hear one more word from you about my character, my lord."

"Pax." Carlton laughed as he backed away from the trembling girl. "I was only teasing you, you know. Come," he continued, drawing her a little away from the others and into a small alcove behind a potted palm. "Let's be private a moment."

He looked searchingly at her. "Have you reached a decision, then?" Susan nodded, scarcely able to look at him. She felt as if she were choking. "I agree that we must marry, my lord," she said faintly.

He was silent a moment then said rather bruskly that he would call to take her driving in the morning . . . that he had thought of a plan.

"Good," said Susan resolutely, feeling a little as if a weight had been lifted from her shoulders now that the decision had been made. "Are you thinking to elope?" she asked.

Carlton raised his brows at her. "What? You would fly with me to the border and be married over the anvil?"

"Do be serious," Susan snapped. "I merely was uncertain when you said you had a plan. It all sounds so mysterious."

Carlton laughed. "Indeed, all will be settled on the morrow. But now we must rejoin the others or tongues will begin to wag.

Chapter 10

The following morning, Lord Carlton called at Spencer House to pick Susan up, as he had promised, and before many minutes had passed, the phaeton turned in at the gates of Hyde Park. There were very few people about, several nannies cautiously guarding their precious charges, but fashionable members of the haute ton were, for the most part, absent. Susan had for many moments been occupied in admiring the skill with which the earl handled his spirited team, and although a show of friendship had not made up any portion of the attitude she wished to adopt, she could not help herself. "You are a capital whip, my lord. I believe I should be honored that you are driving me out. I have heard that it is not at all a thing you do in a general way."

Carlton, a little surprised and gratified by her friendly tone, shot her a quick glance but kept his thoughts to himself.

"My lord," said Susan a few moments later. "I am quite interested in hearing your plan for this marriage of ours."

"Indeed, my dear. But first, you do understand, do you not, that a hasty marriage such as ours must neccessarily be, will give rise to all manner of speculation. Therefore, we must do all we can to scotch any scandal before it begins. Nothing, for instance, would be more fatal to our chances of coming out of this with a whole skin than to elope."

Susan stared back at him. "Well, perhaps you'll be so kind as to tell me then how you perceive our doing the thing. We have no wedding plans made . . . in fact, there has been no notice of a betrothal . . . why, even my aunt and uncle are unaware that we're planning to be married and it's only a few days until we leave for Bath." She shook her head doubtfully. "No, I'm not certain even your credit is good enough to carry this off."

Carlton steadied his team around a corner. "Ah, Susan, how you wound me," he said reproachfully. "And I thought my credit sufficient to carry anything off."

"Now you are teasing me, my lord. In fact, it strikes me that you think this whole thing a comedy."

"No," the earl responded gravely, "a melodrama."

Susan cast him a doubtful look.

"Now here is my plan," he said briskly. "I shall invite you, Alicia, Sophy, and Peter on an expedition to view St. Stephen's Chapel a little north of Hampstead. I trust you haven't yet viewed it?" Susan shook her head. "We shall go to the chapel, where I will have the vicar waiting and he will marry us with your aunt and Alicia to support you."

Susan thought for a moment. "Won't they think it odd in us?"

"Perhaps," replied Carlton with a grin, "but Sophy and Alicia, at least, will think it romantic. As for Peter, he'll be glad to have you off his hands."

Susan smiled at her companion. "What a plumper. Perhaps we shall brush through, however. What would you like me to do?"

Carlton turned his team out the Stanhope Gate and maneuvered deftly through the now crowded street toward Spencer House. "Nothing. I have to leave town for a day or two, and when I return, all should be ready. I shall send Sophy and Peter an invitation for Friday . . . three days from now."

It was to be expected that Susan would pass the following days in a haze. Indeed, at times it seemed as though she was enmeshed in a nightmare from which there was no escape, and at other times, particularly at night, after Sarah had tucked her up in her bed, she felt that all the dreams she had once envisioned were coming true.

Alicia had visited her the day following her carriage ride with the earl and her concern was such that Susan felt compelled to acquaint her with their plans. Alicia had been in wholehearted agreement and vowed to do all she could, when the time came, to smooth things over with Sophy and Peter.

So the day of the expedition to St. Stephen's Chapel at last arrived, and Susan, after dressing carefully in her prettiest muslin, tied the ribbons of a charming bonnet of satin straw under her left ear and glanced once more around her room, wondering if any bride had ever departed from her home taking so little with her.

She joined her aunt and uncle, and a few moments later the earl was announced. After some discussion, it was decided that Sophy and Peter would call up their own carriage as five in any vehicle was most uncomfortable, and Carlton took Susan into his barouche. She had little to say to him, for her mind was in a whirl and the short journey to Lady Brandon's townhouse was passed in silence.

Alicia had been on the watch for the party and she was quickly helped in beside her friend.

"Well, Charles," she said prosaically as the barouche began to move, "I must say I think you and Susan are doing the only thing you could."

Carlton looked pained. "Has no one ever told you you are much too impertinent, my little friend?"

Alicia smiled mischieviously. "My father . . . many times. I thought you would want to know that I approve of this scheme."

"You set my mind at rest, my dear," the earl murmured.

"Don't let him tease you, Alicia," said Susan, shooting a laughing reproach at the tall man across from her.

"No, no," laughed Carlton, "I won't tease her . . . only you, my dear delight."

Susan blushed slightly at being so addressed and Alicia settled into the corner of the barouche feeling very pleased with the way things were turning out.

Little more than two hours had passed when the carriage turned into a pretty churchyard and the whole party was reunited. The ladies walked about for a few moments, shaking out their crumpled skirts and admiring the neat flowerbeds which surrounded the chapel. After the men had stretched their legs, the party entered the little chapel.

They examined the baptismal font, which was said by some to have been a sacrificial stone in druidical days, some very pretty carvings, and a much faded fresco upon one wall. Then Lord Carlton requested that the whole party assemble at the altar. They were soon joined by an elderly gentleman dressed in a black coat and bands, which all of the party recognized at once as a vicar.

Sophy looked quickly at Charles and Susan, a faint smile on her lips, while Peter looked the man over distrustfully.

"We hardly need a tour guide in such a small chapel, Charles," he said, a suspicious gleam in his eyes.

Carlton smiled. "Indeed, Peter. As a guide, Mr. Harwell is unnecessary but as a vicar his presence is indispensable."

Suspicion mounted in Peter's blue eyes. "It sounds to me like you have something havey-cavey planned here, Charles, and let me tell you I'll have no part in it."

"Nor I, indeed," put in Mr. Harwell quickly. "I was asked to come here to perform a marriage ceremony but I will not do so if there is the least impropriety involved."

Sophy's eyes began to twinkle and she drew Susan into her arms, kissing her cheek and whispering how happy she was. She then turned to her bewildered husband.

"What a pretty surprise Charles and Susan have planned for us, Peter. Miss Wentworth, no doubt, was in on the whole, were you were not, my dear?"

Alicia nodded agreement, her brown eyes dancing with excitement.

"Come, Peter," Sophy continued, placing her hand through Peter's arm and drawing him aside. "We must be out of the way a little so the vicar can begin."

Peter removed his wife's hand. "In a moment, my dear. First, however, while you and Miss Wentworth help my niece to tidy herself as best she may, I would like a few words with Charles."

"You will excuse us for a few moments, ladies . . . Mr. Harwell?" asked Carlton imperturbably.

Sophy and Alicia did not respond since they were much too occupied with helping Susan tidy her hair and tying the flowers they had picked from the flowerbeds into a posy for her to carry, but Mr. Harwell nodded, looking anxiously from one gentleman to the other.

"Now, Charles," began Peter urgently, when the two men were out of earshot. "You'll have to explain matters before I'll allow such doings as these to continue."

"It's as Sophy says, Peter. Merely a pretty surprise. I did come to Spencer House this week to ask you for Susan's hand, but finding you gone on business, I decided to put my luck to the touch anyway, and to my good fortune, Susan accepted me."

Peter looked perplexed. "But why must you needs

do the thing this way? No announcement, no balls and parties. Why, my niece is a diamond of the first water, everyone would wish to honor her bethrothal. Not to mention all the friends who would celebrate your good fortune after that other—" A gleam of comprehension showed in Peter's eyes.

"Just so, Peter," said the earl dryly. "I certainly had no desire to go through all of that coming so soon after my engagement with Lady Rockingham."

Peter gave his friend a searching look then smiled warmly and wrung his hand. "I don't know how you persuaded my niece to go along with you on this but then I have always said that you have great address with the female sex."

"Shall we rejoin the others? Mr. Harwell seems to stand in need of reassurance."

"Leave that to me," said Peter quickly, and he went to the vicar, drawing him off to the side while the others gathered around the altar.

In a very few moments the vicar and Sir Peter joined them, a smile wreathing Mr. Harwell's rotund face.

"Everything seems to be quiet in order now, so shall we begin? Lord Carlton, you have the license, I presume?"

Susan glanced in dismay at the earl, for she had not once thought of the need for a special license, but Carlton smiled reassuringly at her as he drew a paper from his coat pocket. "The business which took me out of town this week," he murmured to her.

There being no further obstacles, the ceremony began, and Susan felt her hand taken in a warm clasp then the words of the beautiful, simple service were read. Both responded clearly to the vows although Susan's voice trembled a little, then a ring was placed on her finger, she felt the cool touch of the earl's lips on her cheek, and the wedding was over. Both she and the earl signed their names to the marriage document then they turned and accepted the happy congratulations of Peter, Sophy, and Alicia.

Lord Carlton had reserved the best parlor of a pretty little inn situated not a mile from the chapel and had ordered that a sumptuous supper be prepared. The party repaired there, Alicia joining Sir Peter and Lady Sophy for the short ride.

From the repast spread on a table in the large, airy private parlor, it was evident that Lord Carlton had been painstaking in his arrangements for their enjoyment.

Carlton took Susan's hand and, turning it over, brushed the inside of her wrist with his lips. "Come, my dear wife, shall we be seated?"

Susan felt a thrill chase up her spine and a warmth spread through her body at his words and the touch of his lips.

"Here, here," exclaimed Peter jovially, his blue eyes twinkling. "No more of this lovemaking, Charles. "You'll put us all to the blush."

"Hush, Peter." Sophy smiled as she took her seat at the table. "There is nothing amiss in a husband kissing his wife's hand, is there, Lady Carlton?" She said, laughter in her eyes.

Susan smiled wryly as she sat down. "It will take some getting used to, hearing myself addressed so,

Aunt Sophy."

Conversation was lively throughout the meal, and when they at last rose, it was with the greatest good humor.

Carlton put his arm about Susan's shoulders and faced the other three. "Thank you for joining us today. Susan and I shall remain here tonight and leave for Fairfields tomorrow. I'm anxious that she see it."

"Well, well," Peter exclaimed, a little surprised. "Have you a cloakbag or anything by you, my dear?" he inquired of his niece.

Susan began to shake her head but Carlton interrupted. "I have everything she will need for the journey and perhaps you will have her belongings sent."

Farewells were then said, amongst which a few tears were shed, and at last Susan and Carlton were left to their own devices.

They returned from a stroll in the still evening air to find the landlord and his wife waiting nervously for them.

The landlord drew a breath while his wife wrung her apron behind him. "I never wanted to show him into your private parlor, m'lord, that I didn't," said the landlord. "Said he was a friend of yours and that if I refused him, he would tear the damn . . . begging pardon, m'lady, tear the house down about our ears. Not that he looks like he could do any such thing. I don't hold with such goings on."

"We run a respectable establishment, m'lord," his wife added, "and if there's to be any rumpus raised, we'll have to ask you to take your business elsewhere."

Lord Carlton raised his quizzing glass and stared at the woman, one dark brow raised inquisitively. "Am I to understand," he inquired coldly, "that you are requesting that my wife and I depart?"

"No, no," interrupted the landlord. "No such thing, m'lord. It's just that the gentleman what says he knows you looks fit to murder and we don't like the thought of such goings-on in our establishment."

Carlton smiled frigidly. "I hardly think you have cause for concern, my good man. And now that you have alerted us to our unknown visitor, perhaps you will step aside so we may join him."

The landlord and his wife moved quickly into the narrow passageway next to the taproom, and Carlton ushered Susan into the parlor.

He paused on the threshold. "Good God," he said. "What are you doing here? And what do you mean by frightening our host out of what meager wits he lays claim to?"

Freddie Swithin, who had turned at the sound of the opening door, curled his lip at the earl. "I have come to protect one whose charms and exquisite sensibilities I can only hope one day to call my own."

"Ah," said the earl, strolling easily into the room beside Susan, "I perceive that you have come in the guise of a knight in armor to save your lady love. Do I have that right, Swithin?"

"You may jest all you like, my lord," Freddie said coldly, "but I find nothing to laugh at in protecting a lady's honor."

"Indeed. But is that not a, er, novel position for you to find yourself in?"

Freddie stiffened with rage and his face turned an ugly mottled color. "My lord," he fumed at last, "I must ask you to name your friends."

"Oh, Freddie," interpolated Susan, who had been quietly watching the proceedings, "take a damper. There is no need to talk of duels. And you, sir," she continued, rounding on her husband, who was watching her with amusement. "I must ask you to stop baiting Mr. Swithin."

Carlton bowed. "Perhaps you would like to be private with the gentleman, my love."

"Wretch," she said in a low tone, "don't you dare shab off now."

"My dear," he murmured with a grin, "such language." He walked over to the table. "Sit down then, Swithin, and tell us what has put you in the boughs."

Freddie stood stiffly as Carlton helped Susan to a seat then slouched into the chair he indicated.

"I know what's going on here, you know," he began, rather obliquely.

The earl raised his quizzing glass. "Then certainly you can have no objection."

"No objection?" gobbled Freddie, his eyes bulging. "No objection . . . when with my own eyes I have seen you carry Miss Phillips off to this inn . . . meaning to stay the night. If that ain't a seduction, I don't know what is."

"You sound practiced in the art, Swithin," replied the earl coolly.

Freddie threw back his chair and jumped to his feet. "I don't have to listen to such from you, my lord . . . a practiced rake and a—a libertine."

Susan turned fascinated eyes upon her husband. "Is that what you are, my lord?" she asked demurely, a gleam of amusement in her eyes.

"Miss Phillips!" spluttered Freddie. "How can you take this so lightly?" He seemed bereft of speech, then a look of cunning entered his protuberant eyes. "Perhaps I erred. If so, I owe Lord Carlton my apologies. You don't seem overly upset at a possible seduction, Miss Phillips. Can it be that you are in agreement with the earl's plans? I knew you for a sad flirt, my girl, but—"

At this point, Lord Carlton interrupted. "Careful, Swithin," he said gently, a hint of steel in his voice. "You are speaking to my wife."

Freddie looked stunned then sat down abruptly once again, his mouth half-cocked. "I can scarcely credit it, my lord."

"It's true, Mr. Swithin," said Susan coolly. "Perhaps, however, you would care to tell us what possessed you to ride out here in this way."

Freddie looked wildly at them. "I—I was going to call on you, Miss Phillips . . ."

"Lady Carlton," interpolated Carlton ruthlessly.

"L—Lady Carlton," stammered Freddie.

"Just so," said the earl. "Continue, please."

"I saw the earl's carriage drive up with his luggage strapped on behind and some moments later the two of you drove off. Naturally I hurried back into my own chaise and followed."

"Did you not see my aunt and uncle follow?" asked Susan.

"What . . . no, no, I knew what Lord Carlton had

planned, you see."

"Did you, Swithin?" inquired the earl gently.

"Please, my lord," said Susan impatiently. "Let him continue." She turned again to the fulminating gentleman beside her. "What could you think when we stopped and took Miss Wentworth into our carriage?"

"Why, nothing. I knew that the two of you were as close as inkle weavers and I made sure that she was just lending countenance to your flight from the city."

"Dear me. Then am I also seducing Miss Wentworth?" asked the earl.

"Please, my lord," begged Susan, again trying to repress a chuckle.

"I followed you to Hampstead," Freddie went on, "but I lost you and only by the merest chance discovered that you had stabled your cattle here for the night."

"Ah, that explains it," said Carlton, perfectly satisfied.

Freddie looked bewildered. "Explains what, my lord? I don't see that it explains anything."

"You would not," said the earl at his most urbane. "But I shall enlighten you and perhaps you will leave us in peace. Lady Carlton, Miss Wentworth, and myself had as our destination St. Stephen's Chapel, only a mile or so from this establishment. Sir Peter Phillips and Lady Sophia joined us there. To make a long story short, Miss Phillips and I were married with her aunt and uncle and Miss Wentworth in attendance." He smiled ruefully at his wife. "We desired a private ceremony, you see."

"This all sounds like flummery to me, my lord," declared Freddie. He rose and gathered his coat from the chair where he had thrown it, then turned to Susan. "I don't for one moment believe this ridiculous tale, Miss Phillips," he sneered, "so I will give you a hint. It's said that my lord tires of his mistresses quickly."

Carlton rose at these words and came over to Freddie, anger flashing in his eyes. "I have warned you once, Swithin, and I shall not do so again. Get out."

Freddie bowed but at the door he paused. "I wish you happy in your choice of protectors, Miss Phillips," he said.

He quickly scuttled out the door as the earl came round the table, his fists clenched and his eyes narrowed dangerously.

"No, Charles," cried Susan, stepping between her husband and the open door. "Please, let him go."

After a moment Carlton looked at Susan and grinned a little crookedly. "So much for our hopes of attaching no hint of scandal to our marriage."

"That doesn't concern me," said Susan calmly. "You must know that Aunt Sophy and Uncle Peter will put the notice in the *Times* tomorrow and only a nobody would pay any attention to whatever Mr. Swithin might say."

After a moment's consideration, the earl agreed then a soft light entered his gray eyes and he put out his hand to Susan. "It grows quite late and I think we've had enough excitement for one day. Shall we retire?"

Susan, who had quite forgotten all the ramifications of her marriage, glanced uneasily at the earl. "Retire, my lord?" she stammered.

He took her hand and pulled her gently from the room. "You know, you called me Charles a moment ago. It was the only thing that kept me from planting a facer on Mr. Swithin. Won't you do so again?"

"Yes, Charles," Susan said, blushing.

Carlton drew her inexorably up the narrow staircase. "I know you are uneasy but you wouldn't like to give the landlord any more cause to eject us from the premises so why don't we discuss this in our chamber. His worthy spouse assured me it was their finest."

Their room was indeed a large apartment. A fire burning in the fireplace gave enough warmth to take the chill from the night air, and a patchwork quilt, crimson curtains, and numerous rugs scattered on the highly polished wood floor enhanced its cozy appearance. Susan, however, stood riveted at the door, staring at the four-poster bed which seemed to grow larger and more menacing the longer she looked at it.

Her husband watched her with amusement. "More comfortable than a ship's bunk, I make no doubt."

Color rose in Susan's face and she held her hands to her hot cheeks. "Oh . . . oh, how can you say such a thing?"

Carlton laughed and pulled her into the room. "It won't eat you, you know. Come in now and make yourself comfortable by the fire. There," he said, positioning her chair so her back was to the bed. "Now you don't have to look at it and we can talk."

Susan looked gratefully at him and put her cold

hands to the fire. Her husband poured wine into two glasses that had been placed on a small table and gave one to Susan then seated himself in the chair opposite her, stretching out his long legs. He sipped his wine and sighed comfortably.

"Is there anything amiss?" asked Susan nervously, catching the small sound.

Carlton's eyes smiled wickedly at her from over the rim of his glass. "No, my dear. I was simply thinking what a comfort it is to be seated before a warm fire with my wife at my side."

Susan moved restlessly in her chair and sipped a little of her wine, wondering uneasily how she was to get through the night ahead. Her eyes wandered to the bed.

She jumped a little, spilling a few drops of wine on her dress when the earl spoke. "You keep looking at the bed, my love," he said solicitously. "Are you so tired then?"

"Indeed, no," returned Susan quickly. "I vow I couldn't sleep a wink."

"All the better," murmured her husband, the wicked gleam appearing once more in his eyes. "But I see that you have spilt your wine," he continued, watching her rub furiously at her dress. "Perhaps you would like to change into a dressing gown?"

"No . . . no, it's nothing." A blush rose to her cheeks.

"You know," the earl said contemplatively as he observed her. "You look enchanting when you blush so. Indeed, I find you hard to resist."

Susan's hands ceased their futile occupation and

she looked into her husband's laughing eyes. "Do stop teasing me in this odious fashion," she said.

Carlton chuckled. "My dear delight. How can you ask such a thing?" He put down his glass and studied her. "I've brought along some night clothes for you. Wouldn't you be more comfortable in your nightdress and dressing gown? If you like I could even help you . . . since you have no maid, that is. No, I can see that you wouldn't," he added as she stiffened.

"My lord," Susan said, "after what has gone before . . . I mean . . . circumstances being what they are . . ."

"Yes?" her husband prompted helpfully, his eyes brimming with laughter, as her stammered explanations faded away.

A tiny chuckle broke from Susan's lips. "Sir," she said, attempting to control the quiver of laughter in her voice. "You are no gentleman. You could help me, you know."

Carlton looked hurt. "But my dear, is that not what I offered to do not a moment past?"

"Idiot!" she said, blushing again. "You know that isn't what I meant. This is an absurd situation for both of us and I'm confident you could not wish to take advantage of it."

"Take care," said her husband, wickedly quizzing her. "It never pays to be too confident."

Susan gulped down the last of her wine and Carlton reached for her glass, a tingle traveling up her arm as his fingers touched hers. "Would you care for another glass, or shall we retire?"

"I . . . I'll have another," she said quickly, watching

him nervously.

He poured the wine, his gray eyes alight with mischief. "Now then, where were we?" he murmured. "Ah yes, you didn't wish to be taken advantage of."

"Charles . . . you . . . you wretch," Susan gasped, for he released the glass a moment before her fingers closed on the stem and the contents poured out on her lap.

He quickly withdrew his handerchief and handed it to her. "You would probably not wish me to mop it up for you?" he asked hopefully.

A chuckle again escaped Susan's throat. "You are the most exasperating, unprincipled, idiotish man of my acquaintance, Lord Carlton."

"Not idiotish, my love," he murmured with a grin. "Besides it was spilt for your own good."

"How so, my lord?" inquired Susan acidly as she continued to dab at the large stain.

"Well," returned the earl reflectively as he watched this interesting exercise. "You know you have no head for wine. I recall that too much champagne had the effect of pulling your defenses down somewhat."

"I should think that's what you desire, my lord."

"Perhaps," returned Carlton with a grin. "And the wine may yet accomplish something of the sort."

"You mean that now I'll have to change into the dressing gown you brought for me which, I make no doubt, is completely inappropriate."

"My dear, you wound me. My taste in such things is thought to be quite good. Here now." Carlton placed his wine glass on the mantle and pulled Susan to her feet. He quickly turned her around and began unfastening the tiny buttons along her back. Susan attempted to twist away from him but he took her shoulders between his hands and held her against him for a moment.

"Don't be so fidgety," he ordered softly, his voice a little husky as he resisted the impulse to place a kiss on the spot where he could see a pulse fluttering in her throat.

Susan quieted and remained standing still until he had completed his task. He then went to his portmanteau and withdrew a garment from it. He brought it to Susan and in an instant she could see from the froth of lace and transparent gauze that it was a beautiful but quite immodest dressing gown.

"It's just as I thought," she said reprovingly, holding her dress up with crossed arms. "Not at all suitable for a young lady."

Carlton gave a crack of laughter. "But highly suitable for my wife." He stood before her, a questioning gleam in his eyes.

Susan swallowed nervously. "Well, turn around then."

"Must I?"

Susan nodded and the earl turned on his heel. She allowed her damp dress to fall to the floor and quickly removed her chemise. She then pulled the confection of lace and gauze around her, fumbling with the tiny pearl buttons which closed the front.

"You can turn around now," she said shyly.

Carlton faced her once again and she heard the breath catch in his throat. Her eyes flew to his face. "Is it all right?"

The candlelight at her back shone through the diaphanous material, illuminating her soft curves, and the earl's warm gaze slowly traced the lines of her body.

"Ah, Susan," he murmured, stepping forward and gathering her into his arms. "You're more beautiful than I remembered."

Susan stiffened and turned her face away. "I wish you wouldn't speak of that . . . that night."

He gently turned her face back to his and gazed into her eyes. "You must let me speak of it if only to tell you how sorry I am to have hurt you. Can you forgive me?"

Susan, who knew in her heart that she loved him and had forgiven him soon after the first blind rage of discovery, nodded almost imperceptibly. Her husband saw the slight movement and his arms tightened, pressing her close to him. His mouth descended to her throat and she arched her neck a little, her breath catching as his lips traveled up to her ear and then to her mouth, She responded hungrily to his kiss, her soft lips opening as the embrace became more passionate.

Carlton drew his head back a little, gazing into the deep blue of her eyes.

"Susan . . . my little love," he murmured huskily. His hands went to her head, pulling the pins from her hair, and the soft dark ringlets tumbled around her shoulders. With fingers that shook a little, he smoothed the curls back from her face then picked her up and carried her to the bed.

He laid her gently upon it and, after removing his

boots, began to unbutton his shirt. Susan watched shyly, her breath catching a little when he pulled off the shirt, revealing the hard smooth planes of his chest. His hand dropped to his breeches and amusement flared in his eyes as Susan's eyes snapped shut. He chuckled a little, and when he had finished disrobing, he lay down beside her, taking her chin in his hand and forcing her to look at him.

"My dear delight," he said gently, "there is nothing about me to frighten you, I promise." He pulled her into his arms, forcing himself to hold his passion in check, and she slowly relaxed, finding that she enjoyed the feel of his body next to hers.

After a few minutes, Carlton found his efforts in moderation rewarded as a small hand crept around his neck and Susan snuggled further into his embrace. He sought her lips in a gentle kiss, warning himself that he must go slowly, but a flame of desire shot through him when he felt her eager response. She pulled him even closer to her and her lips parted under the insistent pressure of his. He caught his breath as her hand left his neck and slid down his shoulder, caressing his broad chest then skimming lightly down his arm.

"D—did I hurt you, Charles?" whispered Susan huskily, hearing the quick intake of breath.

"My God, no," he murmured roughly against her hair.

Her hand, which had stilled, once again started moving slowly and gently over the planes of his chest but when it began to trace his rib cage in feather-light movements, he caught it and brought it to his lips

"Enough now." He laughed a little breathlessly, realizing that she still needed his moderation, but that if her caresses continued, he wouldn't be able to suppress his desire.

Stroking her cheek with one finger, he took a long shaky breath. Susan gazed at him, her confusion showing plainly in her troubled blue eyes.

"What is it, Charles? Do you find my touch unpleasant?"

Carlton groaned a little in his throat and closed his eyes for a moment then opened them and smiled at the bewildered girl. His hands went to the tiny buttons of her gown.

"Let me show you how it feels."

Susan's eyes widened as he pushed the material off her shoulders and began gently stroking her skin. His hand skimmed the top of her breast, lightly touching her nipple, and Susan gasped as a hot flame shot through her. Carlton cupped her breast in his hand and lowered his mouth to hers.

"Now, tell me," he murmured, his lips moving against hers, "do you find my touch unpleasant?"

Susan moaned a little in her throat, then pulled him closer, kissing him hungrily. His hands now traveled the length of her back, sending delicious thrills up her spine, then he pulled back and gently removed her gown. She watched him, her eyes deep pools of blue, then closed them again as he began to caress her arms and shoulders. She shuddered with delight as his hands returned to her breast.

His touch at first light as a butterfly's wing became more insistent, tantalizing, and teasing as he explored the soft curves of her body until her heartbeat was drumming in her ears. He kissed her deeply again then his lips dropped to the wildly beating pulse in her throat, murmuring love words as he pressed hot kisses against her silken skin. She gasped as his lips continued down to her breast and her hands seemed to have a will of their own as she curled her fingers in his hair, urging him to continue. Trembling, she pressed herself wildly against him, feeling as if her blood had turned to liquid fire. Charles moved atop her, bracing himself with his elbows on either side of her tossing head. He caught her chin with one hand and kissed her passionately.

"Please, Charles," she whispered raggedly, hardly knowing what she was begging for but desire for him consuming her.

Carlton groaned softly, no longer able to control his own desire, then eased himself into her enveloping warmth.

Later, he lay propped on one elbow, watching the play of moonlight across the face of his sleeping wife. He'd never experienced such an intense feeling of tenderness and love, and he wanted to remain awake for a while savoring those emotions. He reached out a finger and gently brushed a curl off her cheek. She looked so young and vulnerable. He grimaced to himself as he recalled Freddie Swithin's visit earlier. How could the lout think that he would make such an innocent girl his mistress? Although judging from her passionate response, Susan would indeed have made a skillful mistress.

This thought was so unpalatable that he threw back

the covers and strode to the window, staring blindly into the pale moonlight. Finally he crossed back to the bed and slipped in beside his sleeping wife. He lay with arms folded behind his neck staring at the ceiling, then turned his head and looked at the lovely face on the pillow beside him. If only Swithin hadn't come with his insinuations and accusations. He released his breath in a soft sigh. Perhaps it was only the night that was causing all his former suspicions to come so forcibly to mind.

He reached out a hand to caress Susan's cheek.

The following day he woke and dressed quickly in the soft light of dawn then went downstairs for breakfast and to see to the horses, telling the kitchen maid to wake his wife in half an hour and to help her dress.

Susan woke to the sound of light tapping at her door and, after looking quickly around the room for Carlton, called to the maid to enter.

"Y'r husband asked me to help you dress, m'lady," the woman said with a little curtsy.

Susan smiled at being so addressed then stretched with sheer delight. "What a lovely morning," she said cheerfully, beginning to get out of bed.

Suddenly realizing that she had no nightgown on, she colored and slipped back down under the quilt. The maid, however, hadn't noticed her confusion for she was staring at the room, her small eyes opened their widest.

She had crept to the parlor the previous evening, after the landlord and his wife had gone about their business and, with an ear pressed to the door, had heard some of the disagreement between the gentlemen. She was inclined to think Mr. Swithin the injured party for she had been much taken with his fine clothes and London airs and so was eager to judge Susan for herself. She now congratulated herself on her astuteness, for it was obvious from the scattered clothes, spilled wine, and upended glasses that no proper married couple had been in the room . . . and so she would tell the landlord himself.

She crossed the room and picked up Susan's dressing gown, shaking out the transparent folds. "Looks like you and y'r, umm, husband had a right good do here last night, m'lady," she continued with a sly smile and a wink. "Do you want me to be helping you on with this, then?"

The rosy color which had left Susan's cheeks flooded back. "No," she snapped. "Leave it on the bed and see if my dress is in that cloak bag on the floor." Pray to God that Charles has remembered to bring along a dress for me, she thought as the maid began rummaging through the bag. Susan sighed with relief when the maid held up a crumpled muslin.

"Looks like it wants pressing, m'lady," she said with a smirk.

"Well," responded Susan impatiently, "perhaps you can do so while I wash and begin dressing."

The maid nodded and left the room. Susan got quickly out of bed, hoping that she could be at least partially clad before the impertinent maid completed her task. She washed and put on her chemise and dressing gown, frowning at her reflection in the mirror. Little wonder that the maid thought she was the earl's bit of muslin. She seated herself at the small dressing table and, picking up one of her husband's brushes, began to restore some order to her dark curls. The door opened softly, and without turning around, Susan told the maid to leave the dress and go.

Carlton stood transfixed at the door, watching Susan's graceful arms as she slowly brushed her hair. He cleared his throat. "I'm afraid I have no dress," he said, forcing a grin.

His wife swung around, her arms still up at her head and Carlton was a little startled at the picture she made, seated as she was in her dressing gown and lacy chemise with her dark curls tumbling about her creamy shoulders.

Susan, who had started at the sound of Carlton's voice, lowered her arms and smiled nervously. "I thought you were the maid, Charles."

He angrily pushed the door closed, staring at her wine-stained chemise. "Good Lord, Susan," he said sharply, fighting the desire he felt to take her back to bed. "You look like you've been through an orgy. Couldn't you find something more respectable to put on?"

"I brought nothing with me, although there was a dress in your bag. Indeed, you're the one who gave me this gown."

Carlton's hard gaze softened a little.

He crossed the room and dropped a cool kiss on her forehead. Susan suddenly felt a little embarrassed to be with him half-clothed as she was. If only he had taken her in his arms and told her that he loved her.

She was unsure of herself and of how she was to proceed after the previous night, but it seemed that he expected her to behave as if nothing of significance had occurred. She pulled the dressing gown more tightly about her throat then greeted the maid's light tapping on the door with relief. The maid entered and, after casting a sly glance at the earl, laid the dress on the bed.

"Shall I help y'r . . . wife . . . to dress then, m'lord?"

Carlton frowned. "Of course, you'll help Lady Carlton dress," he snapped. Then, after telling Susan that they would be ready to depart in an hour's time, he turned on his heel and left the room.

Chapter 11

Lord and Lady Carlton arrived at Fairfields late that afternoon, after an easy and comfortable journey. Nothing had marred the day, and if Susan noticed a certain tension in her husband's smile, she said nothing, and so it was with some eagerness that she strained for a glimpse of her new home.

The carriage swayed sedately through a small village, which her husband identified as Twickingham, then the road rose slightly and they passed an ancient stone church set among toppled gravestones and protected by a sprawling yew, which looked to be hundreds of years old.

Lurching past the churchyard, the carriage continued a hundred feet or so down the road where it swung right and passed between tall stone gateposts. The posts flanked a smooth, even drive which appeared to lead to a house but Susan was as yet unable to view the structure itself. It wasn't until they had passed through a beautiful wood and the drive turned that she was accorded her first glimpse of her home, a sight which nearly took her breath away.

While not as large as some, the house was of great antiquity and was beautifully situated on a wide sloping lawn. A glimmer of water was seen behind the building, and upon her eager question, Carlton informed her that there was, indeed, a large lake behind the gardens.

The house itself was a handsome structure of mellowed stone, from which bits of an ivy clung, softening the lines. Every windowpane sparkled in the late afternoon sun, and Susan examined the building with pleasure as they drove to the door. Nor was she any less pleased by the interior. Every room she saw seemed to reflect the earl's good taste.

She was introduced to Mrs. Penrose, the housekeeper, and quickly proceeded to endear herself to the smiling woman by complimenting her upon the care she so obviously lavished upon the house. She was no less gracious to the butler or the French chef when she met these worthies, and Carlton managed to hide a grin, contenting himself with a murmured remark that he'd wager she would have the entire staff in her pocket before the day was out.

After an early dinner, in keeping with country hours, Susan and Carlton retired to the smallest and least formal of the several saloons which Susan had been shown earlier in the day and the earl requested the tea tray. After half an hour of conversation in which Carlton was careful to touch upon nothing of an intimate nature, he suggested a game of chess.

"Have you played before, Susan?" he queried as he

walked to a rosewood cabinet and removed the set from a shelf.

A mischievious gleam entered Susan's eyes. "My mother and I would have a game now and again but I've not played for a long while," she replied demurely.

Carlton placed the board on a small table he had put between them, set the pieces in their places, giving Susan the white, then sat back waiting for her to make the first move. She quickly brought a pawn forward and he countered.

The game continued and the earl found that he was having trouble with his concentration as his attention strayed from the board to the intent face of his wife. He made his moves somewhat mechanically, more interested in the play of emotions across Susan's face as she set her strategy than he was in the play of the game.

"Checkmate!" Susan said at last, her eyes brimming with laughter.

Carlton started. "The devil you say." His eyes quickly swept the board.

After a moment he smiled wryly. "I'd say I've been taken like a flat. A few games with your mother indeed!"

He rose and replaced the game in the cabinet. "Shall we play again tomorrow night? I promise you, however, that I won't be such an easy target."

"As you wish, Charles," Susan murmured, and Carlton slanted a swift glance in her direction, hearing the suppressed laughter in her voice. He sat down beside her and took her hand in his, kissing it lightly.

"You play far better than I anticipated but you'd

best be on your guard for the rematch. I'm not accounted a poor player, you know."

"Well, I don't think your heart was in it, Charles," Susan replied candidly. "But I don't despair in being able to give you a game from time to time."

He studied her intently for a long moment and his eyes grew serious. He felt the need to discuss their marriage and wondered if now, while they were easy with each other, wasn't the time. "Susan . . . I . . ." He stopped and shook his head a little. How does one ask one's wife if she plans to be faithful, he wondered cynically.

"No . . . never mind," he continued, reading the question in her eyes. "I think, however, from the smudges under your eyes that you'd better retire. It's been a long day."

"Are you also retiring now, Charles?" asked Susan hesitantly, her eyes suddenly shy.

Her husband looked at her, wishing he could forget the past but knowing that he couldn't. A muscle twitched in his jaw and his brows drew together, then he forced himself to relax, smiling gently at her as he shook his head.

"I'm afraid I can't. There's a great deal of paperwork that Mr. Martin, my agent, has told me I can no longer ignore."

Susan was very much aware of her naiveté and she thought that, however, gently put, she had heard a reproach in his words.

"Please disregard my words, Charles," she said hastily, "I had no right to question you." She moved toward the door, both embarrassed and flustered, then she smiled a little. "I'm a bit tired after all."

The earl's lips tightened. "Do you know the way to your room or shall I call Mrs. Penrose to show you?"

"No, I know the way, Charles, she pointed it out to me earlier." She paused then spoke quietly. "Good night, then, Charles."

"Susan," he said suddenly as she put her hand to the doorknob, "wait a moment."

His voice sounded strained and tense even to his own ears but he walked over to her and stopped only a foot away, keeping his hands tightly clenched at his sides so that he wouldn't forget himself and take her into his arms.

"Yes?" she asked, hardly daring to breathe.

"I . . . that is . . ." He stopped then, with a quick tightening of his lips, continued, "Nothing, it's of no consequence. Sleep well."

He said nothing more so Susan turned and walked quickly up to her room. It wasn't until many hours had passed, however, that she finally heard the soft click of his door in the adjoining chamber and she could sleep.

Two days passed, and under the influence of Susan's warmth and love, Carlton's doubts began to dissipate. Indeed, if Sir Oliver had not chosen that time to rusticate, they might have been spared a great deal of pain.

Oliver, however, had posted north both to visit his mother, for his lands marched with Carlton's, and to offer his felicitations as he had been absent from the city when the wedding took place. He now looked forward to seeing his friend again and he chuckled softly to himself as he rode to Fairfields, unable to picture Carlton in the role of husband. He handed his horse to the groom and, after being informed that the earl would be closeted for several hours more with his agent, joined Susan, who was in the garden.

It took only a few moments for him to discover her, seated upon a small bench set under a tree, fanning her face with a charming villager hat of chip straw and gazing dreamily into the distance.

Oliver grinned and leaned against the trunk of the tree. "Shall you waken with a kiss, I wonder?" He laughed lazily.

At her cry of alarm he pushed himself away from the tree and walked nearer.

She gazed at him in reproach, one slim hand pressed against her heart. "Oliver, you wretch. That was very badly done of you."

Oliver's grin widened as he moved her skirt aside and took a seat next to her on the small bench.

"Never say you're angry, fair princess," he teased as he raised her hand to his lips, looking up at her through the screen of his ridiculously long lashes.

Susan chuckled and rose, withdrawing her hand as she did so.

"Gudgeon. You know better than to flirt with a married lady, particularly one who looks upon you as a brother."

Oliver's wide grin flashed again then he tucked her hand under his arm and the two began to stroll.

"It's not safe for me to flirt unless it's with a married woman and I'd much rather not be called out so I picked you. Indeed, it's far better when the lady treats you like a brother. Besides," he continued thoughtfully, "until my estates are in hand, I can't think of marriage." He was silent for a moment, then his eyes sparkled with mischief. "Not that I intend to grow rusty in the art of lovemaking, fair princess."

He leered at her. "Who better to practice on than the most beautiful young lady of my acquaintance, and one who is married to my best friend and feels herself a sister to me?"

Susan couldn't help but laugh at this piece of nonsense. "Indeed, Oliver. Sometimes, however, I feel that you're just the tiniest bit frightened of the young ladies of the ton."

Oliver's eyes twinkled. "Perhaps . . . although there is one . . ."

His voice trailed off and he gave himself a mental shake, impervious to the laughing question in his companion's eyes.

"But that's neither here nor there," he continued easily. "I did have a purpose in coming today, other than accompanying you on a walk in the shrubbery, delightful as that task is."

He halted and took both her hands in his own.

"What is it, Oliver?" Susan asked and then chuckled. "Are you going to make love to me now?"

"Good God, no!" he said, startled. "Charles is my best friend." He paused and grinned. "Besides, he's a devilish fine shot. No, I just wanted to offer my felicitations in person."

His grin grew a little crooked. "Charles has needed someone like you for a long time, Susan. I think it's hard for him to show affection . . . his parents were cold, formal people, but once you've won his trust, he'll do anything for you. He's a good man to have at your back."

Susan smiled at the intent young man, quite

touched, then acting on impulse, she stood on tiptoe and rested her hands on his shoulders, kissing him lightly on the cheek. She hugged him for a brief moment, tears suddenly appearing in her eyes.

"Thank you, Oliver. I do love him, you know."

Oliver held her chin up with one long finger and his grin flashed again. "Of course you do. I can see it in your eyes every time you look at him."

He gently wiped her cheeks with his handkerchief, then once again tucked her arm under his and they continued down the path.

Lord Carlton stood motionless at the window of his study, his face white with rage, as he watched the attractive couple. He dropped the curtain and turned, hoping to hide their presence from his agent. As soon as was possible, he finished with the man and sent him on his way then shoved his papers aside and strode angrily out of the house, intent upon the stables.

Oliver, who had hoped to speak to his friend, questioned Rollands and, upon making the happy discovery that Lord Carlton had done with his business and was about to ride, followed him to the stables. Before he reached the building, however, he was forced to leap off the path to avoid being run down. He gazed after the earl, startled by the blaze of anger he had seen in his friend's eyes. After he regained his composure, he rejoined Susan for a light luncheon.

"I'm sorry Charles isn't here, Oliver," she said as he seated himself. "He must still be with Mr. Martin."

Oliver took a sip of wine. "Well, he's not with his agent. I just saw him a minute ago. He nearly knocked me off the path."

Susan frowned as she buttered a piece of bread. "I can't think why he didn't join us, surely he knew you were here."

"He's in the boughs about something or other," Oliver continued with a grin. "He looked fit to kill when he rode by me."

"Perhaps he's had some distressing news about one of his tenants."

"Perhaps," Oliver agreed, deciding that she shouldn't tease herself about the matter. "Will you please tell him that I'll ride over tomorrow afternoon." His eyes twinkled. "That is, if my mother doesn't have too many errands for me to attend to. She's already asked me to allow some time for a ride into Twickingham."

"How dreadful for you, Oliver," teased Susan. "How is your mother?" she continued with some concern.

Oliver frowned as he thought about his mother. She had been confined to her bed for some time recovering from a severe bout of influenza and quite alarming him in the process. Although he had wished to see Susan and Charles, she was the real reason he had returned from a tip to Ireland sooner than expected.

"She seems to be making some progress at last and will be fit as a trivet if I can make her follow Dr. Poisenby's instructions."

"That's the best of news, Oliver, and I'm certain you'll see to it that she does exactly as she should."

She was silent a moment then looked at Oliver, her eyes brimming with laughter. "Excuse me, but is his name really Poisenby?"

Oliver grinned. "Strange name for a man of medicine, isn't it? The poor man took some pretty heavy teasing when he first came into the country but everyone's familiar with it now. You must meet him, Susan, he's a fine doctor and a delightful fellow. I'm sure Charles had plans for you to meet all your neighbors, though."

It had better be soon, Susan thought with a flash of humor as Oliver picked up his fork, or the neighborhood will be meeting two of us instead of one.

Susan's pregnancy was not so far advanced as to make her more than pleasantly rounded and not even that was as yet apparent in the high-waisted gowns she wore but she had felt her child move only the night before and could hardly contain her excitement. The thought that Charles was angry wasn't a happy one, however, and as she said good-bye to Oliver and watched him ride away, she hoped that her husband would return in a better frame of mind.

The fact that he had made no attempt to come to her room at night disturbed her tranquillity, and as much as she pondered, she could find no logical explanation for his behavior. She could do no more than hope that her news about their child might restore their intimacy, for she longed to feel his arms about her again.

She dressed carefully that evening, anxious that she should look her best, then sat at her dressing table while Sarah, who had arrived at Fairfields, to Susan's great delight, along with her mistress's baggage, brushed her hair and arranged it attractively. Ringlets curled softly around her face and she stared at her reflection, blissfully unaware of the extremely disquieting picture she and Oliver had presented to her husband that morning.

She was, in fact, much like a lamb going to slaughter as she descended to the small saloon that evening, and as she opened the door, her mind was occupied only with the problem of how to inform her husband that his son was already in a fair way to becoming a bruising sportsman. A blush stained her cheeks at the thought of talking with Charles on such an intimate subject but she had determined that he also had a right to know what was happening with his son. So it was that when she entered the room, Lord Carlton had the opportunity to observe her looking remarkably lovely.

Susan saw the flash of admiration in his eyes then they were carefully shuttered as he continued to gaze critically at her. She paused on the threshold, alarm causing her to grip the doorknob tightly as her husband moved forward. He wished her a good evening in a coldly impersonal tone then pulled a chair comfortably close to the fire and invited her to sit down.

As he handed her to the chair, Susan caught the look of controlled fury he directed her way. "What is it, Charles?" she cried impulsively. "What on earth has occurred to cause you to look so?"

"Nothing," he replied sharply as he turned to the table, upon which rested a decanter and two glasses, and poured them each a little sherry.

She looked at him in confusion as he handed her a glass. "It's obvious that something has angered you."

His brows snapped together as he took a seat opposite her. "Must I repeat myself, ma'am?"

Susan wisely refrained from answering, and as Carlton toyed with the stem of his wine glass, he thought again of the incident he had inadvertently observed that morning. It had taken him the better part of the day to control his rage, and any hope that he had misconstrued what he'd witnessed dissipated as he gazed coldly at the lovely face of his young wife. No, he thought savagely, taking a sip from his glass, he couldn't have mistaken that little scene. His scowl deepened. His wife's improprieties before he'd married her were one thing, but he was truly revolted that she had attempted the same thing with his friend and in his own home.

He drained his glass in a single swallow, wishing it were brandy. He was a fool and Susan had all too obviously succeeded in deceiving him. With an oath, he stood up and began pacing restlessly about the room.

As he rose, Susan glanced up from an apparently fascinating inspection of the patterns etched on her glass.

"I don't know what to think, Charles," she said candidly. "Have I done something or said something I shouldn't?"

"Good God, madam . . ." began Carlton, his voice shaking with suppressed fury. He bit back the remainder of his angry retort as Rollands entered the room to announce dinner, then icily offered Susan his arm. She placed her glass on the table, unable to think of a word to say to the implacable man standing before her.

As they went into the dining room, she gazed questioningly at her husband. Had she married a man whose mind was unstable? It was the only excuse her confused mind could offer for such irrational behavior.

Dinner was an uncomfortable experience. Any conversation Susan attempted was coldly rebuffed and she gave up at last, feeling it all she could do to get through the meal. Her head whirled and she longed for the privacy of her own chamber, hoping that she might then be able to sort things out. From time to time she risked a glance at her husband's face but his thinned lips and forbidding scowl did nothing to cheer her. By the time the last covers had been removed and dessert was served, she had calmed herself enough to realize that her husband wasn't a lunatic but what his problem was she couldn't fathom.

Dessert was a lovely Renish Cream, one of her favorites, but she had hardly taken a mouthful or two before she replaced her spoon and begged to be excused. Charles nodded curtly and Susan gratefully escaped to her room.

No miracles occurred during the night and the situation was much the same on the following morning. Susan delayed going downstairs for as long as possible, anxious that she should not have the misfortune of partaking of another meal with her husband when he was in such a vile mood.

Sarah, who noticed her leisurely progress and attributed it to her delicate condition, suggested that she have a tray brought to her room. For a moment, Susan considered it then berated herself for being a coward. She would not allow Charles to browbeat her and so, with a cheerful smile for the maid, she seated herself at her dressing table and stated that she would be right as a trivet as soon as she had eaten some of Monsieur Charte's excellent omelet.

Sarah brushed the long, silky curls, her brows drawn together as she studied the situation. She had overheard the earl tell Rollands that he would be away from Fairfields for much of the day so he couldn't be counted on to cheer his wife's flagging spirits. Her face suddenly cleared as she recalled Sir Oliver. Perhaps that handsome young gentleman, being the friend he was to both the earl and Lady Susan, could lighten her ladyship's spirits. Hoping to encourage Susan along these lines, Sarah piled the shining masses of dark hair atop her mistress's head and murmured that perhaps Sir Oliver would be by to cheer her up.

Susan's hand flew to her cheek. "I completely forgot to mention to Lord Carlton that Sir Oliver was coming today, particularly to see him. I'll have to go down immediately, Sarah."

She entered the deserted breakfast parlor, and when Rollands came in with a fresh pot of coffee, she questioned him, hoping that her voice didn't tremble.

"Lord Carlton left some time ago in the company of Mr. Martin, my lady," he replied, then, when he saw how anxiously she was watching him, unbent enough to continue. "I believe I heard him mention that he was to pick up his black colt in the village, my lady."

"Did he leave a message for me?"

"I'm afraid he did not, my lady," replied the butler.

Susan smiled faintly at him and picked up her napkin. "Well, no matter." She raised her cup to her lips. "When Sir Oliver arrives, please show him in."

"Very good, my lady."

Susan toyed with her omelet after the butler had quit the room. All thoughts of Oliver vanished and she concentrated once again on solving the puzzle of her husband's odd behavior, which seemed, even in the light of day, to have been queer as Dick's hatband. Her brow furrowed and she concentrated on the problem, going over and over in her mind all the times she had seen Charles the day before.

No logical solution presented itself, and she was still lingering over her toast and coffee when Oliver arrived. Rollands showed him in and the young man's eyebrows rose with amusement when he saw her.

"What's this? I hadn't supposed I'd be interrupting your breakfast, Susan."

Susan smiled at the sparkle of laughter she glimpsed in his eyes. "You've caught me out, Oliver," she said remorsefully as she poured another cup for him. "Now you will think me one of those silly creatures who lie abed all day, rising only when it's time to dress and go out for some amusement."

Oliver laughed as he took the cup from her hand. "Quite right. That husband of yours will have to teach you how to go on in the country. Where is the happy bridegroom, anyway? Never say he's still abed."

Susan carefully began applying raspberry jam to a finger of toast. "I believe he's gone off with Mr. Martin again."

"The devil you say. What's come over him? If I was

at all sensitive, I'd say he was avoiding me."

"It's not you, Oliver," Susan said faintly as she replaced the toast on her plate and began crumbling a corner of it. Forcing a smile, she raised her eyes to his. "Actually, I'm afraid it's my fault that he's not here. I quite forgot to tell him that you were coming."

Oliver looked doubtful. "Well, don't be going into a pelter over that. I'll see him later, no doubt."

He watched her carefully as she finished her coffee, certain that something was amiss. He didn't understand her trouble but he very much wanted to see the roses back in her cheeks.

"Well, I'm off to Twickingham this morning," he said cheerfully. "I've got some things to pick up for my mother." He paused. "You haven't seen the village yet, have you?"

"Just when we drove through from London."

Oliver grinned. "Oh, well, then you've seen about all there is, but if you'd care for it, I'd like for you to go with me. In fact, I need your help."

Susan brightened, suddenly feeling that a visit to Twickingham was exactly what was needed to raise her spirits.

"I'd love to join you," she said quickly. "It will take me only a moment to get my bonnet."

She rejoined Oliver in the foyer, moments later, her charming face set off admirably by a high-crowned bonnet complete with ostrich feathers which bobbed slightly as she walked, and blue satin ribbons tied into a pert bow under one ear. Oliver gazed at her admiringly.

"I vow every lady in town will be watching you from behind her curtains."

Susan chuckled as they walked down the front steps. She felt better already. Her feeling of well-being was short-lived, however, as her companion suddenly exclaimed and slapped his forehead.

"Oh, Susan, I'm the greatest nodcock. I've ridden over, and I can't think you wish to ride in that gown . . . not at all the thing."

He eyed her lovely blue muslin walking dress, with its matching pelisse, and Susan, too, looked down at her attire. "Not only that, Oliver," she said with amusement. "I don't know how to ride."

A frown appeared between her brows. She couldn't like the idea of taking one of her husband's vehicles nor even less the thought of borrowing one of his perfectly matched teams, but her little trip to the village had begun to seem very important to her.

"Perhaps, we could use Charles's curricle, Oliver," she offered hesitantly.

"I don't like the idea above half, myself, Susan, and he's bound to dislike it exceedingly. Perhaps we'd better postpone our outing to another day when I can bring over my own cattle."

Susan nodded and, with a faint smile, turned to the door. Oliver, who couldn't bear to see the disappointment in her eyes and who, for reasons known only to himself, did truly wish her to accompany him, caught her arm as Rollands opened the door.

"Oh, devil fly away with it, Susan, let's do it. I know he won't mind our using the curricle, after all, you're his wife and as for the team," he shrugged and grinned a little lopsidedly, "well, he knows I'm a good whip . . . he taught me."

At this juncture, Rollands gave a discreet cough

and two pairs of eyes turned in his direction.

"I believe the curricle is being repainted, Sir Oliver."

Susan and Oliver gazed helplessly at each other and Rollands again cleared his throat.

"Begging your pardon, my lady, but there is the pony cart."

"Just the thing," agreed Oliver.

"You can't mean it, Oliver," Susan managed with a tiny choke of laughter. "A Corinthian like you in a pony cart? Only think if anyone saw you."

"Not to worry." Oliver grinned. "Anyway, this is much better. Now Charles won't be able to cut up stiff about the curricle and team. Don't mind admitting using another man's cattle without his permission isn't a thing I'd like to do, even if he is a friend."

Susan attempted to swallow her laughter as she pictured her companion, a respected member of the Four-Horse Club, in a ramshackle cart, but she failed miserably. Oliver grinned at her, not in the least put out.

"It'll be a lark, Susan. You handle the ribbons, and if anyone should see me, I'll say it's a wager."

Without waiting for any objections she might raise, he ordered the groom to return his horse to the stable and fetch out the cart immediately.

This was quickly done, and to Susan's delight and amusement, they were soon bowling along the road to Twickingham.

When they arrived in the village, Susan scanned the faces of the people who were about, hoping for a glimpse of her husband, but she didn't see him. By the time Oliver had ordered a boy to mind the cart and had handed her down, she had regained her composure and didn't allow her disappointment to show.

If the thought crossed her mind that a great part of the eager anticipation she felt for her outing had in any way been brought about by the hope of seeing Charles, she attempted to erase it. She was once again uncertain of his feelings toward her, and ever since she'd discovered that she loved him, she couldn't help but feel quite vulnerable.

Oliver offered Susan his arm and they set about on his mother's errands. After an hour or so thus employed, they had completed all the tasks Lady Seaton had set for her son and were driving out of the village.

Susan slanted a mischievous glance at her companion, gazing pointedly at the small parcels he was holding in one hand.

She chuckled softly. "Now tell me why you needed my help today, Oliver. It couldn't have been to carry packages."

Oliver started. "Good God, what a complete idiot I am. Please, turn around, Susan, and drive to the other end of the village."

Susan's curiosity was aroused but she didn't question her companion as she neatly turned the cart and headed it back as Oliver had directed.

They reached the path he wished to take and Susan turned the cart down the lane. It was short and ended at a neat cottage hidden behind a hedgerow.

Oliver indicated that they should halt, then after tying the pony to one of the trees, he handed Susan down. He took her elbow and to her amazement, passed by the front door and continued on around to the rear of the house. They walked through a small flower garden and came to a shed, as neat and well taken care of as the cottage. Susan hesitated, laying her hand on Oliver's arm as he began to enter the building.

"Wait, Oliver . . . shouldn't we ask permission?"

He chuckled at her concern, then explained that the cottage belonged to his old nurse and that she had had to leave quite suddenly to visit her sister, who was ill, but had first requested that he help her with a small problem.

As Oliver continued to talk, Susan became increasingly aware of a noise coming from the shed. She was unable to place the faint, whimpering, scratching sound she heard and couldn't contain her curiosity any longer.

"Oliver," she interrupted. "What's in there?"

He grinned mischieviously and opened the door. "See for yourself."

He stepped back a pace when a small bundle of silky golden fur toppled out. Susan knelt in the soft grass with a cry of delight.

"Oh, Oliver, he's a darling."

The small creature was a young spaniel with a great deal of intelligence, which he plainly displayed when he walked, somewhat akwardly on his fat puppy legs, over to Susan. He licked her hands, then her face as she gathered him into her arms and buried her face in his soft fur. Her eyes glowed when she looked up at Oliver and the young man grinned at the success of his plan.

"Would you like to keep him, Susan?"

She rose, holding the puppy, her eyes alight. "Thank you, I'd love to have him but will your nurse agree?"

"Not to worry. This was the little problem I needed your help with. My old nurse can't keep him any longer, the imp gives her too much trouble and dogs make my mother ill so it wouldn't do for me to keep him either. I'm afraid the only thing I could do was hope to find a good home for him. I hope he won't be any trouble for you."

"Oliver, how can you think such a darling would cause me any trouble?" exclaimed Susan indignantly as she again buried her face in the soft, sweet-smelling fur on the puppy's back. "Oh, I should love having him . . . if . . . if you think Charles wouldn't mind."

Oliver looked surprised. "Charles? Why should he? I've always known him to like animals." He shrugged. "Something in him they respond to, I guess. I never saw anything like it." He offered Susan his arm. "What are you going to call the pup?"

"Troubles," replied Susan immediately, slanting a mischievous glance at her companion.

"Ummm . . . strange name," he murmured with a frown. "Sure you wouldn't like Rover better?"

A ripple of laughter burst from Susan's lips. "Oh, Oliver, you're bamming me, aren't you?"

Oliver grinned. "A little. I guess Troubles is a good name after all. He's been trouble for me, at any rate.

They made their way back to the cart with Susan carrying Troubles in her arms. Oliver took the lines and they were soon out of Twickingham, quickly passing the Singing Swan Inn, which marked the edge of the village. Both Susan and Oliver, however, were much too engrossed in the puppy to be aware of a pair of ice cold gray eyes which followed their progress as they made their way past that establishment.

The gentleman who observed them remained absolutely motionless for a pair of minutes, then swore vehemently and quickly tossed off the brandy he held.

Chapter 12

As soon as the preoccupied couple was beyond the inn, Carlton ordered out his horse and curtly requested that Mr. Martin be informed that he was to follow with the groom and the colt later in the day. Carlton had no desire that the entire neighborhood know of his wife's indiscreet dalliance and so paused a moment to be quite certain that the landlord fully understood the message and that Martin and the groom would not follow for several hours.

He finished with the landlord, and grim thoughts whirled about in his head as he placed one well-polished Hessian in the stirrup and vaulted lightly into the saddle. He left the courtyard of the inn at a sedate pace although the anger he felt was communicated to his mount and the animal jibbed and cavorted nervously until he was allowed to lengthen his stride.

The pony cart had meanwhile come to a halt just beyond the ancient church. The scene which then occurred may have seemed, if witnessed by an angry husband, like an assignation but one moment of eavesdropping would have put that idea immediately to rout.

Susan had removed the blue ribbon from around her smart bonnet and had knelt beside the puppy, tying the satin gently about Troubles's neck while Oliver stepped out of the cart and secured the pony to a bush beside the road.

"Impossible creature," scolded Susan gently as she finished tying the bow. She took the puppy's face between her hands, looking sternly into its twinkling brown eyes.

"Do you really have to make us stop here along the road when we are so near home?" Receiving no answer, she sighed and dropped a kiss on the soft head. "Depend upon it, you will not so easily have your own way in the future." She rose and held the ribbon in her hand as Oliver came round the cart to help her down.

"He has no manners, Oliver," declared Susan with a rueful laugh as she reached for the hand he extended to help her out.

Oliver returned her smile, his eyes twinkling. "He's well named."

At that moment, Troubles, perhaps wishing to redeem himself in his mistress's eyes, spied a rabbit at the bottom of the steep bank which flanked the narrow road on either side and, with a sharp yelp, leapt from the cart and dashed down into the ditch.

Susan felt the ribbon being pulled from her hand and she instinctively tightened her grip but to no avail. She was jerked forward and out of the pony cart, directly into Oliver, who was standing ready to assist her. The impact caused him to stagger and he threw his arms around her, holding her tightly and bracing her body so they would not both tumble to the bottom of the bank.

It was at this most inappropriate moment that the fates chose for the already irate husband to ride up. Neither Susan nor Oliver heard him approach as they were both engaged in the task of regaining their balance. To Carlton, however, it had more the look of a passionate embrace and there was murder in his eyes as he dismounted.

"Unhand my wife, Oliver," he ordered in a voice which sent a shiver down that young man's spine. Two pairs of startled eyes turned to him, and if the earl had taken but a moment to observe carefully, he would have seen no guile in either pair.

Oliver quickly released Susan and attempted to make a hurried explanation but Carlton was not attending. His cold gaze was focused upon his wife, who was hastily attempting to poke up some of the curls which would keep escaping from beneath her bonnet now that there was no ribbon to hold it in place. She looked enchantingly flushed and, to the earl's way of thinking, more than a little guilty with her rosy cheeks, tumbled hair, and heaving bosom.

She, too, tried to explain but Carlton made little attempt to understand her words as they tumbled out one on top of the other. His heart felt heavy and he wondered, rather bleakly, why it should be at this moment that he should discover how very desirable his wife was and how much he loved her.

"Please, Charles," she exclaimed when she comprehended that he had heard none of what she had said. "You aren't listening. Troubles is gone and he is much too little to be off like this. Won't you go after him?"

Carlton stared at her as though she were speaking another language. His attention was quickly riveted upon Oliver, however, who fully realized what was in the earl's mind.

"It's not what you think, Charles," interrupted Oliver, quietly.

Carlton studied the young man. His expression was a mixture of pity and disdain. "If you were any other man, I would call you out but this is more the fault of my wife. She has a certain unsteadiness of character about which you couldn't have been expected to be aware."

Susan gasped and stared speechlessly at her husband, the puppy forgotten.

"You can't mean what you're saying, Charles," protested Oliver, aghast. "You haven't even heard ou[r] explanations."

The earl gestured impatiently, "Spare me thes[e] protestations, Oliver. They don't become you."

Susan moved forward a pace, her eyes wide an[d] incredulous. "Good God, Charles, what are yo[u] thinking?"

Carlton looked at her coldly. "I shall attend to yo[u] momentarily, madam." He turned once again t[o] Oliver. "I want you off my land immediately an[d] you're not to return to visit Lady Carlton. You ma[y] speak to her at social gatherings or in the village [if] you should happen to meet, since it would seem to[o] odd if you were to snub her, but there is to be n[o] other social intercourse between the two of you."

He grasped his riding crop so tightly that his knuckles showed white, but his voice was dangerously soft. "Have I made myself clear?"

"Quite," replied Oliver coldly, realizing there was nothing he could say at the moment which would get through to his angry friend. He turned in disgust and, after murmuring a quiet farewell to Susan, began to trudge up the road to Fairfields.

Susan stood as though she had been turned to stone. Objects seemed to swim before her eyes, and for a moment she was afraid she might suffer further humiliation by fainting.

"How could you?" she whispered at last as she faced her husband, her hands clenched tightly at her sides. "How dare you say such terrible things about Oliver and . . . and about me?" Her eyes filled with tears of rage and sparkled on the ends of her lashes.

"That trick will not work, madame," her husband said contemptuously. "I assure you I shall not succumb to your tears."

Susan closed her eyes and her anger evaporated as she was overcome by the enormity of her husband's accusations. She moved to the pony cart, her slender shoulders slumped with despair, deciding that she wouldn't think of all this now. It would have to be sorted out later when she could think clearly.

Carlton hesitated, struck by the pain he'd seen in her eyes. A muscle twitched in his jaw as he forced himself to resist the compulsion he felt building in him to go to her and take her in his arms. The rigid control he had developed over the years, combined with the horror he felt whenever he contemplated the thought of his name being drawn through the muck of scandal, forced him to remain aloof.

He strode over to his horse, which stood grazing peacefully, and gathered the reins, tied him to the back of the cart. Susan, who had turned as she prepared to climb into the vehicle, regarded him steadily, then spoke quietly.

"You're making a terrible mistake, Charles. I would never play you false, regardless of what you think."

His eyes narrowed and a sneer curled his lip. "Please, madame, no more denials."

Her hand went out to him beseechingly. "Charles, you of all people must know that I . . . that I was innocent when you . . . when you . . ." Her cheeks were stained with scarlet.

"Enough!" He gritted his teeth, fighting to hold his temper in check. "It's not altogether inconceivable that you, like so many of your sex, find it more convenient to be married while you carry on an affaire de coeur with another man."

The bright color drained from Susan's cheeks and lips and her limbs trembled from the shock of his words. "Do you truly believe that, Charles?" she whispered. "For if you do, then I think there is no hope for us."

"That is exactly what I believe."

Susan stared at him, her eyes wide and her hands icy. How could this be happening? Only a few short days ago she had harbored the hope that they would be like any other happily married couple, perhaps even better than most, and now her world was crumbling about her head. Her stomach churned and she felt ill. How could he believe such terrible things of her? What had she ever done to give him such a low opinion of her?

Her mind felt numb. All she could think of as she gazed at him through pain-filled eyes was how much she cared for him and how much she wanted him to take her in his arms, comforting her and telling her that it was all a bad dream. But it wasn't a dream and she couldn't imagine what the future would hold for them.

Her husband spoke, answering her question as though he had read her mind.

"I shall apply for a divorce as soon as the child is born. He will remain with me, of course." He turned from her with an icy detachment.

Susan felt his words strike her like blows. She raised her hands as if to ward them off. "No . . . no . . ." she cried, tears streaming unheeded down her cheeks. She took a step backward and the movement instantly arrested the earl's attention.

"Susan, have a care!" he cried in alarm as she began to lose her footing on the edge of the bank. Her arms flailed as she attempted to regain her balance then her absurd bonnet flew off and she tumbled head over heels down the embankment, coming at last to rest when her head met the corner of a large rock with a resounding crack.

Carlton stood as he was for one heart-stopping minute, then was sliding down the slope, his pulses racing. He gathered his wife into his arms, his face etched with fear. Her skin was white and her lips ashen. When her head lolled against his chest, something like a sob caught in his throat.

"My God, Susan," he grated harshly, "please, open your eyes. Wake up, love."

As he begged her to regain consciousness, Carlton gently smoothed back the dusky hair from her forehead, rocking her and murmuring her name. His words ceased and a cold wave of horror washed over him as he withdrew his hand from the dark curls and gazed at that part of his body as if it didn't belong to him. Blood covered his fingers and was even now beginning to run down Susan's cheek in an ever-increasing stream.

With an oath, Carlton pulled his handkerchief out and gently wiped her face then, with infinite tenderness, parted her hair and dabbed at the blood until he could see the wound.

It was an ugly gash just beyond the hairline. The bleeding had become sluggish, and although it was a nasty cut, a brief scrutiny satisfied the earl that it was not life-threatening. That thought relieved him a little, and he quickly and with no apparent effort lifted Susan into his arms and carried her to the cart.

Carefully cradling her in his arms and with her head resting gently against his shoulder, he urged the pony into a cautious walk. His burden was unwieldly, however, and he had a great deal of trouble maintaining his seat on the cart while he attempted to keep Susan from any further injury, and at the same time restrain the pony from breaking into a jolting trot.

Charles ground his teeth in frustration as the pony

rounded a bend and again began to jog. The frown between his brows lifted and he experienced a wave of relief when he caught sight of Oliver walking rather stiffly back along the track, leading a much bedraggled but obviously happy puppy by a frayed length of blue satin.

Oliver began to address the earl in tones of the coldest formality. "I have Lady Carlton's puppy, my—" He suddenly broke off and stared at the now motionless pony cart in dawning comprehension. "My God, Charles, what have you done?"

The earl favored him with a dark look. "No, I haven't murdered my wife. Stop gaping and come help me." He spoke harshly, causing Oliver to thrust the pup into the cart and go immediately to the pony's head.

"Shall I lead him, my lord?" asked Oliver tightly. Although Oliver was quite obviously concerned, Carlton could tell from his stiff bearing that he was reserving judgment until he had heard what had transpired, and so while Oliver led the animal, Carlton began a rather sketchy explanation of the accident, although he felt both embarrassed and chagrined at the necessity of doing so.

The earl, who had neglected to mention his threat of divorce since he knew exactly how his friend would react to that bit of nonsense, adjusted Susan more comfortably in his arms. He breathed a sigh of relief as he noticed that while she was still unconscious, she seemed easier.

"I apologize for losing my temper, Oliver," he continued remorsefully, "but coming on the two of you like that . . . after seeing Susan kissing you in the garden . . ."

Oliver made a sound of disgust. "She thinks of me as a brother, and how you could read more into it is beyond me."

Carlton could see that he was not to be easily forgiven. "Is this the puppy you were attempting to tell me about?" he asked gravely, realizing that he had misjudged both his friend and his wife.

"Do you really wish to know the truth, Charles?" asked Oliver doubtfully.

Carlton eased Susan into a more comfortable position and assured Oliver that he did, adding that he'd behaved like a complete idiot in the entire matter.

Oliver nodded briefly as he turned into the long track which led to the house. "How you could possibly imagine Susan would play you false is more than I can understand. She loves you too much for your own good."

The earl's lips tightened but he said nothing. He realized at last that he had based his assessment of his wife's character on innuedndo and lies but that realization was of little comfort to him.

They reached the house and Lord Carlton remained where he was while Oliver went for help. His arm tightened around Susan and he dropped a kiss on her brow.

Oliver returned quickly with Rollands, Mrs. Penrose, and several footmen, who immediately fell in to aid the earl in taking Susan up to her chamber.

Much to the dismay of both Sarah and the housekeeper, who were quite naturally distraught, Carlton refused to leave the room until he had seen Susan resting comfortably. After he had placed her on her bed, he went to the door and ordered Rollands to send someone for Dr. Poisenby. When the butler assured him that Sir Oliver had left immediately upon just that errand, he turned back to Sarah and the housekeeper.

Both ladies were hovering over the bed, Sarah attempting to wave burnt feathers under Susan's nose and Mrs. Penrose, looking quite shaken, standing rather helplessly at the abigail's shoulder, wringing her apron and murmuring inarticulate sounds of distress.

Carlton, his face calm but clearly etched with deep concern, strode quickly to the bed and gently moved Mrs. Penrose aside.

"Send someone immediately with hot water, lint, scissors, and clean cloths," he ordered while he took note of the fact that the feathers were not having the desired effect.

After the housekeeper had left the room, he removed the feathers from Sarah's hand. "Perhaps between the two of us we can make Lady Carlton more comfortable."

"Dear God," wept Sarah, raising her tearstained face to his. "Is she going to die?"

"Not if I can help it," he replied grimly. "Now I should like to see her cleaned up and made more comfortable before the doctor arrives."

The girl nodded, and although it offended her sense of what was seemly, she allowed the earl to aid her in removing her mistress's dress and shoes. After this was done, she stood back, her arms folded and brow furrowed, tears once more gathering in her eyes.

"Only pray the babe's not been injured," she gulped with a sob.

Carlton stiffened and turned startled eyes upon the crumpled face of the servant.

"My God, I gave no thought to the child. Will she lose it?"

"I can't say, my lord," the abigail sobbed. Her tears ceased, however, when she looked up and saw the fear in his face. She laid a hand on his arm.

"Everything appears to be all right, my lord," she ventured shyly. She blushed and removed her hand. "I think we would have seen signs by now were she going to lose it."

Carlton closed his eyes and released the breath he had been holding. "Thank you, Sarah."

They both turned to the door as Mrs. Penrose and one of the kitchen maids bustled into the room with the various items the earl had ordered, then Carlton sat down in a chair by Susan's head and with infinite care clipped the hair away from the cut.

"You'll likely never forgive me for cutting your hair, love," he murmured ruefully as he observed his handiwork. He then carefully swabbed the wound, causing it to begin bleeding once again but slowly. He was applying the lint as Dr. Poisenby was shown into the room.

The doctor took in the situation immediately and, after ordering all but the housekeeper from the room, began to set about his work. Carlton, who had no intention of departing, shot a speaking glance in the direction of the good doctor, removed the lamp from Mrs. Penrose's hand, and held it over his wife's face.

Dr. Posienby regarded him from over the tops of his spectacles, his brows raised, but upon correctly interpreting the expression in the earl's eyes, shrugged and doffed his coat.

"If you'll be so kind as to hold the light steady, I'll soon have Lady Carlton's wound stitched and we'll see what's about here."

With these enigmatic words, he set to work and within a very short period of time had set ten neat stitches in his patient's scalp.

"Thank you, my lord," he said briskly as he washed his hands. "I don't think I need cup her, at least not today."

"I should hope not," exclaimed Carlton. "What do you think, Poisenby? Will she be all right?"

The doctor glanced up, smiling sympathetically when he observed the earl's gray face.

"Not a pretty sight, is it, particularly when it's someone one loves who needs stitching up."

He reached for the decanter which Mrs. Pensrose had had the foresight to provide, then filled a glass and pressed it into the earl's hand.

"Perhaps you would excuse me for a moment while I examine your wife?" He nodded his head to the housekeeper, who opened the door for Lord Carlton.

"I'll see you in the book room, then, doctor." Carlton was more shaken by what he had observed than he cared to admit. Susan had looked so young and vulnerable . . . and so terribly white. And it was his fault.

He entered the library and stood by the fireplace, one arm resting on the mantle, his head bowed. He didn't know how long he stood thus, lost in unhappy thoughts, but in what seemed a very short time, the doctor knocked and entered.

Carlton stared at him, his eyes hard and searching. "Well, doctor?"

"Lady Carlton has sustained a severe shock, my lord, but her life doesn't seem to be in jeopardy at this moment." He paused then said delicately, "You did know that your wife is increasing?" The earl nodded curtly, and the doctor continued, "Happily, her fall doesn't seem to have affected her pregnancy."

The earl's eyes had narrowed as he stared at the grave face of the doctor. "What do you mean that her life is not in jeopardy at this moment? Please make yourself clearer."

The doctor sighed. This wasn't going to be easy. "Do you mind if I sit down, my lord?"

Carlton indicated a chair, then waited impatiently while the doctor made himself comfortable.

"Now then, Dr. Poisenby," he said bruskly, "if you'll continue, please."

The doctor looked longingly at the decanter, feeling the need for a bracing drop or two, but decided, wisely enough, that the earl's patience wouldn't extend to his having a bit of refreshment before he began his explanation.

"There is, as I said, no immediate danger, but for some reason, Lady Carlton isn't regaining her senses as quickly as I'd hoped. She's in a state of shock and we can only hope that she comes out of it soon. She's been badly concussed and I don't mind telling you that I'll be glad to see her come around. There's nothing you can do for her, however, other than to keep her warm and comfortable."

Carlton sank into a chair opposite the doctor's and, with hands that shook slightly, gripped its arms, his face ashen and his eyes staring intently at the man.

"You're telling me that she could die." This was said in a flat, colorless tone.

"Now, my lord, I don't like to paint any picture blacker than it is." He sighed and, after a pause, continued, "You must be aware that the longer she remains unconscious, the graver the situation."

There was a long silence, broken at last when Carlton rose from his chair and stood in front of the doctor.

"Thank you, Dr. Poisenby," he said as though the polite words were drawn from him with great effort. "I appreciate both your concern and your honesty. If you'll excuse me now, I'll return to my wife's chamber. Mrs. Penrose will bring you some refreshment before you return to Twickingham." He held out his hand, which the doctor grasped firmly, then turned and made his way from the room.

It was some considerable time later that Elliott knocked upon the door to Lady Carlton's chamber.

"Are you sitting up all night, my lord?" he asked worriedly. "You'll make yourself sick and then what we'll do, I'm sure I can't say. Come now, my lord, let Sarah sit up with my lady."

The earl ran a hand through his dark hair and stared vacantly at the man. "What's that, Elliott? No, no . . . you may leave, I shan't be needing you tonight. I intend to remain with Lady Carlton in case she should waken."

Elliott breathed a deep sigh but didn't attempt to dissuade the earl, for he knew there was little hope of success.

"Perhaps I could bring you something to eat or fetch your dressing gown?"

Carlton looked at the man, surprised to see him still standing in the doorway.

"Please don't trouble yourself on my account, Elliott. I'm perfectly comfortable as I am."

He turned his eyes back to the still figure on the bed and Elliott softly closed the door then positioned himself on a chair immediately outside Lady Carlton's chamber, anxious to be close at hand should the earl want him.

Carlton, however, did not need his valet and even forgot that he had come to the door, so totally lost in thought was he.

He continued to go over the events leading to the accident but couldn't put Susan's distraught voice from his mind. He knew as well as he knew his own name that she had never taken a lover. His insane jealously and pride had ruined their marriage before it had had a chance to succeed and had perhaps killed the woman he loved.

A muscle tightened at the corner of his mouth. He would not let her die, and when she had recovered, perhaps she would forgive him and they could try again. But first he must put all his effort into her recovery.

By midmorning, when the earl descended for a quick breakfast, his mind was considerably calmer although his concern had not lessened. Susan was still unconscious and Carlton had decided to send for Alicia and Sophy, hoping that these level-headed ladies would be able to help him bring Susan round as he was determined to do. Unfortunately, for he could have used the support of his good friend, Peter had left for Spain on government business immediately after Carlton had departed for Fairfields and there was no hope of communicating with him for several weeks at the very least.

Oliver, who rode over to Fairfields not much later, fell into immediate accord with Carlton's plan and prevailed upon the earl to allow him the privilege of escorting the ladies from London. Carlton agreed as nothing short of force would have removed him from Susan's side even though he could not wish Sophy and Alicia to travel without the escort of a gentleman.

Oliver departed without delay and arrived in London after a record ride. Upon receiving the tragic news, both ladies prepared immediately for an indefinite stay in the country. Before more than a day had passed, they were embarked upon the return trip to Fairfields.

Once again the journey was accomplished in record time, and Carlton, upon hearing the commotion of their arrival, came quietly out of Susan's room, leaving her in the charge of Bailey, his old nurse, who had been quite obstinate in her desire to help.

Carlton's face looked pale and tired but his eyes

brightened perceptibly when he caught sight of Alicia and Sophy as they somewhat shakily descended from Oliver's curricle. He went to them with hands outstretched, including them both in his warm smile.

"Sophy, Alicia, thank God you are come. Now Susan may be well." His delightful smile flashed once again. "I daresay you both had your own engagements which you had to make excuses for and I'll never be able to thank you enough for forgoing your own amusements to come to Susan's aid."

"Tut, Charles," said Sophy, removing her gloves. "I have to suppose both Alicia and I shall survive being obliged to miss a few balls. What poor creatures you must think us were we not able to postpone our petty amusements for the sake of dear Susan. Now," she continued in her calm manner as she and Alicia put off their pelisses, "how is my niece? Oliver was a satisfactory companion except that he could tell us very little to ease our minds."

"She's still unconscious but Dr. Poisenby assures me she's in no mortal danger at present." He paused then continued quietly. "I think I need stand on no ceremony with you, Sophy, and so must tell you that I am worried."

He passed his hand wearily across his face as he turned to lead the ladies into the saloon, every line of his body portraying not only his fatigue but also his concern and anguish. "If only she didn't remain unconscious. It's been four days now and I think even Poisenby must admit some worry. I've decided to send to London for Dr. Edwards if she hasn't wakened in another day."

Sophy quickly took off her bonnet and set it on a table. "I cannot but agree with you, Charles. Perhaps, as Dr. Edwards is a specialist of the brain, he'll know more about this sort of case than Dr. Poisenby."

Alicia, who had been standing just inside the door, interrupted somewhat impatiently. "Excuse me but may we not visit Susan? I can't put my mind at ease until I've seen her. Would it agitate her, do you think?"

"No, indeed. She's not aware of anything that goes on around her . . . would that she were." Carlton opened the door and stood aside. "Come with me, please. I don't like to be away so long."

Chapter 13

The earl led both ladies to the room and closed the door softly behind them. Old nurse moved quietly away from the bedside as Sophy and Alicia looked at Susan.

"She's so pale and still," murmured Alicia, gently taking Susan's hand into her own.

Sophy was also a great deal shocked at her niece's appearance and couldn't wonder that Charles seemed so alarmed. However, she attempted to mask the concern in her eyes and said brightly, "Well, now we are here. I feel certain Susan shall soon be on the mend." She smiled and pressed Charles's hand. "Try to be easy in your mind. She shall recover . . . Truly, Charles," she insisted with determined good humor when Carlton gazed doubtfully at her. "Now, you're to leave us to watch Susan while you rest. It's early hours yet and none of us shall be done any good if you should collapse."

"The very thing I've been a'telling the young master," muttered Bailey from her corner, unable to refrain from venting her spleen any longer.

"Yes, and correct you were too, Bailey," declared Sophy kindly. "Now, both of you do take yourselves off. Alicia and I shall manage quite well."

She ushered them gently to the door. "I promise I shall call you if there is any change in her condition, Charles," she added reassuringly in answer to the troubled question in his eyes.

He allowed himself to be ordered out of the room, realizing suddenly how exhausted he was. He entered his chamber and met the disapproving gaze of Elliott directed toward him.

"What is it now?" he asked wearily. "It's fairly obvious you're in alt over something."

Elliott pressed his lips together in a thin line but did not speak. Carlton didn't attempt any further conversation and slumped into a chair as if he could no longer remain on his feet. The valet carefully removed one of the earl's Hessians then reached for the other, muttering under his breath all the while.

"Elliott," sighed the earl, "if you don't explain to me, rather than to my boot, why I'm in your bad graces, you're going to explode. Come now," he urged, "tell me what has put you on your high ropes."

The valet turned injured eyes upon his employer. "I'm certain I'm not on my high ropes when Lady

Carlton lies as she does, but then don't expect me to be forgetful of my position either. If you want the truth with no bark on it, I'll tell you that I can't think it good sense in you to be going about as you have been."

His eyes flicked disapprovingly down the earl's tall frame. "You're ill shaven and unkempt . . . your boots want polishing and your jacket brushing and your face shows fatigue and strain." He sniffed. "I can't wonder that Lady Sophy and Miss Wentworth were more than a little shocked by your appearance."

"I assure you that it wasn't my appearance which upset them."

"Of course they were upset by my Lady Carlton's condition, as they well might have been, but don't you think the entire household would be less at odds were you to attempt to carry on in a more normal fashion?"

Carlton stared at his former batman in amazement. "Is everything at odds, Elliott?"

"I should say it is," Elliott grumbled as he helped ease the earl out of his coat. "The maids do nothing but weep all day, Monsieur Charte is nearly hysterical, and Rollands . . . of whom I would have expected better . . . is going about with such a long face that a body would think he was already hanging the black crape."

Carlton frowned at the valet, his brow knit. "You're right, of course, Elliott. This isn't the Peninsula. I must deal with more delicate sensibilities here and it won't do to upset my staff more than is warranted, but I'll tell you one thing . . . no one is to be hanging crape. Is that understood?"

Elliott nodded quickly then continued to fuss and fret over the earl until he made known his desire for a few hours' sleep. As this had been his wish all along, Elliott gathered up his master's boots and coat and quietly left the room. The earl closed his eyes and, as he retained the instinct of a good soldier, which allowed him to sleep under the severest pressure when need be, was soon asleep.

Alicia and Lady Sophy made themselves quite as comfortable as possible in Susan's chamber but there was very little they could do. Their patient needed no soothing or cosseting so still and quiet did she remain.

It was, therefore, not surprising that before many hours had passed, Sophy descended to take command of the distraught household, leaving Alicia in charge of the sickroom. Sophy peeped into the room from time to time but, upon receiving a negative sign from Alicia, continued her attempt to bring order to a very shaken household.

Alicia, who could always be relied upon when trouble descended, found the task of sitting quietly beside the bed of her dear friend more trying than she had imagined. Her admiration for Lord Carlton rose as she contemplated the hideousness of sitting helplessly beside the person one loved when that person remained as still as if she were already dead.

Alicia's head began to ache from the strain of

watching so carefully for any movement, even that of a finger lifting, but she refused to abandon hope for her friend's recovery.

She felt a measure of relief when Sophy entered the room some hours later followed by Sarah, who carried a dinner tray.

"I thought you might be hungry, Alicia." Sophy smiled, motioning to Sarah to set the tray on a table.

"How very kind, Lady Sophy." Alicia closed her eyes for a moment. "I think this sort of nursing is a deal more tiring than having even a fretful, peevish patient. I vow, my eyes are on fire from watching so carefully."

"Poor dear." said Sophy. "Come over here and eat. I've put the household to rights so now I'll be able to sit up the night with my niece."

"I couldn't allow you to sit up all night, dear Lady Sophy," objected Alicia as she rose and stretched, holding her hands wearily on the small of her back. "You should be fagged to death . . . no, nothing will answer but to share the task."

Sophy began to demur when suddenly there was a slight movement from the bed. Both women hurried over to Susan and exchanged smiles over her while Sophy smoothed her tangled curls.

"Hush, Susan," her aunt soothed, as her niece began tossing her head on her pillow, "all is well."

"Shall I fetch Charles?" asked Alicia in a low tone.

Sophy shook her head. "Wait a few moments, my

dear, until we're quite certain my niece has completely regained her senses. There's no point in disturbing his rest, otherwise."

Alicia nodded and began to bathe Susan's forehead with lavender water, watching her friend's face anxiously. It seemed for a moment that she was slipping back into unconsciousness when quite suddenly her eyes opened.

"No, Charles," she cried hoarsely, grasping her aunt's hand and staring blindly into her eyes. "Please, I beg of you. You cannot mean it."

"Shh . . . sh . . . my dear," Sophy murmured helplessly as her niece dissolved into tears. Her heart had been rent by that anguished plea and she suddenly determined that Charles should not enter his wife's chamber again until she knew more of what had transpired on the road.

"You mustn't upset yourself, love," she continued in a caressing tone. "You've been very ill."

Susan survived her injury, and although the serious nature of it had left her in fragile health, Dr. Poisenby was able to assure Lord Carlton that, provided his patient was not unduly upset or distressed, he entertained the highest hopes for her recovery.

Carlton, much to his chagrin, hadn't seen his wife since she had regained consciousness. He'd slept the night through and had, of course, upon waking the following morning, been made recipient of the welcome news. He had dressed with all haste and would have rushed immediately into his wife's chamber had not Sophy, waiting anxiously outside the door, laid a hand upon his arm.

He favored her with a quick, searching glance. "What's this, Sophy? Has Susan suffered a relapse?"

Sophy indicated that her niece had not and was, on the contrary, making a splendid recovery.

"It wasn't on that head I desired to speak with you, however, Charles. May we please go into the saloon for a moment before you decide when you will see Susan?"

The earl's eyes narrowed and his lips were pressed tightly together, but he nodded and escorted Sophy into the sunlit room.

"Now then, this is much better," said Sophy, nodding. "I detest being overheard by servants, no matter how well I may like them."

She settled herself, then glanced up at the earl, who had remained standing by the door.

"Well," she said kindly, "shall you sit down and hear what I have to say or continue to stand there glowering at me like a bear?"

His frown lifted and a smile touched his pale face. "Do I glower, Sophy? I don't mean to, I assure you." His gaze became questioning. "Will you tell me now what this is about?"

Sophy regarded the earl thoughtfully. "You shall not like what I have to say but you must hear me out." She paused. "I think it would be better if you did not see Susan just now, Charles."

His brows snapped together and his mouth tightened as he gazed at her.

"Pray do not interrupt," Sophy said calmly, reading his intent in his eyes. "I've had a chance to talk to Susan and I don't believe she is ready to see you."

"Has she said so herself?"

"No . . ." Sophy said, placing the tip of her finger against her lips and frowning with concentration. "She has not exactly said that she will not see you, but when I mention your name, she becomes quite agitated . . . I should almost say frightened if it were not so nonsensical."

She looked at him sharply. "Is there any reason she should be afraid of you, Charles?"

Carlton returned her steady look although inside he was cursing himself bitterly, conscious of how strongly his accusations and his talk of divorce had affected Susan. Would that he could take back every word, but that was patently impossible. He sighed. Sophy was right — he would have to wait until Susan was stronger before he spoke with her.

"I assure you, dear ma'am, my wife has no cause to fear me." He paused and the expression in his eyes hardened. "If you think it best that I stay away from Susan, I shall, of course, bow to your wishes."

Sophy flinched slightly as the earl continued, "I would be immensely grateful if you could keep me informed of Susan's progress, however."

"Would you care to tell me why my niece feels as she does, Charles?" Sophy inquired searchingly. "Perhaps I may be able to help."

"No," he returned roughly, his voice taut with emotion. He gestured to the door without looking at her. "Please, for God's sake, go now, Sophy. You have my word that I shall not upset Susan with my presence, but I must talk with her when she's stronger."

Sophy, who realized that she had pushed the earl as much as he would tolerate, murmured her thanks and left, closing the door gently behind her.

Susan, with all the resiliency of youth, began at first to make a rapid recovery, particularly when she'd heard from Dr. Poisenby's own lips that her child was in no danger.

As the days passed, however, it began to be evident to Alicia and Sophy that she was far from recovered. Indeed, where she had initially looked eagerly to the door whenever a visitor had entered, she now didn't bother to turn her head. She was listless and uninterested in any of the gossip Sophy and Alicia offered, and those two ladies began to exchange concerned looks over her bed.

Susan could have told them why she'd lost interest in the inconsequential chatter they hoped to amuse her with, and in the healthful foods they pressed upon her, had they inquired. Sophy, however, was much too tactful to pry and it's doubtful that Susan's pride would have permitted her to explain that she wished only to see her husband one last time before he proceeded with a separation. Even the scandal divorce would cause her didn't alarm her as much as did the possibility that she might never see Charles again.

By the end of the second week following her accident, Susan seemed to be making no progress whatsoever and Sophy was becoming quite alarmed. She said nothing to Charles of his wife's lack of improvement however, hoping instead that the next day would find her niece improving once again.

Susan obediently ate what was served her, determined that her baby would thrive but she was content to lie abed all day, staring unseeingly out her window. Visitors, other than Sarah and Mrs. Penrose, were denied, although there were a considerable number of messages delivered to the house from friends in London. Even those failed to engage Susan's interest.

Alicia read one of these cards to Susan and smiled as she showed her patient the lovely grapes which had accompanied the note.

"That was nicely done of Sir Oliver, Susan. Do you think perhaps you'd care for some of his fruit with your luncheon?"

Susan turned her gaze from the window and looked indifferently at her friend. "I'm sorry, Alicia. I wasn't attending. Did you wish something?"

Alicia felt her heart torn for her friend and she decided she could stand no more.

"Susan," she began softly, seating herself on the bed and holding one of Susan's hands between her own. "Won't you tell me what's upsetting you so?"

The pale girl on the bed looked at her friend, hope flaring in her eyes, then it was gone. "It's nothing, Alicia." She turned her head back to the window. "You can do nothing . . . no one can."

Alicia couldn't bear the sorrow in Susan's bleak tones. "One can always do something, Susan. Perhaps Charles could help." This she offered rather tentatively, knowing that Susan's aunt didn't wish the earl's name mentioned.

Sophy had explained in her calm manner that they were having quite enough trouble effecting Susan's recovery without upsetting her by mentioning the earl. She meant well, but misunderstood entirely the reason for her patient's apathy. She had talked to Oliver in London immediately following the accident, and while neither friend believed for a moment that Charles had had a hand in Susan's fall, the fact that he had been angry and that harsh words had been exchanged was enough to convince Sophy that any reference to him would be detrimental to her niece. Susan had questioned no one concerning her husband, certain as she was that he'd already departed for the city and Alicia dared not contradict Lady Sophy's express wishes by bringing the subject up.

So it was, that Alicia was completely unprepared for the flash of joy in Susan's eyes at the mention of her husband's name. It was gone as swiftly as it had come but Alicia had seen it nonetheless and she began to think that perhaps Lady Sophy had been wrong.

"Susan," she said urgently, "don't turn away from me, please, I beg of you." When her friend had turned toward her once again, she continued a little helplessly. "We all . . . that is, Lady Sophy . . . I mean . . . well, we all thought you didn't wish to see Charles but you do, don't you?"

Susan's blue eyes filled with tears. "Oh, Alicia," she begged, "please don't tell him so when you return to London."

Alicia looked startled. "London? What's London to do with anything?" She suddenly felt quite stupid.

Susan gripped Alicia's hand tightly. "Do you mean he's not yet gone off to London?"

"Good God, no. Why should he do such a ramshackle thing as to shab off to the city when you've been lying here near death?"

"I thought . . . that is, I was certain . . ." Susan's eyes began to fill with hope. "Alicia, has he inquired about me at all?"

Alicia gaped at her, eyes wide with astonishment. "Inquired about you?" she repeated faintly. "Why, who do you suppose sat day and night with you until your aunt and I arrived? Good heavens, Susan, we were fairly tripping over the man when we first arrived. If Lady Sophy hadn't ordered him to his chamber, we should all have gone quite mad."

Alicia hugged Susan a little convulsively. "He's been wild about you." She paused and pulled away slightly, her hands on Susan's shoulders. "Have you thought he deserted you?" she inquired intently, brows drawn together. "Yes, I can see that you have."

"But, Alicia," ventured Susan when her friend had released her. "I don't understand why he hasn't visited me."

"He was only following Lady Sophy and Dr. Poisenby's orders that you weren't to be upset or agitated. Would you like me to send Sarah for him?"

"I . . . yes," replied Susan, rather faintly, her hand at her throat.

Alicia rose but was stopped immediately when Susan placed a hand on her arm. "Wait . . . oh, wait please, Alicia. He can't see me like this."

She pushed the covers back and would have been out of the bed if Alicia had not stopped her.

"I need a prettier bedgown, Alicia, and my hair must be brushed . . . and . . . and I'm quite certain I'm pale beyond anything."

"You remain in bed, Susan, and Sarah and I shall have you looking fine as a fivepence before the cat can lick her ear."

Susan slipped back beneath the quilt while Alicia rang the bell for Sarah. Before long, Susan was clad in a lovely gown with a lace wrapper over her shoulders. Alicia handed her a mirror as Sarah finished brushing her hair.

Susan looked into the glass and couldn't repress a gasp.

"Good God, Alicia," she asked in a strangled

voice, "what happened to my hair?"

She turned her neck this way and that, attempting to determine the extent of the damage done by the earl's panic-striken hand.

"I look like a half-shorn sheep."

Alicia tilted her head and looked her over critically. "It's not as bad as all that, Susan. One does become accustomed, you know."

Susan looked askance at her friend and Alicia began to laugh.

"Perhaps I could even it out a bit, if you'd like, Lady Susan," suggested Sarah, picking up the scissors.

Ignoring Alicia, Susan agreed to the idea then sat quietly, albeit nervously, as Sarah snipped. After a quarter of an hour passed, she began to become alarmed at the amount of hair on the floor.

"Have you done much of this sort of thing, Sarah?" She frowned.

Sarah stopped for a moment, regarding her mistress, her tongue between her teeth. "I was used to cut my brother's hair, ma'am, and I did do a fine job of it, if I may say so myself."

She resumed her work and Susan remained silent for a little longer then spoke again. "You aren't cutting too much, are you?"

Sarah placed the scissors on the table and stepped back a pace. "Guess I'm in the habit of clipping boys' heads, my lady."

Susan's eyes widened and her hand flew to her head.

"I think it looks quite lovely," Alicia said, staunchly, "It needs only a little getting used to." She pressed the mirror to her bosom. "You may be a little shocked but I assure you this style is all the crack. Not many young ladies could carry it off half so well."

"Pray hand me the mirror, Alicia," asked Susan in a strangled voice.

"In a moment, dear. Just bear in mind that Charles did such a poor job, hacking here and there like he did that Sarah could do nothing less than cut it all off."

These words didn't increase the little confidence Susan retained in Sarah's abilities and she held out her hand.

"I'd like to see for myself, Alicia."

The mirror changed hands and Susan gasped when she saw her reflection. Gone were the long dusky ringlets and in their place soft curls, none more than two or three inches in length, covered her head.

"No use to fly into the boughs, Susan." Alicia's eyes twinkled. "You look enchanting . . . you know you do. Besides, who could possibly object?"

"Aunt Sophy, for one, Alicia," replied Susan dryly, still gazing at her reflection and running one hand through the springy curls.

"Pooh, she'll love it. It's just how Caro Lamb affects her hair and she's very good ton." Alicia paused then added irrepressibly, "Well, perhaps no such very good ton right now but she does se style."

Susan nodded absently as she continued to peruse her new coiffure. "Actually," she murmured at length, "I do rather like it."

At this, Sarah, who had been all but forgotten by the two young ladies, breathed a sigh of relief and proceeded to tidy up the room.

When the maid had finished and had departed, Susan straightened her wrapper and smiled tremulously at Alicia.

"Well, Alicia, would you be so kind as to inform my husband I should like to see him when it's convenient."

Alicia pressed Susan's hand and nodded then ran lightly out of the room.

Susan waited, her heart pounding and her pulses racing. When she heard the earl's footsteps outside her door only moments later, she squared her shoulders and murmured a fervent prayer that Alicia had been right.

Lord Carlton entered his wife's chamber hardly daring to breathe. His cool reserve, which had been badly shattered during Susan's convalescence was lost completely when he gazed at the vision in the large silk-draped bed.

"My God, Susan," he exclaimed. "What have you done to your hair?"

A look of uncertainty flickered in Susan's eyes. Had Alicia been mistaken? Her husband didn't sound much like a distraught lover.

"D—do you dislike it so much, Charles?"

He walked quickly to the bed and took her hand, holding it gently. "You look absurdly young to be a wife and mother."

Susan's eyes brimmed with laughter. "I had no other recourse, my lord. My last barber made rather a sorry botch of the job."

Her husband grinned appreciatively. "I shouldn't ask him to cut your hair again." His grin faded and he sat on her bed. "Can you ever forgive me?"

Susan felt a thrill of relief and her voice shook a little as she spoke. "For cutting my hair in such an absurd fashion . . . of course."

Carlton smiled tenderly at her. "You know I don't wish to be forgiven for cutting your hair. Besides," he continued, regarding her shining curls thoughtfully, "you should be thanking me. I believe it was my hand which began this transformation."

Susan smiled and gazed lovingly at the handsome man sitting beside her. "Shall you now become my lady's maid and always cut my hair?"

"I'll do anything you ask, Susan," replied Charles simply. "I wouldn't blame you if you held me in such contempt that you wished me gone forever. I can't condone nor explain any of my actions other than to say that I've been bewitched by you, so much so that all rational behavior has been driven from my mind. I wouldn't admit until it was almost too late that my insane jealousy was caused by my love for you. Your accident has brought me to my senses at last."

He paused, his expression rueful. "I almost lost

you, but I shan't let that happen again."

Susan raised her eyes to his. "I love you, Charles," she said a little shyly.

He said nothing more but enfolded her in his strong embrace and her arms went about his neck. He held her for a long moment without speaking then took one arm from about her and cupped her chin with his hand then bent his dark head to kiss her.

A few moments later there was a light tap on the door and Sophy entered the chamber. She hesitated and then smiled as Susan raised a rosy cheek from her husband's shoulder.

"I see I intrude," she murmured cheerfully, as she turned to leave.

"It's quite all right, Aunt Sophy," said Susan mistily.

Sophy observed the two glowing faces with satisfaction. "Yes, my dears, I can rather see that it is."

Without another word she left the room, her eyes sparkling as she pictured her husband's reaction to the news that Lord and Lady Carlton had finally made their peace.

ZEBRA'S REGENCY ROMANCES
the Lords & Ladies you'll *love* reading about

THE ROGUE'S BRIDE (1976, $2.95)
by Paula Roland
Major Brandon Clive was furious when he returned to England to find the wrong bride foisted off on him. But one look at Alexandra, and Brandon instantly changed his mind.

SMUGGLER'S LADY (1948, $3.95)
by Jane Feather
No one would ever suspect dowdy Merrie Trelawney of being the notorious leader of smuggler's band. But something about Merrie struck Lord Rutherford as false, and though he was not in the habit of seducing country widows, it might make an interesting change at that . . .

CRIMSON DECEPTION (1913, $2.95)
by Therese Alderton
Katherine's heart raced as she observed valuable paintings mysteriously disappear, but her pulse quickened for a different reason in the Earl's company. She would have to get to the bottom of it all — before she fell hopelessly in love with a scoundrel.

A GENTLEMAN'S MISTRESS (1798, $2.95)
by Mary Brendan
Sarah should have been grateful that Mark Tarrington had hired her as a governess. Instead the young widow was furious at his arrogance and her heart's reaction to him. Sarah Thornton was obviously going to require patience which was the one quality the earl had little of.

FARO'S LADY (1725, $2.95)
by Paula Roland
Jessamine arrived at a respectable-looking inn — only to be mistaken for a jade that night by a very drunken gentleman. She vowed revenge and plotted to trap Hugh Hamilton into a marriage he would never forget. A flawless plan — if it hadn't been for her wayward heart.

Available wherever paperbacks are sold, or order direct from the Publisher. Send cover price plus 50¢ per copy for mailing and handling to Zebra Books, Dept. 2076, 475 Park Avenue South, New York, N.Y. 10016. Residents of New York, New Jersey and Pennsylvania must include sales tax. DO NOT SEND CASH.

THE BEST IN GOTHICS FROM ZEBRA

THE BLOODSTONE INHERITANCE (1560, $2.95)
by Serita Deborah Stevens

The exquisite Parkland pendant, the sole treasure remaining to lovely Elizabeth from her mother's fortune, was missing a matching jewel. Finding it in a ring worn by the handsome, brooding Peter Parkisham, Elizabeth couldn't deny the blaze of emotions he ignited in her. But how could she love the man who had stolen THE BLOODSTONE INHERITANCE!

THE SHRIEKING SHADOWS OF
PENPORTH ISLAND (1344, $2.95)
by Serita Deborah Stevens

Seeking her missing sister, Victoria had come to Lord Hawley's manor on Penporth Island, but now the screeching gulls seemed to be warning her to flee. Seeing Julian's dark, brooding eyes watching her every move, and seeing his ghost-like silhouette on her bedroom wall, Victoria knew she would share her sister's fate — knew she would never escape!

THE HOUSE OF SHADOWED ROSES (1447, $2.95)
by Carol Warburton

Penniless and alone, Heather was thrilled when the Ashleys hired her as a companion and brought her to their magnificent Cornwall estate, Rosemerryn. But soon Heather learned that danger lurked amid the beauty there — in ghosts long dead and mysteries unsolved, and even in the arms of Geoffrey Ashley, the enigmatic master of Rosemerryn.

CRYSTAL DESTINY (1394, $2.95)
by Christina Blair

Lydia knew she belonged to the high, hidden valley in the Rockies that her father had claimed, but the infamous Aaron Stone lived there now in the forbidding Stonehurst mansion. Vowing to get what was hers, Lydia would confront the satanic master of Stonehurst — and find herself trapped in a battle for her very life!

Available wherever paperbacks are sold, or order direct from the Publisher. Send cover price plus 50¢ per copy for mailing and handling to Zebra Books, Dept. 2076, 475 Park Avenue South, New York, N.Y. 10016. Residents of New York, New Jersey and Pennsylvania must include sales tax. DO NOT SEND CASH.

BESTSELLING HISTORICAL ROMANCE
from Zebra Books

PASSION'S GAMBLE (1477, $3.50)
by Linda Benjamin
Jessica was shocked when she was offered as the stakes in a poker game, but soon she found herself wishing that Luke Garrett, her handsome, muscular opponent, would hold the winning hand. For only his touch could release the rapturous torment trapped within her innocence.

YANKEE'S LADY (1784, $3.95)
by Kay McMahon
Rachel lashed at the Union officer and fought to flee the dangerous fire he ignited in her. But soon Rachel touched him with a bold fiery caress that told him—despite the war—that she yearned to be the YANKEE'S LADY

SEPTEMBER MOON (1838, $3.95)
by Constance O'Banyon
Ever since she was a little girl Cameron had dreamed of getting even with the Kingstons. But the extremely handsome Hunter Kingston caught her off guard and all she could think of was his lips crushing hers in feverish rapture beneath the SEPTEMBER MOON.

MIDNIGHT THUNDER (1873, $3.95)
by Casey Stuart
The last thing Gabrielle remembered before slipping into unconsciousness was a pair of the deepest blue eyes she'd ever seen. Instead of stopping her crime, Alexander wanted to imprison her in his arms and embrace her with the fury of MIDNIGHT THUNDER.

Available wherever paperbacks are sold, or order direct from the Publisher. Send cover price plus 50¢ per copy for mailing and handling to Zebra Books, Dept. 2076, 475 Park Avenue South, New York, N.Y. 10016. Residents of New York, New Jersey and Pennsylvania must include sales tax. DO NOT SEND CASH.